Not a Norman Rockwell Christmas
Stories for the Holidays

Robert Mauro

2

This book is dedicated to my wife, Bernadette who has shown me that all things are possible. And to my four children: Heather, Nick, Sean and Zach who are sources of constant inspiration. Finally, to our Old English sheepdog, Bailey, who constantly tests my sanity but also keeps my sense of humor alive.

Table of Contents

Always Someplace to Go

Chapter I

He sat at the counter in the little bodega and watched the steam rise from the grate outside. A couple of people were rushing past the window returning home from work or finishing up last minute holiday shopping. Almost all had their collars turned up against the below freezing temperature and the wind that was howling. The city streets became wind tunnels that whipped the wind up one street, while the next street was relative calm. Snow had fallen earlier in the day but had lost its luster to the cars, busses and trucks, turning the streets slushy, and what little snow that remained was banked on the sidewalks, a grimy shade of grey.

The man stirred his hot chocolate with a peppermint candy cane, a sop to memories of years past in places long gone. Much had changed since the time the man had last been on this street. Owned by an Irish couple when he was a child, this soda shop now belonged to a Hispanic woman with a sweaty brow and a greasy apron. Shelves that used to hold Dutch Masters cigars and penny pretzel sticks were now stacked with dusty bricks of Bustello coffee. Sacks of arroz were pushed up against the corner, and the news racks no longer held the New York Times, the Wall Street Journal, and the Post, but the El Diario La Prensa, Hoy Nueva New York, and CNY Latino. Decades ago, he sat at the counter drinking a twenty-five cent egg cream or buying a pack of cigarettes for his mother. A stop after church each Sunday to pick up the Daily News and the Mirror for his father brought him here. These memories etched indelibly in his mind were at variance with what he viewed through his old eyes. This little store had served untold numbers throughout the years long after his family had moved on from the city in the exodus of humanity during the urban flight of his youth.

"Hey, Papi, I'm closing soon."

"I'm sorry, said the old man. I didn't mean to hold you up. I'll be finished in just a minute."

"It's Christmas Eve, Papi. I have got to get home to my kids."

"Yes, yes, I know. It is Christmas Eve." He put on his hat and coat, pulling up the collar and wrapped the scarf around his neck. The cup rattled shakily in the saucer as he brought them over to the woman.

"You got somewhere to go, Papi? It isn't a good idea to go walking around here at night if you don't know where you are going."

"Oh, I have somewhere to go. Everyone has somewhere to go on Christmas Eve, don't they?" He smiled and left a five dollar bill on the counter. "Keep the change," he said, placing his hand on the handle of the door. "You and your family have Merry Christmas."

Street traffic had thinned out by the time he left the bodega. The wind had picked up making it feel much colder. Store lights had begun to be extinguished as the doors were locked and heavy meal gates were drawn down over the plate glass windows. Pages from discarded newspapers were scudding down the sidewalk, wrapping around light poles and parking meters. The only lights to be seen in the lowering darkness were those of the few cars moving down the avenues, the street lamps, and the occasional restaurant.

He walked slowly up the street until he came to the nearest intersection, where he turned. Buildings, sidewalks, and streets that were all familiar to him although he had not seen them in years. Again, his memory harkened back to when people were sitting out on the stoops during the summer; kids playing stickball or running through an open fire hydrant to ease the baking heat of summer in the city. Of course, it was not summer. People no longer sat on stoops for fear of violence. And even if it had been summer and the people were not afraid, the accents would have been different. Thick Italian and lilting Irish voices had been replaced by the lyric Spanish of those from Puerto Rico and the Caribbean. Children no longer played stickball, but were inside their apartments playing video games. No matter how much he wanted things to have remained the same all these years, he knew that much had changed. Better to remember things as they used to be, than it is to focus on what everything had become.

After about fifteen minutes slowly walking, the man reached his destination. The church appeared smaller than he had remembered. Age that had wizened him had similarly affected the building he stood before. There was now an iron fence around the rectory that had not been there in time past. Cracks and crevasses lined the façade of the church, becoming a mirror image of the old man's face and hands. He saw himself in the weary old building but felt a sense of comfort and serenity in knowing that they were both standing and had survived, at least temporarily. It was an arbitrary triumph over the passage of time.

Turning slowly, he looked toward the school that was attached to the church. In his mind's eye, he could envision the children gathering from the surrounding streets to begin their day. They jostled and laughed, played childlike games in the cold winter air, amidst the sounds of cars and trucks rumbling down the road. When Sister Mary came outside and rang the bell, the children would form up in two separate lines by gender and grade and the lines would begin to slowly snake into the school. He could remember the last day of school before Christmas Eve; the sugar cookies and the hot chocolate and the peppermint candy canes that he would receive from the Sisters. One year, just before the children were to be dismissed, it began to snow and it was difficult to keep his mind on anything else but the clock reaching three o'clock and dismissal. Once released, he raced all the way home as the snow swirled; large fluffy flakes that resembled feathers from a torn pillows being shaken from the rooftops. Christmas, at that time, in that place, when he was a child, was a memory that stayed with him all these years, and frequently returning regardless of the season.

The old man turned as his memory of past days faded to black, and he climbed the few steps to the door that led into the vestibule of the church. He walked through the entry, past a small bank of candles that were lit as offerings of prayers to the departed. Little had changed over the decades, save the updating of vestments and the occasional painting of walls. Somehow, the church appeared smaller than his memory recalled. Undoubtedly, this was the circle of memory, when as a child everything appears larger than it actually is. As we reach middle age, the same scene revisited may appear proportitate to our actual size because we have grown. Finally, as one approaches the conclusion of our time, the object or place reverts back to the illusion of immenseness. So it was true for the old man.

Suddenly, he could not recall particulars of the church. It was not clear to him whether the pews were the same, nor the altar, nor the tabernacle. The ceiling seemed lower, but he realized that this could not be. On each side of the church were seven stained glass windows, each representing one of the scenes of the Stations of the Cross. How many hours had he sat staring at these marvelous windows during the boredom he felt on Sunday at Mass as a child? His memory now coming back into focus, the windows were as familiar to him as a well-worn pair of slippers or as his plaid bathrobe. Finding a pew near the back, he genuflected, made the sign of the cross, and sat down.

Intermittently, the door at the back of the church would open and people would come in and sit down. Although only shortly after 8 o'clock in the evening, the final service of the day would shortly begin. Midnight Mass on Christmas Eve no longer was being held in most areas of the country. Giving in to the wishes of affluent suburban parents who wanted to get their children home and into bed early so that Santa could make his deliveries earlier, churches began holding the traditional Christmas Eve Mass in the early evening. What became a convenience for those in the suburbs became necessity of safety for people who lived in the inner city.

The church was almost full to capacity when the service began. Many years ago, when the old man was an altar boy, the Mass was sung in Latin. Reflective of those now sitting in this church on a cold and windy Christmas Eve, the Mass was said in Spanish. Though unfamiliar with the language, the old man knew the Mass well enough to follow along. He made the responses to himself and felt perfectly at home in, what to others, would seem to be a foreign place. His heart was uplifted by the singing of the Christmas hymns by the small children's choir. Even the occasional sound of a child off-key did not affect his fulfillment. Looking at the pews, he could see that they were filled with families, including grandparents, aunts and uncles. They were dressed as fashionably as their meager resources would allow; a garish Christmas tie here, a well-worn hair ribbon there. There were patches on the knees on a child's jeans in one row, a hand-me-down little girl's dress on a pretty child in another row. Many of the men wore the clothes they had put on to go off to work that morning, the difference being that they were freshly shaven and their hair was slicked back in the style of the day. Regardless of the clothes that they wore or the poverty that had befallen them, all sang their hymns with fervor and joy, completely immersed in the coming of Christ child's birth. It did not matter the material things that were denied to them by the cruelty of life, they were joyful to be together on this holy and happy time of the year.

One by one, row by row, the people stood to line up to receive Holy Communion. When it was his turn, the old man stood and joined the line and slowly made his way toward the altar. Cupping his hands, he held them forward to receive the Host, the priest saying "el cuerpo de Cristo," to which the old man replied. "Amen."

He made his way back to his seat and knelt in prayer. Thoughts of his children and grandchildren drifted into his head as he prayed for his own peace and theirs as well. More than that, he prayed for those around him that they could carry forth their joy and love throughout the year.

The organist began to play the recessional to signal the end of Mass. Men and women, families, began to file out of the church, yet the man remained kneeling. When the last steps had receded he rose from his knees and sat back in the pew. Darkness increased as the church lights were lowered, until all that remained was the flickering of the candles and a small light illuminating the altar. Deep in

13

thought, the man remained as the bell in the steeple tolled the hour, and then tolled again the half hour. Still, the man remained in the pew.

Sometime after the last bell had rung, the vestry door opened and a man in a black robe wearing a cross around his neck made his way down the side aisle of the church to the entryway. Keys could be heard jingling as he locked the doors of the church for the night. After finishing this task, the priest began to walk up the main aisle when he noticed the old man sitting alone in the pew.

"Excuse me, Senor, the priest said, but the church is closed for the evening. I am afraid that you will have to leave now."

"Oh, I beg your pardon. I am sorry, apologized the old man. I was just sitting here awhile after the service. It was very beautiful."

"Thank you. Do you understand Spanish, Senor?"

"No, no, the old man replied. When I was an altar boy many years ago the Mass was said in Latin, so I could follow along fairly well. I am sorry to have caused any problems. I'll be going."

"Are you okay, Senor? I do not remember ever having seen you here before. Almost all of our parishioners are known to me."

"No, I'm not from around here. I was walking by and the church seemed to be such a peaceful place that I thought I would come in and rest my soul for a while."

As the old man began to rise to leave, something about him struck the priest. He walked with the man toward

14

the back of the church and put a hand on his shoulder. "Senor, are you alright? Do you have somewhere to go?"

Smiling, the old man said, "Father, one always has a place to go."

The words intrigued the priest in a way that he could not quite put a finger on. It was not a particularly unusual or ominous rejoinder. Maybe it was the smile on the old man's face or the tone of his voice. The priest didn't know, but it was just his instinct to keep the conversation going.

"Senor, it is very cold outside, and I do not know where your journey is to take you. But why don't you come with me to the rectory and join me in a cup of tea and we can chat for a bit before you go?"

"I think that I would enjoy that very much, Father."

The walked together through the sacristy and down a short hallway that connected the church to the rectory. The priest escorted the old man into a small but comfortable sitting room. On the mantle were many Christmas cards. A not insignificant number of them were hand drawn cards from the children of the parish school. They were adorned with stick figure angels or scenes from the Nativity. A couch and a comfortable overstuffed chair, a few bookcases and an artificial Christmas tree were the only other accoutrements in the room. "I'll go get the tea ready. Make yourself comfortable." In a few minutes, the priest was back with a tray containing a teapot, some mismatched teacups, and some sugar cookies cut in the shapes of trees, stars and bells.

"You know Senor, I apologize that I have not properly introduced myself. I am Father Emilio Santos, the Rector here. What might your name be?"

"My name is Raymond Taft. It is a pleasure to make your acquaintance Father."

"Where are you from, Mr. Taft? Surely you are not from around here?"

"No, I am not from around here. I live about 200 miles north of here.

"That is quite a long way. Are you here visiting family?"

"My family lives close to where I live up north. No relatives here. I went to school here some 70 years ago. If you take a look at one of those books on your bookshelf, you might even find a photograph of me in Sister Mary Debra's second grade class."

Father Santos rose from his chair and went over to the case that held the school yearbooks. Finding the book from the year the old man mentioned, he opened it and flipped through the pages. The pages were brittle and yellow with age, and the pictures verily faded. After scanning for a minute or two, he brought the book over to Mr. Taft and pointing to a child in picture said, "that is you, is it not?"

"Yes, that was me when I was in the second grade. Those were wonderful days. Unforgettable days. I remember the days close to the Christmas holidays the most. That is why I came here today. I have not been back to this church in 70 years. It was so long ago, but it seems like yesterday."

"If you do not mind my asking Mr. Taft, why are you not with your family this holiday evening?"

"Oh, it is a long and not very interesting story, Father. I do not wish to bore you with it.?"

"Surely you will not bore me. And if it is a long story, then we will definitely need some more tea to see us through it." Father Santos poured some more tea into their cups. Then he went to a small cabinet under one of the bookcases and removed a decanter. "Maybe you would like a little sherry to go with the tea, eh Mr. Taft? I save this for special occasions, and your visit on the eve of the birth of Christ would count as a special occasion, I think."

The old man accepted both the tea and the glass of golden liquor from the Father. "I don't know how special this occasion is, but I am surely humbled by your kindness and hospitality."

"Now, tell me your story, Mr. Taft."

The old man set the sherry down on the table next to him. "I have a fairly large family. There are three sons, one daughter, nine grandchildren and two great grandchildren. My oldest child is forty-nine years old. For all those past forty-nine years we have been together on Christmas. When the children got old and married, sometimes a couple of them would come on Christmas Eve, and the rest would arrive on Christmas morning. As they got older the holidays seemed to stretch out over more and more days as people would come and go. There were times when we would have as many as twenty or more people at our house for Christmas breakfast because of the girlfriends, boyfriends, husbands and the wives. Our door was always open for whoever knocked upon it. This year it was different.'

"What changed?"

The old man arose from his seat and poured some more sherry into his glass. "Two years ago, my wife passed away. We were married close to fifty years. Needless to say, it was difficult on all of us, especially around the holidays. The year after her passing, all of the children, grandchildren, and great grandchildren came to the house for Christmas, just as they would always do. There were a few tears on Christmas morning, because Mom was not with us. But in all other ways, it seemed to me to be as good as it always had been. Everyone laughed and joked and we had our usual large breakfast before going to church, and the large dinner that evening. I guess I was wrong that everyone was enjoying themselves."

He sat down and continued. "About a week ago, one of my sons called. He had been chosen to tell me that everyone was going to be off doing their own thing this year and wouldn't be coming to spend the holidays at the house. Everyone had been was too depressed the previous year, and it wasn't the same without Mom being there. They all needed a break, he said. I told my son that it was tradition, and that we had always been together for Christmas. He told me that it was time for everyone to start their own traditions, and for me to become a part of theirs. As far as they were concerned, Christmas tradition of coming to my home ended when their Mom passed away. So, for the first time in almost fifty years, I was going to be alone."

"Didn't any of your family invite you to their home?"

"No. Some of them decided to go on holiday trips. The grandchildren are too young to want an irascible old curmudgeon like me hanging around. So with nowhere to go, and nobody to be with, I went to the one place I remembered having some of the best holidays as a child."

"It must be very painful not being with your family at Christmas?"

"Yes, it is. I guess that I believed that we would always be together at the holidays. It never occurred to me that they would want to go their separate ways at Christmas. My wife kept us all together, so with her gone I suppose that glue that bound us to one another is no more."

Father Santos rose and refilled the old man's glass. "What about your church back home? I do imagine that you are a member of a parish? Would it not have been easier on you to have been part of your parish family for Christmas and not traveled so far?

"I have kept up with the doings of your church for a number of years. I found the school website and have been receiving your newsletter. As I mentioned, I attended school here a long time ago and remember that time very fondly. When my family decided not to get together, I didn't want to be at home by myself, so I checked the website and saw the time for Christmas Eve Mass, and thought I would come down and see this place for myself once again."

The old man looked around the room as if he remembered something. The thought, whatever it was, left him too soon. He wished that he could latch on to the image longer, but the fatigue of a long day was beginning to overtake him. Placing his glass down on the coaster beside his chair, he started to rise. 'Thank you very much Father, for the tea, the sherry, and for your hospitality. While some things of your church have changed, many others have not. Certainly, as I am sure that you can understand, I would have preferred to have spent this day with my children. But this is definitely a suitable substitute."

Father Santos put a hand on the old man's arm. "My friend, it is a long way back to your home and it is very late. I fear for your safety driving such a distance at this hour. There is a very comfortable room here at the Rectory. Stay with me this night and rest. Tonight, there is a room available at the inn."

"No, no, I really cannot impose on you any longer. You have things to do in the morning, and no need for me to get in the way. I will be fine driving. A little coffee and I will be wide awake and alert."

"Why take the chance? I insist that you stay. You have been good company and I would definitely enjoy it again at lunch tomorrow. Come. I will not take no for an answer. Sleep the sleep of the just and not the troubled, and then you can be on your way in the sunshine of the day of the Lord's birth."

The old man saw that good sense would overcome any of his arguments. And he had to admit, at least to himself, that he was really tired. Had he persisted in leaving, he knew that he would have had to have stopped somewhere along the way home to take a nap or to have gotten a room at a hotel. "You are very persuasive, Father. I will do as you ask, and I am thankful for your kindness."

They walked together out of the small office and down a hallway to a bedroom at the end. Father Santos reached for a wall switch and turned on the light. Neatly furnished, the room had the scent of not having been used in some time. Against one wall was a single bed, a night stand with a lamp and a bible. A dresser and an ancient armchair occupied the opposite wall. To the side of the bed was a window that overlooked a garden of reflection that as about the size of a postage stamp. The room appeared comfortable in a Spartan sort of way, somewhat more than a monk's cell, but not as large as a typical guest room. Having stood for more than one hundred years, the room, as did the rectory, was showing its age.

"Maybe not what you are used to at home, Mr. Taft, but I think that you will be comfortable here for the night. There are some books in the closet should you choose to read for a bit; the bathroom is across the hall, and the kitchen is the room next to my office. Should there be anything else you require, there is a small buzzer by your bed. Just press it and I will come to you."

Sitting on the bed, the old man looked up at the Father. "No, I don't believe that I will be needing anything other than a good night's sleep. I have no doubt that I will get that here in this room." Taking the Father's hand, he said, "thank you" again. "You have no idea how much this evening has meant to me."

"Somehow, Mr. Taft, I believe I do have an idea what this night has meant to you. I have no doubt it has been a difficult night for you. Sleep well, and I will see you for coffee before you leave."

The door closed and the old man began to undress, neatly folding his clothes and placing them on the chair. Climbing under the covers, he rolled over and looked outside at the small patch of grass outside his window. There by a bench, stood a statue of the saint the school and the church were named after. Mumbling a few prayers as he closed his eyes, the last thing the old man remembered before falling off to slumber was the whistling of the relief valve on the steam radiator across the room.

Chapter II

The morning sun shown clear and bright through the bedroom window as the old man opened his eyes after a long sleep. A light breeze blew the remnants of a dusting of snow from the outside window sill, the flakes becoming a prism of colors in the sunshine. He rose from the bed and began to dress, not being sure of the time of day until he noticed the small alarm clock on the night stand. Almost 11 a.m., he thought, a much longer slumber than he expected.

Once dressed, he moved down the hall to the kitchen. Father Santos was already there, sipping from a mug of coffee. The aroma of freshly brewed strong coffee removed the last vestiges of sleep from his head and awakened his senses. It was Christmas morning.

"Good morning, my friend, I trust that you slept well," said Father Santos. "Please sit down and let me fix you some coffee. It may be a little stronger than you are used to, but it will open your eyes fully to the day."

"I slept very well, Father. Thank you. I would love some coffee. Black, if you please."

They both sat in silence for a number of minutes, the Father wishing to give the old man time to fully wake up. "I take it you will be leaving soon? What are your plans when you arrive home?"

"Plans? I have no plans. I imagine that I will make a light meal, build a small fire in the fireplace, and read. That is what I do most evenings. At my age, excitement might me a little detrimental to my health," he chuckled.

"Before you head back, I would like to show you something. It should not take very long, and will not delay your departure by very much time. Would you do that for me Mr. Taft?"

"After the kindness you have shown me, how could I refuse? It would have been a long and difficult ride last night had I perinsisted on leaving. I am glad that you insisted that I stay, and would gladly do as you wish."

"It was my pleasure having you, sir. It is not often that I am blessed with a visitor. But do not hurray, please, finish your coffee and have another up if you so desire."

Without hurry, the men continued to make small talk as they drank their coffee. After they finished, they got their coats and headed out of the Rectory. The late morning was cold, but not unpleasantly so as they walked past the church and the school. People were hustling to their destinations for a Christmas lunch or to spend the day with relatives. Many stopped to shake Father Santos' hand, wish him the best the holiday had to offer, and then they went on their way.

After a few blocks, the father turned into the courtyard of an apartment building. A snapshot taken some forty or fifty years ago would have shown an attractive entryway to a fashionable address. Time and neglect had weathered the stone and brick masonry, as if its once attractive face had decided to forgo make-up after many years of putting on a pretty face. Now, half measures of repair hid the worst cracks, only adding to the sadness of what was once must have been a grand building.

The pair of visitors were met by a broken elevator and walls covered in graffiti. In places the urban painting was so old, that it too was chipped and peeling. The smells of the apartments that the old man once knew; the boiled cabbage or frying garlic was replaced by an assault on olfactory nerves of dried urine and stale cigarette smoke. They began their ascent up the stairs steering clear of the trash and the detritus of drug use. Fortunately, their climb was not long, as they only had to travel to the third floor. There they stood before an apartment door decorated with a paper cut out of a smiling Santa Claus bearing the words "Merry Christmas" on a banner under his red bag of toys. Father Santos raised his hand to ring the doorbell when the old man touched his shoulder. "One moment Father, why are we here?"

"This family are parishioners of my church. The boy goes to the parish school. They asked me to stop by on Christmas morning. Since you are my guest today, I thought you might like to come along."

"Father, I need to be getting back to my home soon. And I do not need a substitute family," the old man said with a hint of annoyance in his voice.

"Oh no, Senior, I did not mean to offend you. My visit here with you to this wonderful family is not meant as a substitute. I am not trying to replace your family with these wonderful people. Please accept my apologies if I have offended you. Certainly, we may leave and I can escort you back to the Rectory if you do not wish to stay. Then I will return after you have left; you do not have to stay if you do not want to"

The old man did not say anything, but he did not make any movement away from the apartment door either. He tilted his head toward the door as a signal that the priest should knock. The priest knocked, and within a few seconds footsteps could be heard. A chain stopped the door from opening completely, and pair of brown eyes peered

24

questioningly out. Seeing the Father standing on the landing, the door closed momentarily and the chain was slid from the lock. Once the door was opened, a pretty Hispanic woman stood on the other side. She had a pretty smile and beautiful brown eyes. Dark circles under her eyes from fatigue were the only thing to detract from her appearance.

"Feliz Navidad, Father, how good of you to come this afternoon."

A short conversation in Spanish ensued between the priest and the woman, the contents of which the old man could not understand. Standing there with a smile on his face, he felt a little foolish. Clueless as to what was going on, he finally stuck out his hand and said, "Merry Christmas. My name is Paul Taft. It is a pleasure to meet you."

"Dios mio, exclaimed Father Santos, how inconsiderate of me. Anna, this is my friend who has been so kind as to spend Christmas Day with me. Mr. Taft, this is one of our parishioners, Anna Cruz."

"It is so nice to meet you Mr. Taft. Please gentlemen, come in and let me take your coats."

Both men handed Anna their things, and she put them on a small table that was behind the door. They walked down a hallway; to the left was a small kitchen and to the right was the living room. Sitting in front of a television was a child of about eight or nine year of age playing a video game. The boy took no notice of his mother or the visitors when they entered the room.

"Enrique, where are your manners? Stand up and say hello to Father and to his friend, Mt. Taft."

Enrique rose with a look on his face of someone who has taken a bite out of a lemon, and said in a voice laden with indifference, "Hello Father, Hello Mr. Raft," mangling the old man's name. He walked over to the boy and stuck out his hand. "Why don't you call me Paul, okay? We old folks will get out of your way so you can get back to your game." Grateful that he was not going to be shanghaied into the kitchen, Enrique grinned and sat down. Immediately, he was absorbed back into his video world.

"Come into the kitchen and have come coffee, gentlemen."

They sat down at the small circular table in the kitchen. Ms. Cruz bustled around getting cups and saucers placed, made sure that there was sugar in the sugar bowl, and retrieved a small, cheap cut glass creamer for the milk from a cabinet. She was a whirlwind of controlled chaos, measuring out coffee, putting the water in the kettle on the stove, placing cookies on a plate with a paper doily underneath. In no time at all, the coffee was being poured and conversation was beginning to take place.

His mind was elsewhere, and his answers were perfunctory only. What he expected when he entered the apartment was not what he found, especially considering the appearance and the condition of the hallway and stairway leading to this apartment. The floors were immaculate, polished to a gleam that was almost blinding. While the furniture was certainly well used, it was not worn, containing no holes or stains. The kitchen was spotless, there were no dishes in the sink and there was a sparkle to the stove. A small artificial Christmas tree was sitting on top of a table in the corner of the living room. Family photographs were placed on a particle board bookcase. His powers of observation, honed from years at his profession still were high functioning, and he noticed

26

one common denominator in the photographs that was not present in the house.

The old man was brought back to the present when Ms. Cruz asked him if he would like some more coffee. Just as she set the pot down the telephone rang and she excused herself to take the call. In a lowered voice, he asked the question that was on his mind. Father Santos looked at him for a moment, then, making sure that Enrique could not hear him said. "Victor Cruz was Anna's husband, and Enrique's father. He owned the small grocery store that we passed on the corner as we were coming here. The store sold beer, cigarettes, lottery tickets, sodas, and a small selection of groceries. Victor was good to the people, giving their kids jobs delivering things for a few dollars; extending credit, slipping a few extra things into the bag for the old people who couldn't afford more. It was a small store that made just enough money to afford this apartment, and to send Enrique to our church school, and for a few special things on occasion. This past summer, one of the kids he gave a job to tried to rob Victor as he was closing his store for the evening. The boy stabbed Victor nine times when Victor would not give up the day's receipts; a total of a little more than one hundred dollars. Victor was left out on the street, and by the time the paramedics arrived, he had bled to death. Now, Anna works in the store so that she can keep Enrique in school. We help as we can, but we are a poor parish. Like you, this is their first year without a loved one at Christmas."

The old man said nothing. What could he say? His children not being with him this year was nothing compared to the pain this woman and her son must be going through. At least he had his family; he knew where they were. He could call them whenever he wanted. He would see them again. To look at the young boy playing his game, the old man could not understand how Enrique was not visibly suffering from his loss of his father. It was inexplicable that he was enjoying himself on Christmas, while the old man was still feeling sorry for himself.

Getting up from the table, he walked into the living room. "Do you mind if I watch you play for a little while, he said?" "It's okay," the boy answered. Looking down at the table, the old man noticed the video game box. "Did you get the game as a Christmas present," he asked? "Uh huh," Enrique responded. It was apparent from the cover of the game that it was not the newest version and had been purchased used.

"You like baseball," the old man asked?

"I love baseball. My father used to play catch with me all the time. Mom tries to do it with me now, but she isn't very good. She doesn't have the time either. She is always at the store."

"What is your team, Yankees or the Mets?"

"The Yankees"!

"Well, I am a Red Sox fan."

"The Red Sox suck. I hate the Red Sox.

"Enrique! That was very rude and not very nice. You know better than to use that language. Apologize to Mr. Taft right now."

Laughing, the old man said, "That is okay, Mrs. Cruz. No self-respecting Yankee fan likes the Red Sox. There is no offense taken." Turning back to Enrique, he asked, "Have you ever been to Yankee Stadium, it is not too far from here. I used to live here when I was very young; in this apartment building as a matter of fact. My

Dad used to take me to Yankee games all the time when I was your age."

Enrique put down the game controller. "No, I have never been there. Papa always said he was going to take me. Maybe Mama will take me some day, or maybe when I am older."

The old man had no words left to say to the child. He could sense without looking that Father Santos and Anna had been observing their conversation. Whose sadness was greater? Was it a man whose family no longer wanted to share the holidays with him, or a child who had no father to share Christmas with? For Enrique it would not only be this Christmas. It would be all of the holidays; birthdays, Fourth of July, and Christmas' to come. All of them. Nor just today but tomorrow, and the day after that, but all of Enrique's tomorrows. In comparison, what did the old man have to complain about?

"Mrs. Cruz, could you kindly tell me where the rest room is," he asked?

"It is down the hall; the door on the left right by the table with your coats."

"Thank you very much. I will be back in a moment."

Conversation between the priest and Ms. Cruz continued. After fifteen minutes or so, it became obvious that the old man had not returned to either the kitchen or the living room. Father Santos went down the hallway and tapped on the bathroom door. There was no response. As he put his hand on the doorknob he looked over to the table by the front door. The old man's coat and hat were no longer there. Opening the front door, the priest looked down the hall and then walked over to the stairs. There was no sign of the old man at all. Ms. Cruz was walking toward the priest as he was closing the door. "What is the matter Father? Where is Mr. Taft?"

"I don't know Anna. It would seem that Mr. Taft is gone."

Chapter III

Night was beginning to fall as Father Santos made his way back to the Rectory. The suddenness of the old man's departure from the Cruz apartment worried and confused him. Everything had seemed to be going well. The old man was chatting with Enrique, and then he was gone. There was little that Father Santos had not seen in his years as Pastor, but this disturbed him in a way different from other encounters he had with people. Maybe it was that the old man seemed to be so wanting of company, or maybe it was the season of the year. Whatever the reason, in all likelihood, Father Santos would never know why he left the apartment so abruptly.

The grounds of the church were quiet, and only a few lights were on in the Rectory as the priest approached. Opening the door, he noticed an envelope on the floor. Somebody had slid it under the door while he was out. Nothing unusual about that, parishioners frequently left notes or messages. Sometimes they even left donations. He put the envelope in his shirt pocket and hung his overcoat in the closet.

Time passed as the priest busied himself with a few things in his office. Feeling a little weary from the day, he went into the kitchen and warmed up some left over coffee and took it into his study. As he sat down in his chair, he felt the crinkling of paper in his pocket. He had forgotten all about the envelope that he found on the floor by the front door. Taking the letter opener from the table beside him, he slit the envelope open. Inside was a letter and another envelope folded in thirds. Putting on his reading glasses, he unfolded the letter and began to read.

Dear Father Santos,

I cannot begin to tell you how grateful I am for your loving kindness to me. You have been the life preserver that I needed at a time when I was beginning to believe that there was no more reason for me to continue my work. These past few years, there have been few outward signs of true giving and of people understanding the true meaning of the commemoration of the day of our Lord's birth. You have renewed my faith, that, more often than not, people do remember what this day is all about, and that we are all one family so that there is always a place to go.

I also wish to apologize for leaving Mrs. Cruz's apartment so abruptly. Had I not done so, I would not have had the opportunity to complete something very important. Enrique and his mother have a quiet dignity in the face of tragedy that is almost overwhelming. That they made a complete stranger like me feel at home and part of their family is a very special quality. And I know that your counsel has helped them on their quest for healing.

That being said, I want you to accept the enclosed gift with certain conditions. Use it to make sure that Enrique may complete his education at your school through high school. With your help and guidance, he will go far. This will also take some of the burden from the back of Ms. Cruz. I would also like you to take Enrique to a baseball game to see the Yankees. You will not be a substitute for his father, but do it in memory of him.

You will notice the name and address on the check. I am sorry for the deception, but I would not have been able to do what I needed to do had I told you my real name. And I realize that my appearance does not coincide with the usual conception. All I can say is that I am all things to all people, and that when I do appear it as who I am, not as how some want me to be.

So Father, please continue your good works. I'll be watching. Merry Christmas!

Father Santos opened the second envelope and unfolded a check for a large amount of money. The funds would easily cover Enrique's continued education with much left to spare. The name and address startled him, and for a time, he did not believe that the check was real. However, the next business day, he contacted the bank that the check was drawn upon. To his astonishment, the check was real and the funds were available.

Mr. Taft never visited the church or Father Santos again. He returned to his home up north, and told the story to his family. Since that time, his family began again to spend the holidays together. Sometimes they were at his home, sometimes they were at the homes of his children or grandchildren. Regardless of which home the celebration of Christmas was held, they all had a renewed spirit of the holidays and what it meant to be together as a family.

Some years later the old man passed away, as all old men eventually do. At the funeral, his family finally met Father Santos who filled in the blank spaces of the Christmas visit of the father. Along with Father Santos was a tall, very handsome Hispanic man. Enrique told the old man's family how much it meant to have met their father. That serendipitous visit enabled the young man to complete high school and to begin college. For that, Enrique would always be grateful.

That Christmas holiday in the Bronx that one year meant so much to so many people. They learned the importance of giving, and to sharing, and community.

Even in two very different places people come together and hold out their hand in friendship and peace. As long as there people like Father Santos and Maria Cruz, there will always be someplace to go on Christmas.

Our Traditional Thanksgiving

Chapter I

The blood trail began at the open tailgate of the station wagon and continued down the driveway. From there it wound its way through the garage, leaving a wide swath of blood on the cement floor. Up and over the step leading from the garage to inside the house the path of blood remained unbroken. The trail of gore finally ended upon entering the kitchen. Lying on the kitchen table was the body, its leg missing and the head lolling over the side of the table with the eyes still open in a hideous leer. There on the table, with blood dripping over the side was our dinner. On the table was the Thanksgiving turkey that had been blown to bits by dear old Mom so that we could have a "traditional" Thanksgiving. Lest the reader become confused as to what a one-legged, blood drenched, partially de-feathered turkey has to do with "tradition," we need to step back a few days back in time to see how we arrived at this point.

Approximately one week prior to Thanksgiving, our family of six was sitting down for dinner. Mom had just set down a platter of meatloaf on the table, which my father began to pass around so that we could serve ourselves. Out family of six consists of Mom, Dad, me, and my three brothers. I was the eldest of the siblings; a junior in high school as I remember it. Everyone was chattering away at their own conversations; this was a typical Wednesday night dinner.

During a pause in the various back and forth chattering, my mother cleared her throat. "I've been doing some thinking about Thanksgiving," she said. Immediately, everyone stopped eating. We all knew from past experience that when Mom has been "doing some thinking" that something was afoot. Whatever Mom's plan entailed one could be sure that my Dad was going to bear the brunt of the work. It was not that he wanted to be involved; it was just that Mom figured that if she was going to be the brains then Dad was going to be the muscle. Whether he wanted to or not. Even as Dad rubbed his forehead in advance exasperation, we all knew that whatever idea Mom had in her head, this was not going to be your typical Thanksgiving.

"What is there to think about? We do the same thing every year. We go to the football game, come home, put the bird in the oven and eat. Is there something I am missing," Dad asked? An inquiry such as this inevitably led to Dad's downfall. Asking my Mom about her plans or ideas rarely led to a good outcome, especially where my Dad was concerned. Far better to not say anything and hope that Mom will get the clue that nobody is interested and we can all go on eating. No such luck today.

"This year, Mom said, we are going to have a traditional Thanksgiving." Sitting next to my brothers, my first thought was that she was going to make us dress up like Pilgrims and Indians and eat outside. No, that wasn't it, I decided. I couldn't see Dad dressed up like John Alden. Then I began picturing Charlie Brown and Snoopy passing out a Thanksgiving dinner to his friends consisting of popcorn, pretzels, and buttered toast. It wouldn't be that either. Every year we had turkey, stuffing, cranberry sauce, mashed potatoes and gravy, and pumpkin pie with whipped cream. Except for the year my youngest brother threw his already chewed piece of spearmint gum into the potatoes. We all wondered why the spuds had a vaguely green tinge to them, and had the telltale aroma of Wrigley's gum. Eighty-six the spuds that year. Other than that one hiccup, how could a Thanksgiving be any more "traditional" than what we'd been having as long as I could remember?

Apparently, Dad and I were on the same page. "What exactly is a traditional Thanksgiving, and how does it differ from what we've been doing?

"Well, this year, everything is going to fresh and natural. Nothing will be frozen or store bought. I have been doing extensive research, and I want that day to be just like it was on the first Thanksgiving."

A few seconds of silence passed while we all digested what Mom had said. If history was any indicator, her statement that "I have been doing extensive research" was code for "I read an article while waiting at the dentist's office and you can be assured that what I am about to say is preposterous and not particularly well thought through." Then she would spew indecipherable facts and other disconnected thoughts in our direction to the point that Dad would eventually lose his mind. When my Dad was ready to pop his cork, there was usually enough of warning so that we could all take cover. He would either suck in such a large breath of air that plates, utensils and the salt shaker began to be swept towards him by the negative air pressure being created, or his face would turn really red and a vein in head would begin to throb. I looked for some external indication to see if Dad was going to explode, but he was gazing off over the top of Mom's head as if he were watching ships on the horizon while he was seated alone on a tropical beach. No doubt that was what he was wishing that he was doing at that moment. Wanting to get a little skin in the game, and hoping to egg Mom on at the same time just for grins, I decided to venture into the uncharted Thanksgiving waters.

"Mom, you realize that turkey was not served at the first Thanksgiving. Not only that, Thanksgiving was not even a holiday until sometime in the 1940s. Are you saying that we are not going to have turkey and all the other stuff, but that you plan to serve corn, fish, and whatever it was that the Pilgrims ate that day? "

"Of course we are going to have turkey. And we are going to have stuffing, and mashed potatoes, and gravy, and all the rest of the things that we always have. The only

38

difference is that everything will be fresh and not frozen. There are farm stands where I can get everything I need; all the fruits and vegetables. Nothing will be store bought; if I can't get it at a farm then it will not be part of our dinner menu. It will be the best tasting, freshest Thanksgiving meal we have ever had. Just think, Mom mused, fresh squeezed apple cider; pumpkin pie made from a fresh pumpkin; stuffing made from fresh…" Her voice trailed off as it became obvious that she had not researched where to find farm-grown bread. "It will take a little longer to get things done, so I won't be able to go to the football game, but missing the game will be well worth it when you all taste how wonderful fresh food really is."

Everyone breathed a sigh of relief. This didn't seem to be all that bad. Although Mom's research did not include where the farm stands were or whether the stuff she wanted was even in season, it wasn't such a departure from our usual Thanksgiving fare for anyone to be particularly concerned. No doubt that Dad would have to do a little more running around to all these farm stands to get the vegetables and other food (wink, wink, nod, nod), but in the grand scheme of Mom's usual grand schemes, this appeared to be one of the more benign ones. That was because Dad had no intention of going anywhere but to the grocery store and buying everything there without telling her. He'd just put everything in brown paper bags so she would never know the difference. Unfortunately, as with any of Mom's simple plans, appearances can be quite deceiving. There was just one more major food item that needed to be addressed.

We all resumed eating, safe in the knowledge that we would not be roasting venison over a roaring bonfire on a spit in the back yard next Thursday. "Since you want everything fresh and not frozen, what day do you want me to go to the butcher to get the "fresh" turkey," Dad asked?

"Oh you do not have to go the butcher; I am going out into the woods next Wednesday to shoot a turkey."

"That's nice dear," Dad mumbled as he stuck another forkful of meatloaf into his mouth.

We all kept eating. Like the four second delay built into live television programs, all of us just sat at our places devouring meat, potatoes, and vegetables. Then it happened. Almost in unison, forks, knives or spoons went clattering to the table and we looked over at Mom. We all expected a "gotcha." Or an "I was just kidding." Or "you really don't believe that I said I was going to go out and shoot a turkey, did you?" Nothing of the sort was forthcoming; she continued to eat as if nothing unusual had occurred.

"What did you say? Did you just say that you were going to go out into the woods and shoot a turkey?" Dad was looking at her as if she had been speaking in tongues.

"Yes dear."

"Yes?" That is all you have to say? Just that you are going to go out, find a turkey and kill it? That's it? No different than you taking a stroll down the driveway to get the mail? Are you out of your friggin mind?" Man, this is going to be fun I thought.

"Well, that is really all there is to it. What is so difficult to understand?"

"Are you de-ranged? We live in a Levitt development; there aren't any woods around here for miles; how's that for starters? Look around you, there are hardly any trees in the entire neighborhood. Do you think that you are going to find a turkey hiding behind the dog house (The dog house in our backyard is the residence of our golden retriever, Mickey.). Oh, how about the fact that you have never fired a gun in your entire life? Even if you were an expert Marksman and are the reincarnation of Annie Oakley, we don't own a gun for you to use on your wild game expedition. Other than that I can't think of anything difficult to understand."

"Can I go with you, Mom? I want to go and shoot a turkey too? I have never shot a turkey before," seven year old Jack asked?

"Nobody is going anywhere and shooting anything," Dad said, his voice rising in decibel level as he continued. I don't know where you get these loony ideas from, Kate, but this one isn't going to fly."

"Turkey's don't fly, Dad. We learned that in school today when we were talking about Thanksgiving," ten year old Donny piped in. We all started to giggle because we could see that Dad was just getting warmed up. He ignored the giggles and kicked his voice up one more notch.

"There have to be places where you can go to get a fresh turkey without doing the killing yourself. The butcher has fresh turkey. Didn't that ever cross your mind?"

"Of course it did, dear. But it wouldn't be as fresh as one I shot and killed the day before Thanksgiving, would it? "

The coloring of Dad's face took on the hue of an overly ripe tomato. "How do you plan to do this? Like I said, we don't live anywhere near a place where you can hunt for turkey. And you don't own a gun, nor do you have a hunting license. Forget all of that stuff for a moment. What are you going to do with a turkey on the off chance you did shoot one? You are going to have to pluck the feathers, gut, and clean the bird. Do you even have a clue as to how one goes about doing that?"

"I've got it all worked out, Mom replied. I talked to Bill Yager about it this morning and he is going to loan me one of his shotguns or a rifle, or whatever it is, and show me how to use it. He also told me about a place he knows where I might find some turkeys. There is no need to worry about plucking and cleaning the turkey, I'll read up

on all of that before I head out early Wednesday morning."
Before Dad could say another word, Mom smiled, got up
from her chair and began to clear the table. This meant that
the conversation was over. Case closed. No more
discussion allowed. Everything was settled as far as Mom
was concerned and nothing more needed to be said.
Everyone knew that this scheme would turn out like all of
the other "ideas" that Mom dreamed up, which was
nowhere. Come next Thursday, the Butterball would be on
the table and Dad would be swearing about how and where
to begin carving. The holidays were safe.

A few days later on the Saturday before
Thanksgiving arrived, Dad and I went to the A&P to begin
to get the fixings for the following Thursday. These were
the kind of items that could not be procured fresh from
farms at this time of the year in New Jersey, such as sweet
potatoes, gravy, processed flower, pumpkin pie mix,
lemons for the lemon merengue pie, Bells Turkey
Seasoning, bread for the stuffing, onions, celery, and
chicken broth. In other words, everything was purchased at
a grocery store, just as it had been every year. All except
the turkey. There was no mention made of buying a turkey.
Nobody said anything more about turkey shoots or all
natural anything. Presumably, there was a contingency
plan in place once Mom realized the absurdity of her plan,
and that eventually she would send Dad out buy the turkey
at the A&P, and have it on the table at around 5 p.m. on
Thanksgiving. Little did we realize that we should have
asked a few more questions about the appearance of the
main attraction on Thanksgiving. Were we ever in for the
surprise of our lives.

Chapter II

There wasn't any inkling of what was to come later that day when we awoke on the morning before Thanksgiving. All of us kids arose at the usual time, which was about 6:30 a.m. and began the daily process of getting ready for school. After dressing and engaging in a few moments of hand-to-hand combat trying to get into the bathroom, we piled down the stairs and into the kitchen for breakfast. We were in a better mood than usual as we only had a half-day of school that day. Dad was going to come home early from work, pick us up, and keep us out of Mom's hair long enough so that she could finish cleaning the house and complete some prep work for the next day. She was bustling around trying to get us fed before we went out the door for school, getting out milk and cereal bowls and trying to keep her hair rollers from falling into our cereal. Dad was having his first cup of coffee. For the most part, an outsider would view this as a typical weekday morning at our house.

"What are your plans for the day, babe," Dad asked, seeking intelligence data. We had heard nothing about the shooting of turkeys since last week. I didn't think his attempt to gather information was too subtle, but Dad was not a subtle kind of guy. Mom was up for the task.

"I'll be going to the grocery store to pick up some odds and ends, and then I will be getting the bird ready for tomorrow."

Dad gave me a wink that implied everything was back to normal and we had nothing to fear. "I am going to take the boys out to bowl a few games after I pick them up from school. I figure that we should be back somewhere around four, will that give you enough time," Dad asked?

"Oh, that will be perfect. I should have everything done by the time you guys get home."

Dad never suspected anything amiss, although he should have. In retrospect, all the signals of covert action were in place. First, when Mom stops talking about something and goes silent, that is exactly when he should have become suspicious. All he had to do was take a short trip down memory lane to the time that she thought it would be a wonderful idea to pack up everyone and everything and move all of us to Australia (we were living in New Jersey at the time). She harped on Australia for a couple of weeks regaling us of tales of carefree days of warm weather and beaches. Australia was Shangri-La; the perfect place to raise the family. And then she seemed to have forgotten the entire idea. We heard nothing more of Australia, kangaroos, or the sweet little Qantas koala bear. That was until my Dad received a phone call at work a few weeks later from the Australian consulate wanting to schedule our entrance interviews. So he really should have been wondering what Mom had up her sleeve when she seemingly had given up on her idea of going off on a turkey shoot.

Second, there still wasn't a turkey anywhere in the house, alive or dead. Not in the refrigerator and not in the chest freezer in the laundry room was there even a package of chicken legs. Dad may have assumed that she was going to buy the turkey when she went off to pick up the "odds and ends" at the grocery that morning. There was a fatal flaw in his reasoning. Back in the day, as the kids liked to say, around 1968 to be exact, most turkeys purchased at grocery stores were frozen as hard as boulders. The only place one could purchase a "fresh" turkey back then was from a butcher shop. However, a fresh turkey purchased from a butcher was very expensive. And "organic" or "free range" turkeys did not yet exist; only rock-hard frozen ones, and they needed days to thaw out. But Dad would not have known that because he was a 1960s husband and father who never went near the stove unless it was to get a cup of coffee. He knew nothing about cooking a turkey and even less about where Mom put one after it was bought. So unless the bird rolled out of the fridge and landed on his foot, he wouldn't have thought twice about there being no turkey around- if he thought about it at all.

Finally, Mom was dressed differently that morning than usual. Think Elmer Fudd minus the hunting hat. She had on jeans (not unusual), a flannel shirt (unusual), and heavy boots almost akin to construction boots (very unusual). Dad being Dad, he wouldn't have noticed a truck rolling through the living room until after his second cup of coffee. Warning bells were going off everywhere, but he must have figured that the storm had passed. Either that or he was deaf.

We finished up our breakfast, grabbed our books and took off to catch the school bus. Dad was right behind us, heading to work. A little after noon, Dad picked us up from school instead of us taking the bus home. We stopped for a quick lunch at the local diner and then to the nearby bowling alley to bowl a few games. Nobody bowled particularly well, but there was quite a bit of laughing and good-natured jabs at each other to make for a fun afternoon. We all piled into the car for the ten minute drive to our house. It was about 3:30 p.m. Now we pick up where the story began.

I was sitting in the front seat of the car as we made the turn into our long driveway. We could see the back of Mom's car as we pulled. The tailgate of the station wagon was down, and there was something on the ground trailing into the garage that I couldn't make out. All of a sudden Dad jammed on the brakes and screamed, "Oh my God." Four very surprised children ricocheted around inside the car (no seat belts in those days) as a result of the panic stop. Dad turned the engine off and raced out of the car as fast as he could. Dazed yet knowing something serious was happening we spilled out of the car and ran after him. Then we saw the trail going from the back of Mom's car into the garage. There was no question that what we saw on the ground was blood. My father was screaming my mother's name as he raced through the garage. There was a bloody smear on the door knob leading into the laundry room, and another one on the door knob from the laundry room into the kitchen.

We barreled through kitchen door only to be brought up short by our father blocking the way a few feet inside. I knocked into him first, followed, in turn, by my three brothers. All except Dad fell to the floor. When we got to our feet we saw the reason for all the blood. There on the table, with its head hanging over the edge was our bloody, partially feathered, one-legged Thanksgiving turkey.

"KATE, my Dad thundered. WHERE ARE YOU? COME DOWN HERE THIS MINUTE."

Mom walked into the kitchen with a smile that exuded utter satisfaction. It was the look of accomplishment mixed with an "I told you so" grin. "Good Lord, John, what are you yelling about?"

"What am I yelling about? I am yelling about this, pointing to the kitchen table. What the $@*& is that?"

"Well, what does it look like," came Mom's reply?

"It looks like road kill that you found on the side of Kennedy Boulevard."

"I told you last week I was going out to shoot a turkey for Thanksgiving dinner. You know me John; I always do what I say I'm going to do."

My youngest brother lifted his head up to get a better look at the bloody mass on the table, turned his head and promptly barfed on my father's shoes. Looking down at the mess that had splattered Dad's shoes, my twelve year brother, Greg muttered under his breath just loud enough for me to hear, "that yack doesn't look any worse than the bird."

46

All of the color was beginning to drain out of my Dad's face. Instead of yelling back at Mom, he turned to me and said, "Help me get this mess cleaned up before a police car drives past our driveway and thinks that a murder has been committed." Greg started to mumble, "Well, a murder did take place…" but Dad pointed a finger at him before Greg could get any more words out. I just nodded and went outside and got the garden hose to begin spraying down the driveway and washing down the station wagon while Dad took care of the inside stuff. As a parting shot, Dad spun around as he was going to the garage to get a bucket, "Kate, I'm not finished with you, not by a long shot. We are going to sit down and talk about this once I have cleaned up this House of Horrors." Greg inched closer to Dad and said, "Cool, kitchen table or the living room?" The icy cold stare he received from Dad quickly disabused Greg that he was going to part of the post-slaughter discussion.

About twenty minutes later the garage was cleaned. The carcass had been placed on a large tray, covered in newspaper and put on top of my Dad's workbench out in the garage. Dad had no intention of letting the decedent reside in the fridge next to the edibles. Being that it was close to freezing in the garage, Dad figured what was left of the bird would stay there until he figured out how to dispose of it. All of us kids were hanging around in the garage looking at our holiday bird when he told us to go upstairs and play; he was going to have a talk with Mom and he did not want our inquisitive ears around. Upstairs we went, but we had no intention of missing out on the battle that was about to rage downstairs.

My room was located directly over the kitchen. I carefully removed the heat register in the floor. In the kitchen, there was heating grate on the ceiling close to the kitchen table. If someone were to stand under the grate, you could look directly down from the upstairs register and

47

see them. Down on our hands and knees, we would be able
hear every word that was being said. I probably could have
dispensed with the stealth activity. Dad was yelling loud
enough to have heard him had we been down the street.

"How did this happen, Kate? How did you manage
to find and blow apart a turkey in the seven or so hours
since me and the kids left the house this morning?

"That was easy, Mom replied. I drove out to
Colonial Park and walked around the woods. I was out
there for quite a while without seeing any turkey." It must
be explained that Colonial Park is a municipal park, where
hunting and fishing are not permitted. The most daring
activity in which one can engage in at the park is tennis.

"You took a shotgun to roam around Colonial
Park?" Where kids are being pushed around in strollers?
And people are hiking the trails? Walking? And riding
bicycles?

"Oh, there weren't any people around; the weather
is too cold for that. Besides, it is a school day. What
would kids be doing there on a school day when they were
supposed to be in school?" Dad began to massage his
temples. Mom continued to tell her story.

"I was walking for hours not seeing anything. Then
I heard it; the sound of a bird close by. I moved closer and
there it was. Tied up to a fence post in the yard near a farm
just outside the park was a big, fat turkey. It was just
standing there. So I went up to the front door and knocked.
When nobody answered the door, I went out back and shot
the turkey. It took all of my strength to drag that sucker
back to the parking lot and heave it into the wagon."

Dad looked up, the color already having left his
face. "Wait a minute. You walked into somebody's
backyard and shot their turkey? Just like that? And
dragged it away? No questions asked? Just amble up, see
a bird, shoot a bird, and drag the dead bird away?

"No, I knocked on the farm house door first. I told you, there was no answer. You didn't expect me to stand around there all day in the cold and wait for whoever owned the place to show up, did you?"

"No, no, of course not, Dad replied. Mom never noticed the sarcasm in his voice. "By the way, how did the turkey manage to lose its leg? I mean, I know that you shot the thing, but how close were you? When I picked it up to bring it to the garage, shotgun pellets fell out and were rolling around the garage floor."

"I was about five feet away. Let him have it with both barrels. I wasn't going to let it get away."

"No. No. There was always the chance it could have untied the rope and made its escape." Dad got up from the table. "Good. Good. You go out to a public park with a gun that doesn't belong to you. You don't have a hunting license. Then you trespass on someone's land and knock on their door, I presume to ask the occupants if you could go into their back yard and blow their turkey apart. When they don't answer, you decide to steal their turkey, shoot it at almost point-blank range with a double barrel shotgun, blow off its leg and fill it with enough buck shot so that we'll all get lead poisoning, drag it back through a public park and heave it into our car, drive home, take it out of our car leaving a forty foot long blood trail in your wake, and dump the bloody carcass on our kitchen table. Is that about right?"

"I think that about covers it,"

Dad moved his seat back from the table, got up from his chair and left the room. Dazed wouldn't begin to describe the expression on his face. "Where are you going," Mom asked?

"I am going out to the store to see if I can find something to put on the table for dinner tomorrow afternoon."

"It's six o'clock, dear. All the stores are closed now. The stores will not be open on Thanksgiving Day. They will not reopen until Friday morning. Besides, we already have a bird for tomorrow. All I have to do is clean it"

Upon hearing that, Dad took off his coat and went and got himself a glass from a kitchen cabinet. Next, he went to the fridge and dumped a handful of ice into the glass. He opened another cabinet door, found a bottle of Johnny Walker and pored himself a healthy shot. Leaning against the kitchen counter, he looked at his glass, and back at the bottle again and poured more scotch into the glass. Heaving a sigh he drained the glass in one gulp. He left the glass on the counter, took the bottle and climbed the stairs up to his office muttering something about "I'd turn her into the cops, but they would never believe me." Then he closed the door to his office. We did not see him for the rest of the night

Chapter III

It was a very quiet evening that night before Thanksgiving. With the exception of Dad, who stayed in his office all evening, we all ate dinner in silence, wondering what the next day was going to bring. The body of the deceased Thanksgiving dinner lay in repose in the frigid garage; all of us afraid to take a step in that direction for fear of one or the other parent screaming at us. When all of us kids went to bed that night, we did not know what kind of dinner we were going to have the next say.

One of our "traditions" on Thanksgiving Day was that the entire family went to see the football game at the local high school. Dad had gone to Summertime High School and played on their football team, so we tried never to miss a holiday game. I was a junior at Dad's alma mater, but did not follow in his steps regarding football. Mom would usually come along, but today, she stayed behind, responsible for our dinner, whatever that was going to be.

The day was grey, cold and windy; not unusual weather for that time of year. Dad was huddled up under his car coat and hat clutching a cup of hot coffee. Usually he was yelling at one player or another, however, today he was unusually quiet even though Summertime was doing what it did best when it came to football, which was losing. When I tried to talk to him about the game, he would only reply with one word answers or with a grunt. This was a signal that I knew all too well; that he was really pissed off at someone or something, which, given the stuff that went on the day before, really should not have come as much of a surprise. The best thing I, or anyone else, could do was to keep their trap shut and leave him alone.

Our high school was losing miserably that day and the cold, damp weather began to get to all of us. Midway through the fourth quarter when it became painfully obvious that there would be no comeback, my brothers, Dad, and I made our way to our car. Everyone was unusually quiet as we did not want to say anything to set Dad off, or to aggravate him any more than he seemed to be.

We pulled into our driveway. It was difficult to put the scene of yesterday out of our minds, so we were just a bit apprehensive. Fortunately, the station wagon was on the driveway, tailgate shut, and there were no blood trails. The garage door, which Dad shut before we left for the football game remained closed, another good sign. Everyone exhaled a sigh of relief.

Dad reached down, grabbed the handle to the garage door and pulled it up. Stepping inside the garage, we noticed that there were remnants of white feathers wafting through air, almost like down snowflakes. We all looked to where Dad had left the dead bird. It was gone. In its place was a mound of feathers on his work bench. Next to the feathers were the electric clippers Mom used to trim our second dog, an Old English sheepdog named Gus. Off to side of the work bench was a clear plastic bag, the contents of which were bloody and nasty looking. It appeared to my untrained eye that Mom had used the clippers to shave the turkey. She also apparently gutted the bird, leaving the entrails in the plastic bag by the bench. Everyone stood there for a moment before Dad muttered, "Christ on a crutch," and stomped into the house.

The first thing that we noticed when we got inside was a haze of acrid smoke hanging about three feet from the ceiling. We saw the smoke rising from the chimney as we were pulling into our driveway, but assumed that Mom had started a fire in our fireplace. And we could hear the "popping" of the wood. So it was obvious that she had the fireplace going. The second thing we noticed was that there wasn't the usual campfire wood type smell coming from the fireplace. The scent that assaulted our noses smelled like a mixture of rancid fat laced with old gym shoes. The final thing that we noticed was that all the windows in the kitchen and the den were open, which was unusual given that it was cold enough to snow outside.

Fighting off the onset of apoplexy, Dad marched into the living room, where the fireplace was, with a determination usually reserved for Olympic athletes; or kamikaze pilots. We were all close behind. We found Mom sitting in a chair close to the fireplace, a glass of brandy and water in one hand and a rotisserie crank in the other. On a spit in the fireplace was the turkey, now minus its head in addition to the one leg. What was left of the feathers was burning off as we watched, and the bird was blackening before our eyes. Rendered fat dripped on to the logs intensifying the flames giving the impression that one was looking into the bowels of Hell. Dad looked at Mom as if he was ready to toss her into the fireplace along with the turkey carcass. I was waiting for him to lose it so completely that the next time that I saw him would be in a padded cell. To my utter surprise and as calmly as I have ever seen my Dad, he quietly walked out of the room. He didn't say one word to my Mom. Not one syllable. A few minutes later, he returned with a garden hose that he had snaked from the outside through the open kitchen window and into the living room. "Bye, bye turkey," Dad said as he aimed a stream of water into the fireplace and onto the turkey and the logs. Now it was Mom's turn to go ballistic.

"WHAT ARE YOU DOING TO MY TURKEY? YOU HAVE RUINED OUR DINNER."

"No Hon, I probably just saved six lives. That's not a turkey; it is a creation from Hell. But hey, let's all play make believe, even though I wouldn't feed it to either Mickey or Gus. So, you go out and blast your garden variety turkey. Next, you shaved the turkey with dog shears. The bird has a heavier beard than Santa. Even I know that the way to pluck poultry is to stick it in boiling water and then pull the feathers out. You don't use clippers on it as if it were grooming a poodle. After the "plucking", you make a contraption to cook it on in the fireplace. Then you try to cook a one-legged, buckshot filled headless bird in our living room fireplace. That is, of course, assuming that the house didn't burn down in the process, leaving us all homeless. I do have to give you credit for the gizmo you put together to turn the thing so it can be charred equally on all sides. It is pretty ingenious. Rube Goldberg would have been proud"

You could just see the steam building up and ready to blow out of both of Mom's ears. Before she could start to yell, or to say anything, Dad began laughing. It started off as a chuckle and built to such an extent that he was bent over laughing. Tears were coming out of his eyes. I was worried that he had finally lost it; that the last two days fractured his sanity past the point of no return. Not quite knowing what to do and seeing Dad like this, the rest of us started laughing too. Five people were standing around a fireplace that was smoldering and dripping with a combination of water and turkey grease. In less than a minute, Mom's face softened into a smile, and then she too began laughing. With such a mess throughout the house and seemingly, no dinner for Thanksgiving, what else was there to do?

It was a little after five o'clock when we sat down for Thanksgiving dinner. All of us were in a good mood, laughing and joking with each other. Mom poured Dad and herself a glass of wine. We filled our glasses with either soda (a real treat) or apple cider (an even bigger treat) while I set the table and Mom got the food out of the oven (not the fireplace) and set it on the table. She sat down at the table and placed her napkin on her lap. "Time to say Grace, she said."

We bowed our heads and thanked God for the food. We also thanked him for not letting Mom burn down the house. Or get shot in the woods. Or for us not having to eat the bird she shot. We said Amen together at the end of the prayer. Dad looked lovingly at us all and said in a bright voice, "Okay troops, let's all dig in. With that, we carefully turned back the foil on our Swanson's Turkey TV dinners. Turkey, stuffing, mashed potatoes with butter, and green beans all in one small tin tray. It was not a "traditional" Thanksgiving dinner by any means. And we were all extremely thankful for that.

Ghosts of Christmas Past

The presents have all been opened, the wrapping paper secured in the trash can. Outside decorations have been removed and put into the upper reaches of the attic to be retrieved next year. All that remains of the Christmas tree is a pile of pine needles on the rug awaiting the assault of the vacuum cleaner. Another Christmas has come and gone and now comes the time when I sit back in my comfortable chair and assess the season's success.

To be sure, there is no bigger kid than myself when Christmas comes around. I love the lights, the bright wrapping paper, and especially going to church in the weeks leading up to Christmas day. There is something about the mystery of religion and the birth of the Lord Jesus which fills me with a wonder and warmth that only strengthens my joy at the coming of the season. I cherish the silly Christmas carols and the holiday television specials. Not a year goes by where I do not watch every version of Charles Dickens' A Christmas Carol at least once. And nothing can beat the look of shear happiness on the faces of my children, and now my grandchildren, when they open their presents from Santa on Christmas morning. But this year, and, to be honest, for the past few years, I have become more and more disillusioned with the holiday season. Not the usual low-level depression that tends to follow the orgy of parties and gift giving, but the sense that something in the season of lights and wonder has lost a bit of its luster. It wasn't until I walked into a local merchant's shop a few days after Christmas this year that I began to get a handle on what had been missing seasons past. And this small little shop in a little town renewed my joy of the holidays.

We all have our memories of Christmas past. I suspect that for most of us, our memories of Christmas' of our youth seem sweeter than those of the present. Kind of like our parents telling us about how good "the good ole days" were (now we tell our children the same thing), even though the good ole days weren't really all that good. These memories of Christmas seasons of our youth shape the traditions we share with our children, bringing a little bit of the past with us as we go along. But I digress.

As I was saying, a few days after Christmas, I wandered into a small shop along the main street in Bel Air, Maryland, a few miles from where I live. Evergreen potpourri scent filled the air as I entered, giving off the aroma of pine fragrance that our fresh cut hybridized, genetically engineered Christmas tree lacked. Moving from small room to small room, I glanced over the reproductions of faux Victorian merchandise on sale for half of the cost that they were a few days ago, when something caught my attention. It wasn't anything that I saw on one of the store shelves, but it was a smell that seemed to be out of place with the rest of the scents that were bombarding my senses. I couldn't immediately place the smell, but it was vaguely familiar; something that I had definitely experienced before. The smell was not unpleasant, but it was very distinctive, and I wracked my brain trying to place where I had encountered it before. As familiar as it was, I could not reach back far enough into my memory to identify it. Taking a few more steps, I recognized the originator of the scent and understood immediately why it had made such an impression on me. It was a steam radiator hissing along a back wall of the shop. As odd as it might sound, this sight, sound, and damp smell recharged my joy of the season. Does it sound just a touch preposterous? Come with me and I will explain how and why it made me so happy.

For the first nine plus years of my life, I lived in the Bronx in a fairly old five storey apartment building. In the corner of every room, there was a radiator which provided the heat for that particular room. You could always tell when the heat was coming on by sound the steam pipes made as the steam began to course through the pipes. After a while, you could hear the whistling of the relief valve on the radiator. Not only did one have to contend with the noise the relief valves made, but also with the necessity of placing a small pan or bowl under each one to catch the water that dripped from them. One of my earliest chores in the winter was to go around every few days collecting and emptying the pans. Mom often would drape clothes on the radiator to dry, especially coats, scarves and mittens. After they finished drying, the garments always felt so toasty and comforting when you put them on to go out in the winter cold, as if you were the filling of a fruit turnover being wrapped in warm pastry dough. And then there was the smell that the radiator gave off.

The smell was one of heat, a damp smell that was unique to itself. It was not a harsh smell, but one that seemed to be complimentary to any other aroma in the house. I always associated it with Christmas, when the radiator's warmth melded with the aroma from the Christmas tree and filled the entire apartment with the fragrance of evergreen. In the days before Santa's arrival, I would rush home from school with the anticipation of what new smell would be mingling with that of the tree and the radiator. Would it be the sugar cookies Mom made while I was at school, cut into the shapes of stars, or Christmas trees, dusted with red and green sprinkles? Or maybe today there would be Toll House cookies baking. Those were my favorite because I could always manage to swipe a few chocolate morsels when Mom wasn't looking. Other times it was the aroma of hot cocoa that hit my nose upon my arrival. I would sit down and do my homework sipping the cocoa while Mom finished up the last of the Christmas cards. She would look up from her cards and laugh, going to the sink to get a wash cloth to wipe away my "marshmallow mustache." In the days before video games and cable television, the season was not as visceral, but more olfactory. We experienced the holidays with all five of our senses. Yet the one sense that always seemed to remind me of yuletide past was my sense of smell. We went to bed on the nights leading up to Christmas with the aroma of cookies, peppermint, and evergreen in our heads. There was the distinct scent of our church during Advent; the aroma of frankincense and myrrh. The Italian grocery stocked Christmas cakes and cookies that you could only get during the season. They had an aroma all their own. Yes, smell was the sense that made Christmas real to me as a child.

Anticipation of Christmas morning began weeks in advance, when the first holiday decorations went up in the stores the day after Thanksgiving. Each shopkeeper would decorate their shop in their own unique style, unlike the cookie cutter decorations found in today's malls and big box department stores. There were no LED lights, or plastic ornaments; they were made of real glass and would shatter if dropped on the floor. Real evergreen and holly garland was hung in the stores. The only colors you would see were green, red, and the occasional gold unless the storekeeper had bubble lights. And all the lights would be blinking. Going into the toy store or the hobby shop as a child (not a Toys R Us in sight back in my youth) was a treat because you could be sure that you would be given either a candy cane or a Christmas cookie by the man or woman who owned the store. My mother always was the one who did the Christmas shopping. She did it during the week and it was always at night after my Dad came home from work. When I was old enough, probably around the age of five, Mom took me along on her holiday shopping outings. And although it couldn't possibly have been snowing each time we went out to do the shopping, it seemed as if it was, just to make the atmosphere a little more festive. I could never figure out, at least not until I was a teenager, how the store owners could decorate the inside of their establishment with real snow because real snow melts; and theirs never did, staying pearly white the entire season. Little did I know that it came out of a can? Hot chocolate was my reward for carrying the bags that held those secret treasures that would magically appear under the tree on Christmas morning. And no matter how hard I tried to find those presents, and believe me I tried, I never discovered the hiding places.

Another sign that Christmas was nearing was me and Dad going out on a frosty Saturday morning to buy our Christmas tree. Unlike today, we didn't get our tree from a parking lot located in a strip mall or from Home Depot. Dad and I went to the train rail yard in Hunt's Point in the Bronx and bought the tree right off one of the freight trains that brought the trees in from one of the New England states. Even though it seemed to be bitterly cold on those December mornings it never had any effect on us, because we would stop and warm ourselves by the fires burning in the 55 gallon oil drums interspersed throughout the rail yard. Although we were walking around a massive train yard in New York City, I felt as if I was in an evergreen forest. The scent of fresh cut pine was so strong you believed that the smell stayed on your clothes for days afterwards. Dad seemingly spent hours choosing the perfect tree, and they always were perfect in my eyes, no matter what they looked like. Mom always had some comment to make about the tree. It was either too big or too small, or too skinny or too fat for the apartment. This would be the signal for Dad to get out the saw and start hacking away until Mom approved. Then he would drill holes in the walls and string wire around the tree so it wouldn't topple over. We tried not to laugh as the living room became a wasteland of pine branches. No matter how hard he tried, the tree always had a list to it that would have made the Titanic proud. Somehow, the tree would make it through the holidays without hitting the floor. And I definitely learned some new words that mom told me not say anymore and would never tell me what they meant.

Our excitement peaked on Christmas Eve. After dinner, we would all sit in the living room, the tree ablaze with light, ornaments in place and the floor strewn with the plastic silver icicles that had fallen from the branches. Mom would make everybody hot chocolate with marshmallows, bring out the homemade cookies and we would sing Christmas carols or watch that absurd Yule Log on television. All this was her attempt to tire us out and get us to bed so she and my Dad could become the real Santa Claus. As hard as she worked at, Mom could never get us kids quite settled down. We would go off to bed with one eye open and one eye closed, trying to get a glimpse of the shadow of the big red fellow who was going to reward us for being good all year. Eventually, the other eye would close without us ever getting a glance of St. Nick.

Christmas morning came all too early for my parents and none too early for us. The floor under the tree, only a few hours ago barren of gifts was now covered with brightly wrapped presents. While it seemed as if there were hundreds of boxes in all shapes and sizes to open, the joys of the morning lent to numerical exaggeration. My parents were not poor, but neither were they rich, so our vision of the number of presents was greater than reality. No matter. We opened our three dollar model airplanes and our two dollar jumble of army men and were happy beyond imagination. We groaned when the package contained clothes, gifts from our grandparents and other relatives, but the stern stares from Mom and Dad put a quick end to any complaints. After a while, there were no more presents left to unwrap, so Mom and Dad went out to the kitchen to have their coffee, while we played with our toys, warmed by the heat from the hissing radiator behind us. It was only when I had my own children that I finally realized why Santa never seemed to bring presents to my parents. It was a question that I always wanted to ask them, but I never did because, quite frankly, I didn't want to hear that they had spent all of their money on us, and had nothing left over for themselves.

Times change; we grow older and we exchange our childhood toys for the trappings of responsibilities. Simpler times have been replaced by two income earner families, with hardly enough time to think about Christmas' past, let alone time to enjoy the Christmas present. Mom and Pop toy stores and hobby shops are long gone and forgotten, their places being taken by Toys R Us, Target, and Wal-Mart. Nothing is unique anymore; you can purchase the same item in a big box store in Miami as you can in Seattle. And if you don't want to be bothered with the crowds in the stores, not to worry, you can always shop from the comfort of your home on the Internet.

Christmas now begins with stores being decorated for the holidays by the middle of October. By the time Thanksgiving rolls around we have been bombarded with so many ads on television, and Christmas catalogues in the mail that all we can wait for is for the whole thing to be over and done. The Christmas cookies that we bake, if we bake any at all, are more likely to come from a pre-made roll or from a tube we squeeze onto a baking sheet- already fully decorated- than from a mixing bowl. The Christmas trees we put up in our house, if not artificial (visions of aluminum trees from Charley Brown's Christmas are dancing in my head), have been cross pollinated and hybridized to the point that they have virtually no scent at all. But don't let that disappoint you. You can always buy a can of pine scented Febreze to substitute for the real thing. Without question, few if any homes are still heated with steam, where the end point is the whistling of the relief valve.

The gifts that we give can no longer be purchased for less than twenty dollars. Parents are bludgeoned by media that they are somehow "less than" if they do not have the latest, four hundred dollar video gaming system under the tree for their child on Christmas morning. Along with the gaming system it is required that you purchase sixty dollar video games and expensive add-ons until the once reasonable holiday has become a six month debt payment or a precursor to bankruptcy court.

Yes, Christmas was different when I was a child more than forty years. Still, as I walked out of that store a few days after Christmas, I left with a smile on my face. Too often we do not enjoy the present for what it gives us, rather we celebrate the things we remember as a child with a reverence that is unreasonable. We cannot go back to those days; they are gone forever. But if you combine the joy you take from the holidays with your own children now and remember the joys of your past put into perspective, the holidays will be what you want them to be. I know that my children look forward to the traditions that my wife and I have introduced over the years almost as much as they look forward to the loot, and hopefully they will pass on some of these traditions to their children, and add new ones that they come up with along the way. Now, if only I could pass along to them a radiator and scent of steam heat, what glorious Christmas' they will have.

Your Goose is Cooked

Mmmmm. The aroma of thyme, sage, and rosemary float through the house in waves. All of the hustle and bustle. Cabinet doors opening and closing. Refrigerator door slams as someone yells, "Get me another beer." "Hey Grandma, when will dinner be ready?"

I sat down in a chair in my in-laws house early in the afternoon of Christmas Day, watching and trying to stay out of the way of all the craziness. Presents had already been opened and a light lunch consumed. Before too long, plates of food would be placed upon the table for the traditional Christmas dinner. Hoards would descend upon the dining room, battling for food. The tussle for grub would be so frenzied that it would have been a good defensive measure to outfit the children with football helmets to insure against head injury. I would wait until the second wave, content in the knowledge that I would not be singled out this year as "The Man Who Messed up Our Dinner." It was only one short year ago that I had not been so fortunate. Just sit back and listen to this short story. See if you decide to help out and cook something for your next big family dinner.

Christmas is a time of tradition. There are the Christmas carols, the festive lights, Christmas cookies and holiday parties. We decorate our houses, visit friends and relatives, exchange presents, and watch our favorite movies. The traditions are as distinctive as the people involved in the tradition making. I have a friend who decorates her Christmas tree in a New York Yankees décor. Gauche, but she lives in New Jersey, not an area high on the list of taste consciousness. Some other friends of mine travel out into the wilderness and cut down a fresh tree. They make a day of it, bringing a picnic basket full of wine and some cheese. It is a ritual that so far has not resulted in the loss of fingers. It is also theft, since they do not go to a tree farm, they just wander off into the nearest forest and use a saw to cut down a tree that will fit into their living room, then they lug it back to their car, hoping that they do not get caught by the local constabulary. They have been doing it for years.

Many other holiday traditions revolve, unsurprisingly, around food. The tradition may be the type of food, a specific recipe, or date determined gathering. Some Italians follow the traditional seven-course Christmas Eve meal which leans heavily on seafood. Turkeys and hams are also a popular choice for Christmas day meals, as more of these two types of meat and poultry are sold from Thanksgiving through Christmas than at another time of the year. A peculiarly Maryland tradition is to serve sauerkraut with the holiday meal. Along with the ubiquitous Three-Bean Salad and sauerkraut, no Maryland Christmas dinner would be complete without the Berger cookies, which consists of a tasteless white cookie topped with an entire can of chocolate frosting. You think that I am kidding? Come on down here to Maryland, where I live, and you'll find Berger cookies in almost any grocery store.

Holiday traditions abounded in my family, most of them far too dreary to be the subject of a Christmas story. My first wife and I did start a holiday tradition that lasted as long as our marriage did, which was about ten years. We decided that we would split the holidays with our respective families; we would spend Christmas Eve with my family and Christmas day with her family. Owing to this new tradition and a complete disability in her family's ability to produce edible food, I learned how to cook.

I am going to add a little background information here that is important for the reader to understand all that follows. Names have either been changed or omitted to protect the innocent, as well as for my own safety.

When I first married I was only 21 years old, and hardly a gourmand. Neither was my bride. And to be completely generous, she needed complete instructions, along with diagrams and schematics, on how to boil water. Now, my mother was a fairly good cook. She was inventive and had a certain flair for the dramatic. There were, however, a few flaws in her culinary arsenal. First of all, she had a penchant for getting into the cooking sherry a little early in the day. Consequently, she might only get to the stove a few times a week, and when she did, there tended to be a measure of inconsistency to the cuisine. The other problem was that once Mom latched on to a recipe that she liked, we got it almost daily for the foreseeable future. One can only eat so much Turkey Tetrazzini before it becomes unpalatable, no matter how masterful the dish is. To this day, some thirty years after leaving home, I have never touched Turkey Tetrazzini again, nor will I ever let it touch my palate for as long as I live. Just thinking about Turkey Tetrazzini gives me the shivers and an unmistakable surge of bile makes its way into my throat.

When it came to my then mother-in-law, her approach to cooking was to be as inventive as possible and then cook everything to the consistency of burnt tree bark. Part of this had to do with the fact that her husband would not eat anything that was not well done. Actually, that is being way too generous. It had to be charred before he would touch it. It did not matter whether it was meat, rice, potatoes, chicken, pudding, oatmeal, or reheating leftovers, everything was overcooked. Even the coffee was burnt, having the consistency of the stuff that burps up from the La Brea Tar Pits. Smoke would rise up from the coffee cup like witches brew and it had a propensity to melt things. Like spoons and dental fillings.

Given that my wife couldn't (or wouldn't) cook, it was left up to me to learn how and take on the task of preparing the nightly meal. Either that or go broke going out to eat every night. I took out a subscription to Gourmet magazine, watched cooking shows, browsed through cookbooks in bookstores. Little by little and through trial and error, I began to learn the basics of putting together edible meals. In very little time, I could rival my mother-in-law (not a particularly difficult task), and was catching up quickly on my own Mom.

The point of this story is not, however, my journey to becoming an accomplished cook. This is about how holiday traditions can rear their ugly head and bite one in the backside. This story is about a tradition that never was and a goose that never should have been cooked. Thoroughly confused? Follow closely.

From the time my Christmas memories began until the time of my first marriage; probably a span of about sixteen years or so, there was no traditional Christmas meal at my family home, at least not one that I can remember. Without question, we all did sit down to eat together, but, for the life of me, I couldn't tell you what was on the menu or who was there to eat it. We probably had turkey a number of years, or possibly a ham on occasion. But we could have had steak, pot roast, or roast beef as well. Heck, it is also possible that we had cereal and milk a time or two. It is also possible that one year we had goose, but somehow I doubt it. The point is that we did not have any one singular traditional dinner menu for Christmas. Believe me, if we had the same thing sixteen or seventeen years in a row, I would have remembered what it was that I had been stuffing down my throat all those years.

Once married and Christmas day dinner shifted to my in-laws, there was no traditional meal either. The only rule was that no turkey would be served because everyone in the house detested turkey. A charred standing rib roast was more likely, but whatever the unrecognizable carbon encrusted thing on the serving platter was, it definitely was not going to be a turkey.

Fast forward a number of years and to Wife Number Two. She could cook very well and we really enjoyed cooking together. We loved to spend an entire afternoon working in the kitchen together trying out some new recipe. It was fun. It was cheap. No restaurant required. We were both in college at the time and money was tight, so we had to be inventive with both money and menu.

As was expected, I had to meet the in-laws before getting married. The time for the visit was to be at Thanksgiving, so not only would I be meeting my wife's mom and dad, I would be on display before a good chunk of the rest of her family. To say that this was going to be uncomfortable would be quite the understatement. Meeting new people has never been a problem for me, and I am generally not concerned about making a good impression. In other words, I clean up well. But when you have about twenty or more pairs of eyes watching your every move, your style can get moderately crimped. I figured that a good ice breaker might be to bring along something that I had made to be included in the Thanksgiving feast. One of my delectable winter desserts would endear me to the family, hopefully to my future wife's mother.

I decided to make a cranberry pie, a dessert that I had made many times before. In fact, I had made this pie so times that I no longer needed to consult a recipe. Cooking with cranberries can be a tricky thing. Anyone who has ever popped an uncooked cranberry into their mouth knows that it is sour and tart. Cranberries need sugar in order to make them edible. Thus, the cranberry pie contained brown sugar, regular sugar, and for good measure, maple syrup. Not a problem. Even though I was somewhat rushed getting everything together because of last minute school papers and exams, the pie looked beautiful when it came out of the oven. This was going to be a wonderful dinner and the pie was going to be the star attraction that would help endear me to my wife's family. I was going to make a great impression. Or so I thought.

A boisterous and noisy crowd greeted us when we walked through the door. My wife's mother is a sweet woman of Italian heritage. That meant that all of the furniture in living room was encased in plastic. My future wife has three younger brothers, all of whom are married. I was offered a beer, which definitely helped with the nerves, and ushered into the living room where the men were watching football. I was introduced all around, and began to think that this was going to be a snap. Then I met my wife's father.

Although Don is at least two inches shorter than I, he was one imposing dude. He had a deep bellowing voice that evoked images of a drill sergeant. That made sense as he was a retired Master Sergeant, having served over twenty years in the Air Force. I introduced myself and held out my hand, waiting for it to be crushed. I definitely was not disappointed; my hand feeling as if the finger nails were going to shoot off the ends of my digits. His eyes narrowed, and the first words out of his mouth were not "How are you doing?" or "Pleased to meet you." They were something much more welcoming. "What the hell is cranberry pie? Bernie's Mom told me that was what you were bringing and I thought she was pulling my leg. I have never heard of anything as asinine in all my life. Pumpkin pie, cherry pie, those make sense. What is a cranberry pie anyway?"

Wanting to say it is a pie and there are cranberries in it seemed to be just a touch snide and definitely would not have gotten me off on the right foot. I began to say that it was something that I made for the holidays and that it looked festive. But I was so flustered that I couldn't get the words coherently. I was making these guttural sounds that were not words. Don looked at me for a couple of seconds and shouted "Bernie, (that is what he called his daughter) you bring home a guy who stutters? I ask him a simple question and he can't speak, all he does is make noises like he is choking to death. I thought that I was going to have to perform the Heimlich maneuver on him." With that, he waved his hands in a sign of dismissal and walked back to his recliner and plopped himself down and turned his attention to the television. I sat down and stared at the football game and did not make one sound.

After what seemed like an eternity, it was time to find our places at the table for Thanksgiving dinner. I managed to keep a low profile during the repast, making small talk with a couple of my wife's siblings who were sitting on either side of me. After we finished the main course, I helped washing the dishes in the hope that I would make amends for the rocky start. Once this was done, the various pies and desserts were placed on the table and all were called back. I was keeping my fingers crossed that I was going to come through this final stage of dinner unscathed and I could depart having successfully passed the familial scrutiny.

My wife's mother commented on how lovely my pie looked. She passed up on the traditional pumpkin pie to sample a piece of my dessert. It was obvious to me that she was making this gesture to be kind, and I was very grateful. Unfortunately, almost immediately upon her taking the first bite, I could tell that something was wrong. Her jaws were moving slowly as if she were trying to identify exactly what she was eating. I had no doubt that had she not been in a room full of people she would have spewed the contents of her mouth across the dining room table. "My, oh my, this pie is certainly tart. She was definitely not kidding. I immediately put a piece of the pie into my mouth and it was almost more than I could do not to gag. In the rush to make the pie, somehow I had neglected to put any sugar in it. I yakked the pie into my napkin and sputtered, "There's no sugar in it; I forgot to put any sugar in the pie."

Needless to say, I began to apologize to my wife's mom, who was downing water to get the taste out of her mouth. That wasn't good enough for Don. "What the hell are you trying to do, kill my wife?" Yes, that was my plan all along, to bump off my future in-laws with a killer cranberry pie. "Oh Don, he didn't do it on purpose," his wife said trying to diffuse everything. "What do you expect anyway? Who the ever heard of making a cranberry pie anyway," Don continued on. Having heard this question a few hours earlier I already had a pithy reply on the tip of my tongue. Only my wife's fortuitous placing her hand on my arm and squeezing it until it went numb prevented the overturning of chairs and the table, and possible injury to innocent bystanders. After another five minutes or so of invective, Don ran out of steam. Coffee was served, and had it not been that I had no stomach for being arrested for drunk driving, I would have downed the contents of the liquor cabinet. The only safe thing to do was to beat a hasty retreat, which we did as soon as we finished coffee.

Christmas was only six weeks away and another trip up north to visit my wife's parents was in the offing. I had no doubt that I was probably the last person that Don would want to find under his Christmas tree on the 25th of December. Under no circumstances would anyone with any intelligence even think of proposing to cook something for Christmas dinner after the cranberry pie fiasco. But alas, I am not just anybody, and few friends or relatives would consider me to be the sharpest tool in the shed. So when my wife and I were sitting around our apartment discussing Christmas at her parent's house a couple of weeks hence, the thought of my cooking anything for Christmas dinner was perhaps the farthest thing from her mind.

"You know, I began, I was thinking of cooking one of the traditional dishes from my childhood for Christmas dinner at your parents. Being out here in California, I miss the holiday traditions my family had when I lived in New Jersey. I thought doing one of them for your folks would be nice."

To say that my wife was skeptical would be mild. "Didn't you have enough grief with the pie? I know that your heart is in the right place, but I'm not so sure about your head; it might not be on your shoulders if you show up there with any food that is not store bought."

"This won't be like the pie; it is much easier than that. All I have to do is put it in the oven and roast it. As a matter of fact I'll cook it at your mom's house so it won't have to be reheated and I won't run the risk of it being dried out."

He color returned to my wife's face. "Oh, you are going to do a bird? That's a relief and actually, it will be a real help to my mom. She always has so many people over for the holidays that she is cooking for days before and is exhausted by the time dinner is over. Just promise that you are not going to be baking any pies. Please."

"You have nothing to worry about (which, was when she should have started worrying, especially when I didn't tell her that the "traditional" dish was a roast goose, not a turkey, but, then again, she didn't ask.). I will take care of everything." Little did I realize that finding a goose would be so difficult? I went from grocery store to grocery store; nobody stocked either fresh or frozen goose. Meat department managers routinely broke out in paroxysms of laughter when I inquired. Nobody knew where to order one from; they had never had a request for goose before. Needless to say, my frustration began to build.

Finally, after a few days of driving all over the greater Sacramento area, I was able to find someone who would order a goose for me. There was only one problem; a fifteen pound goose cost more than seven dollars a pound. That was over one hundred dollars for a relatively small bird. And, we're not talking about 2013 prices; this was back in the early 1990s, when a turkey cost about thirty-nine cents per pound when it was on sale. That means I could have purchased about two hundred seventy pounds of turkey for what I spent on a fifteen pound goose. But hey, Christmas only comes around one time a year, right, and who the hell wants to eat two hundred seventy pounds of turkey anyway?

I picked up the goose from the butcher the day before we were to travel to my wife's parents, which was going to be sometime in the early afternoon of Christmas Eve. To be honest, I didn't look at the bird when I picked it up. It was a fresh goose, cold and wrapped in that plastic that all poultry is comes in when you purchase it at a grocery store. I gave the money to the butcher and he gave me the goose in a brown paper bag. Once home I put the bag in the refrigerator and didn't think much more about it. The next day, we loaded the car, including the goose, which was placed into an ice filled ice chest. Upon arrival at the in-laws the bag was put into fridge. We went on to enjoy a very happy and fun evening with all of my wife's relatives. Needless to say, the job of getting children to bed and keeping them there while the adults finished wrapping presents was quite the chore. In all of that time, I gave no thought to the bird residing quietly in the kitchen. Why should I? Tomorrow was going to be a snap. I was going to wish that I hitched a ride on Santa's sleigh returning to the North Pole.

Watching children open their presents on Christmas morning, I believe, is the greatest joy of the entire holidays. Their expressions are priceless. At least for the first half hour or so, until the first toy is broken, or the realization hits that something requires batteries and there a none to be found. Anywhere. Then there arises a cacophony of screaming, crying, and foot stomping. Somewhere within the first ten minutes into the bedlam, I turned to my wife and asked, "How long do you think it will take for the bird to cook?" "It is a fifteen bound bird and figure twenty minutes or so per pound," she replied. Doing the calculations in my head I said, "It should be done in about five hours. We should get started on it now."

I took the bag containing the goose out of the fridge and set it out on a counter and turned to grab a roasting pan. My wife moved in behind me and took the bird out of the bag, instantly notice the sticker on the outside. "You paid over one hundred dollars for a fifteen pound turkey? Have you lost your mind," she said in a not so quiet voice? "Shhhhh. It's not a turkey, it's a goose. Nobody has to know how much we paid for it. Yes, it was more than I wanted to pay for it, but it'll be worth it." She glared at me with heat that would have melted the polar ice cap. "Wait a minute; you bought a goose instead of a turkey? What possessed you to buy a goose?" Without waiting for my response, she continued, "It better be worth it. If it isn't the best piece of poultry anyone has ever tasted, I am going to carve you up and use you for cat food when we get home."

Deciding that there was no way I was going to win I prepared the roasting pan and my wife began cutting up onions and celery for the stuffing. I cut the plastic outer wrap off the goose and was about to grab it to rinse it off, when something didn't seem quite right. For the most part, the bird had the appearance of any other turkey, chicken or duck. It had two legs, two wings, and a large hole in its caboose where the stuffing was supposed to go. Unlike other poultry that I had cooked in the past, the goose was long and squat, its appearance more like a low-rider car without the bounce or the wheels. I turned to my wife while holding the bird by one leg and said, "Does this thing look a little strange to you?"

She looked at the piece of poultry I was holding like she was examining a diamond through a jeweler's loupe for flaws. Then she poked it a couple of times. "I don't think there is much meat on this thing, she said. There might be enough meat to make a couple of sandwiches, but that would be pushing it."

She was correct in her assessment. A Cornish game hen has more meat on its bones than did the goose I was holding. Conservatively speaking, there was about thirteen pounds of bone and maybe two pounds of meat on the goose, and that was really pushing it. There was virtually no breast or thigh meat anywhere to be found. This was one lean goose. It was also not going to feed anywhere near the ten to fifteen people who were going to have Christmas dinner.

My wife was standing next to me with her head on the counter shaking. I wasn't sure at first if she was laughing or crying. Between spasms of laughter she asked me what I was going to do now, and then something about me being in a world of shit, followed by the suggestion that I might want to start running away before her dad found out and came after me with his shotgun. Needless to say, I did not find her comments either helpful or funny.

There was nothing really left to do but to stuff the thing and put it into the oven and to slink away hoping that nobody would look to see how the cooking was coming along. Unfortunately, I was going to have to face the music once the goose was cooked and put onto a serving platter. Of course, I was delegated to carve it in front of everyone, and visions of Chevy Chase cutting into the turkey on "Christmas Vacation" and not sugar plums were dancing in my head. My wife's mother, my wife, and I were working in the kitchen getting odd and ends ready to put on the table when I thought it might be a good time to apologize in advance for everyone going hungry on Christmas Day.

"Mom, I am really sorry about the goose. I didn't know that they were so lean when it came to meat. I have never seen such a skinny bird."

"Oh, that's okay Bob. I didn't want to say anything to you because Bernie told me that it is one of your family's holiday traditions. Don used to go hunting for goose all the time when we lived in Michigan. Always knew there wasn't much meat on them. We used to have to roast at least two of them at a time so there would be enough for everyone. Since I knew that there wasn't going to be much goose to go around, I asked Pat's wife to do a turkey. She is bringing it over, so we'll be fine.

At that moment Don stuck his head into the kitchen and grinned. "I had a feeling that you didn't have a clue about goose. A family tradition my ass. I think you have seen A Christmas Carol one too many times? I just hope that you are not going to saddle my daughter with any more of your family traditions. She'll wind up as skinny as a rail and will blow away with the slightest gust of wind."

I breathed a sigh of relief for having dodged a bullet. More likely a shotgun shell. When I sat back and thought about it later, I had to admit that the "goose tradition" had never been a tradition at all. Christmas at my house lacked any tradition; unless, perhaps it was my Dad yelling and upsetting everyone on Christmas morning. Now, that was a tradition all of us kids could count on like clockwork. When I was growing up, all I wanted was for our family to have the type of Christmas that all of my friends had. Theirs was one of people opening presents, enjoying themselves, eating dinner together and having fun, just like in one of those Norman Rockwell pictures. I inserted the goose as a tradition for the dinners at Christmas that were always so painful for me; where nobody would talk to each other and we couldn't wait for everyone to finish eating so we could scurry away from the table as fast as humanly possible. Over the years, I selected bits and pieces of holidays I had watched on television or read about in books. I then morphed them into a happy Christmas household, complete with a holiday goose.

Christmas at my wife's house was a blast. We all laughed at my goose and how scrawny it was. After tasting a small piece, I decided that turkey was vastly superior. And by unanimous vote it was determined that I would no longer be permitted to bring food to any future family gathering. Too bad. I was going to do my traditional whole suckling pig for their next Fourth of July picnic.

Turning a New Page

Chapter I

They were everywhere you looked. On shelves, piled on end tables, in the cabinets where the dishes should have been. That was just on the first floor. The stairs leading down to the basement were lined with them as was almost every inch of the basement. Bookcase upon bookcase, shelve upon shelve. The stairs leading up to the basements were loaded too. Two bedrooms had been taken over, crammed floor to ceiling with books. Books were everywhere. There was Dickens, Poe, Trollope, Hemingway, and Carroll. The shelves held Serling, Bradbury, Huxley, Orwell, and King. There were books about presidents, kings, dictators, and emperors. There were books on war, and on peace (as well as War and Peace), and every subject in between. Shelves upon shelves contained fiction, the classics, history, biography, political science, sociology, philosophy, natural science, law and religion. Some of the books were old and others recently purchased. There was hardback and soft cover. Thousands upon thousands of books, bought by, given to, and collected by Oliver Tremlow.

Mr. Tremlow (Ollie to friends and family), had lived the better part of his seventy-four years in the quaint Massachusetts town of Newburyport. For many years, Ollie drove to work every weekday, and some weekends too, into Boston. He was an attorney, now retired, and he loved his work and he loved the city. In short order he realized that Boston would be too expensive a place to live, and not the place to raise a family. After some searching and researching, he decided on Newburyport, a small hamlet by the sea roughly 35 miles from Boston. Housing prices had not yet skyrocketed and the T had not yet been extended to its furthest reaches. It was perfect place to raise a family.

Besides being an attorney, a husband, and father, Ollie's passion was reading and collecting books. When not either reading or adding to his collection he was a devoted baseball fan, alternately cheering and cursing his beloved Boston Red Sox. As far as books were concerned, he had been a voracious reader since childhood, losing himself in science fiction and history. Over the years, his choice of reading material became more eclectic, adding biographies and books on such diverse topics as rats, whales, pigeons, bananas, and Hostess Twinkies to his collection. Ollie did not collect rare books, mainly because he believed that his books were living breathing things. He did not want his books to be perched behind glass not to be touched, nor the pages to be turned, nor the words not to be examined and enjoyed. Keeping books under lock and key, he believed, would not serve the purpose for which they were intended.

Having a family of small children meant that, in the beginning, older books were boxed and put into storage as newer ones were purchased so that there was room for the bipeds (and a few quadrupeds) who inhabited the three bedroom house. No books were ever discarded; even children's books were donated to various charities so that their usefulness could continue as his children outgrew them. One of the favorite places to go on a family road trip was to the local bookstore. Ollie would never say "no" when one of his children asked for him to buy them books. "You are never alone when you have a book," Ollie would tell them. It was a statement that he truly believed.

The years swept by, certainly quicker than he would have liked. His four children grew and moved out of the house. Two of them moved to other states, and the other two stayed on in Massachusetts. No sooner had the house emptied of children did his wife pass away, leaving the house neither as warm nor as lively as it had once been.

Most days, Ollie would sit in his worn chair by the window and read. He liked being able to watch the passing of the seasons during the pauses in his reading, a fire in the fireplace when the weather turned cold, and his cat, Micawber, on his lap. Winter was upon Newburyport; a thick carpet of snow lie upon the ground. The grey sky was threatening more of the same. Soon it would be Christmas-in about three weeks- and the downtown area not far from where Ollie sat was decorated with the usual display of lights and pine garland to draw shoppers in to the quaint shops and cafes. In the years when the children were younger, and the books did not create barricades that blocked most of the living area, Ollie and his wife would host the family Christmas celebrations. Ask any one of the children and they could relay all the scents that made Christmas in the Tremlow house so special. Ollie was too old, and his house too cluttered to be hosting the holidays anymore. His oldest son, Nick, would pick him up a few days before Christmas and take him to his home to celebrate with the entire family. Ollie preferred it that way. No cleaning. No muss and no fuss. He didn't even have to bring presents. They would already be at Nick's home, ordered by Ollie online and delivered free of charge. Wasn't technology great, Ollie would chuckle to himself?

Ollie loved the holidays. He loved his children, their wives and his grandchildren just a bit more than he loved his books. The Tremlow's were a close family- they always had been that way. Ollie and his wife instilled in the children the importance of family. Friends come and go; the only people you can, or should ever be able to rely upon was your own family. Of course, there were family spats from time to time, but they usually blew over quickly with no lasting damage. The family was a fun, practical joking bunch to be around. There was quite a bit of laughing, foolishness, eating and drinking going on when the Tremlow clan got together.

Truth to be told though, on occasion Ollie was feeling alone. His books were a source of comfort, but they could not replace the closeness of human contact. While the pages could make him laugh, feel sad, enrage him, or even bring him to tears, they did not have the warmth of another person. They could not listen to him, touch his shoulder, or pat him on the back. He had Macawber, but that cat was in a world of his own. Macawber would spend hours going from room to room with a pencil in his mouth. Should one of the ceiling fans be on, he'd spend the entire afternoon with his head going around in circles watching the blades spin. No, Macawber was not the answer to Ollie's occasional loneliness. Maybe it was just the time of the year, or possibly just a passing thought that leaves as easily as it enters. He pondered that as he watched the snow began to fall again, afternoon leaving and the evening taking over in its place.

Ah, it's not so bad, he thought, as he got up and made his way to the kitchen. Putting the battered kettle on the stove he mused, at least I have my health and my family. And my books; I'll always have my books.

Setting his mug of tea down on the kitchen table, Ollie looked up at the books stacked all around. He remembered what he had told his children years ago. "As long as I have books to read, I will never die." Everyone laughed and though that Dad was just being his inscrutable self. That had been his mantra for more than forty years. If the family wanted to laugh at him, so what, he paid them no mind. His saying was a take-off on an old episode of the original Twilight's Zone television series called "Ninety Years Without Slumbering." In this episode, and old man owns a very old grandfather clock. He believes that if he cannot keep the clock running and it were to stop that he would die. Ollie felt the same way; if he did not have his books, he would stop ticking too. Nobody but Ollie took this seriously, and in the end of the Twilight's Zone episode even though the clock did stop ticking, the old man did not die. Ollie was a much more fatalistic soul, realizing that he was closer to the end than he was to the beginning. Or maybe Ollie was just trying to convince himself that since there would always be an endless supply of books that he would be immortal.

Ollie was brought out of his reverie by the sound of something moving across the kitchen table. He looked up to see Micawber lapping tea out of his tea cup. This cat simply has no brains, he thought. "Hey dumbass, get your nose out of my tea and get off the goddamn table before I toss you into a pot and make stew out of you." Micawber responded by taking a flying leap off of the table, skidding across the kitchen floor right into the kitchen trash pail, which overturned spilling used tea bags, milk cartons and other detritus across the kitchen floor. Ollie was going to give the cat a well-aimed boot to its rear, then thought better of it, slowly rising from his chair to clean up the mess. "Thanks a lot, Pal. I have nothing better to do than to get down on my hands and aching seventy-four year old knees to pick your mess. Then I'll get stuck and not have one of those ""I fell down and I can't get up"" contraptions to call for help. Nice going pinhead." Finally realizing that he was having a one sided conversation with an animal that was unlikely to do anything more than look at Ollie with a dumb expression, Ollie got a plastic bag from the pantry closet and began cleaning up the wreckage.

Finally finished sweeping up the trash knocked over by the cat, he boiled more water and made another cup of tea. Going into the living room and seeing no trace of

Micawber anywhere nearby, he set the cup down, put another couple of logs on the fire and stoked it. Micawber slowly poked his out from behind a pile of books and began slowly slinking toward the rug in front of the fireplace. Realizing that Ollie was not going to toss anything at him, the big cat fell asleep, comfortable in the warmth given off by the blazing fire. In a short time, Ollie became drowsy as well, and as he often did from the combination of being mesmerized by the leaping flames from the fireplace and the sedating effect of the herbal tea, fell off to a comfortable nap in his leather chair.

Chapter II

Ollie was awakened by the sound of footsteps crunching on the snow outside. He pushed aside the window curtain and peeked outside and saw a bundled up figure hurrying up to the front steps of his house. Having forgotten to turn on the front porch light, he could not make out the identity of the figure, and soon heard the knock at the front door. "Who in blazes is coming out here at this time of night in this crappy weather," he thought.

Calling out for the identity of the visitor, he heard the familiar voice of his oldest son, Nick. He opened the door, and Nick walked past him and quickly to the fireplace without even taking off his coat.

"You come here to see me, or to roast marshmallows, Ollie asked in a slightly irritated voice? You created more wind rushing past me than I'd find in a South Sea typhoon. To what do I owe this pleasure?"

"Ah, that's what I love about you, Pops. Always ready with a loving welcome. What's the matter with you today, no book delivery?

"You're a real fresh breath of Artic air. I'll have you know that I have not ordered any books in two weeks. There are at least a few more new ones to read before I need to restock. Take your coat off and set your sorry ass down and get warm. Then you can tell me why you decided to visit me in the middle of the night."

"It is not the middle of the night Pops, looking at his watch. It is only a little after 7 o'clock. I wanted to talk to you about Christmas, so I figured I would stop by on my way home from work."

"It'll be the middle of the night soon enough for an old fart like me. And here is nowhere near your home or your school. So don't make it sound as stopping here isn't out of your way. Let me get you something warm to drink and then you can go on to your Turkish delight about Christmas." Ollie puttered around the kitchen for a few minutes and came back with a couple of glasses and a bottle of scotch. He poured out a few fingers in each glass and then handed one to Nick. "This'll get you to stop drinking those girly drinks with the little umbrellas in them," Ollie said, as they both sat down and touched glasses.

"Every time I come here we have a scotch, and every time you say the same thing. You definitely need new material."

"You'd fall off your chair if I didn't say the same shit every time we have a drink together, so quit complaining and drink up," the old man chuckled.

This was the usual bantering that went back and forth between Ollie and his son. In fact, it was the way he bantered with all of his children and grandchildren. He had been sticking it to them since they were little kids and they all knew that he never meant anything by it. They expected to get razzed, and were expected to dish it back. Ollie never saw it as a sign of disrespect; he loved his family dearly and talking smack to each other was their way of showing affection. The time to worry was when they didn't give each other a ration of crap.

Nick was Ollie's oldest son and lived about ten miles away. He had a wife and three children and was employed as a history teacher at a school nearby. Ever since he was a young child, Nick and his father would trade harmless insults back and forth. Nick was a frequent target of Ollie's penchant for practical jokes, most of which had their origins in slapstick and thus, were older than Ollie. Whether it was a whoopee cushion or an exploding cigar, Nick always fell prey to his fathers never ending antics. His Dad had not tried a cattle prod or a joy buzzer on him yet, but he figured that there were still some good years left in him to trot out that wheezy joke yet.

"Okay dude, what is so special about this Christmas that you felt that you had to make a trip out here to speak to me about it this much in advance? Not like I haven't been enduring all those children caterwauling, those sorry-assed off-key Christmas carols, and suffering through terrible cooking at your place for the last five years," said Ollie.

Ever since his wife died, Ollie spent the holidays at Nick's house. The holiday season for the family started about four or five days before Christmas day. All of Ollie's family, his daughter, his two other sons, their spouses and children would arrive and they all would finish up their shopping, pitching in to help bake cookies, and share in trimming and decorating the tree. For the most of the activity, Ollie occupied a plush armchair in the living room issuing orders to whoever might pass by, or telling someone to fetch this or that for him. Invariably, his orders were ignored and he would have to get up and get whatever he wanted himself. The house was wall-to-wall people, with lots of laughing and eating, all culminating with everyone up on Christmas morning for the adults to exchange their gifts and the children to find out what Santa had brought for them. Being with his family on Christmas was the time of the year that Ollie looked forward to and cherished the most of all the holidays.

"Well Dad, we'd like you to stay for Christmas and...."

"Of course you'd like me to stay for Christmas. What else did you think I was going to be doing? I always stay with you and Diane, and the rest of your teenage terrorists. Just tell me what day you want me there."

"Dad, if you would just let me finish. We want you to stay after Christmas. Actually, what I am trying to say is that Diane and I want you to come live with us."

Ollie looked as if he had been hit by a thunderbolt from the heavens. There had never even been a hint from Nick that he wanted him to move in. "You been hitting the sauce a little too hard these days, fella?" Ollie asked. What makes you think that I want to or need to leave my home of forty some years and move permanently into that insane asylum of yours?"

Look Dad, you have been out here all by yourself ever since Mom has died. Not to piss you off, which I know I'm going to do anyway, but you are getting older and..."

"Stop right there, Sonny. Yes, I am getting older. I walk with a cane. And it takes me longer to get up and take a whiz when nature calls than it did when I was your age. I also get myself to my own doctor's appointments and I can still do my own grocery shopping, the laundry, and if I had a broad I could have a merry old time without the little blue pill. So, I don't feel like, or want to go anywhere, thank you very much. I like my home just fine and I am going to stay right here."

"Pops, this place is a firetrap. If a fire started in here this house would go up in flames in an instant; you'd never get out. I know that you love your books, but they are everywhere. You can't have more than a couple of people over here to visit you at one time because there is no room.

That's just on the main floor. You have gotten rid of the beds in our old rooms and filled them with books, there are books in the bathtub, books in the linen closet, and I won't even try to put a number to the amount of books in the basement." You need to be in a place where people can take care of you and where you'll be safe."

"You are officially starting to piss me off, Junior." Nobody tells me how I am going to live whatever amount of time that I have left," Ollie's voice rising. "Those books keep me company; they keep me alive and give me a reason to get up in the morning. There is always another book for me to read. Neither you nor anybody else is ever going to take away my books. Take them away and I die!"

"Pops, either you agree to come and live with us or I am going to call the Fire Marshall. I have already spoken to him and described what is going on here. He told me that all I have to do is call him and he would come over and I have no doubt that he would certify this place a fire hazard. Then you will have no choice. I don't want to do that, but I will if you refuse to listen to reason. We want you safe, and we don't want to continue worrying about you."

Ollie rose from his chair and thundered, "You get your ass out of my house right now before I throw you out. If I were you I would begin to worry about your own safety. I may be old but I can still take this cane and knock your head over the Green Monster from here."

"But Pop...."

"I don't want to hear any more about moving out of this house from you. Not one more sound. You know how to let yourself out and don't let the door hit you on the ass. If you persist in anymore of this horse crap, I'll swat you

94

down like the annoying gnat that you are. I'll write you out of my will and donate your inheritance to Amazon. Now scoot, I'm going to bed"

"What inheritance? Nick chuckled. You've spent it all on books."

Ollie waved his hand at Nick in a gesture of dismissal and moved toward the stairs leading up to the second floor. Both sides of the stairs were lined with books so that the handrail was partially blocked. None of these piles were particularly stable, wobbling with the slamming of the front door. It would be so simple to trip over these piles, or to put a hand on a wobbly stack and to fall.

This is exactly what occurred less than thirty seconds after Nick left the house. Ollie's shoe hit the underside of the fifth step and he lurched to one side. He put his free hand down on one of the stacks to steady himself, but the pile gave way, sending him bouncing down the stairs along with a cascade of books that he brought down along the way. The thought Ollie had before darkness overtook him was, "Ain't this a kick in the head, I hate it when that damn fool kid is right."

Chapter III

Ollie regained consciousness a short time later to find himself flat on his back staring up at the ceiling of his living room. His right leg was very painful, and he had great difficulty attempting to get up to a sitting position. Hearing the noise from outside the house, Nick had rushed back into the house in to find his father lying underneath the fallen stack of books. Ollie resembled an upside down turtle attempting to right itself, without success. While Ollie was swearing like a drunken sailor at his son, Nick decided that an ambulance and a visit to the hospital would be necessary.

To say that Ollie was agitated when he arrived at the hospital would be an understatement. He abhorred doctors and hospitals with a passion, and avoided both at almost any cost. Years earlier, Ollie had ignored a cyst on his shoulder that eventually grew to the size of a small lemon. It wasn't until a friend had slapped him on the back with some measure of force that the cyst ruptured, consequently becoming infected and needing medical attention that Ollie went to see his doctor. When his physician asked why he had waited so long to be seen, Ollie told him that had his friend not slapped him on the back, he wouldn't have been seeing a doctor at all. With his disdain for the medical profession, it was a miracle that he had made it to seventy-four relatively unscathed.

After a battery of tests, cursing, more tests, more swearing, and an x-ray, it was determined that Ollie had suffered a non-displaced fracture of the tibia. In other words, Ollie broke his leg. Because the fracture was relatively minor as broken legs go, and the risk of surgery involving plates and screws would be significant in someone Ollie's age, the orthopedist decided to cast Ollie's leg instead. Predictably, this brought about another round of swearing and cursing by Ollie. It would not have mattered what decision the orthopedist made, cast or surgery, the old man was not going let anything pass without being as surly as possible. The doctor decided to admit him to the hospital overnight for observation, just to be on the safe side, which did nothing to lessen the temper tantrums. Eventually, when it became apparent to Ollie that he wasn't going home anytime soon, he dialed everything back to his usual state of low-level, garden variety irascibility. Better to save his outbursts for something he could actually influence, he figured.

After a couple of hours he was wheeled up to his room. Given that he was miserly in most things, save his family, friends, and, of course his reading material, he had no intention of paying for a private room. A semi-private room, preferably with a roommate who was comatose would suit him just fine. The lights were off so Ollie could not see his roommate. He hoped that it would not be a wailer, a moaner, or someone who snored so that he could get some sleep, suddenly being very tired. Ollie groaned from the discomfort in his leg, which had been somewhat relieved by the shot of morphine he received in the ER, as an orderly moved him from the gurney to the bed. Once settled in, he fell off to sleep within minutes.

His eyes had been closed for what seemed to be only a few seconds when he awakened to the sounds of nurses and the general bustle of the day. Searching with his eyes, he finally found a clock on the wall that showed that he had been asleep for more than nine hours. A breakfast tray had been left on the stand next to him, and picking up the lid, he could see that it must have been sitting there for a few hours. "I'm not eating that crap," he mumbled. "Damn, am I hungry? If I wait for a nurse to show up get me some grub all she'll find is a cadaver. I'll just have to get up and find some real food myself. All I have to do is figure out how to get these rails down and I'm outta here"

The mumbling caught the attention of Ollie's neighbor in the next bed. The man was an elderly gent close to Ollie's age, with a handsome face and a pleasant demeanor. He turned toward Ollie with a grin that evoked sunshine and said, "Hi, neighbor. I'm Clarence. What are you in for?"

"What am I in for?" You make it sound like I'm here serving a prison sentence. I'm here because my fool son convinced an idiot doctor that I should take up space and a hospital bed for a leg bruise. So, why are you here, Clarence? Perforated hangnail? Ruptured hair follicles? You certainly are sunny enough that you can't possibly have anything seriously wrong with you? "

"Nope, nothing too awful; had a hip replacement a few days ago. I fell on some ice outside of my house while shoveling snow and busted my hip. Once I get out of here and finish rehab, I am going to an assisted living center in town so that I won't be doing anything foolish like shoveling snow again."

"Assisted living, Ollie snorted, I'd rather poke my eyes out with a screwdriver. Nothing but a bunch of old farts complaining about who changed the television channel and climbing on the short bus "for gum your food day" at Bob Evans."

"Oh, it isn't anything like that at all. I have my own apartment and it is furnished with my own things. There is a dining room if I want to take my meals there, or I can cook my own food. The most important thing for me is that there is companionship. I can be with people my own age and talk to people who have had the same kind of life experiences that I've had."

"What do you mean people who've had the same life experiences as you? Incontinence? Liver spots? Best denture adhesive? Is your erection lasting more than four hours? Thanks, but no thanks."

"Don't you ever get lonely? Don't you ever miss being around people and having someone to talk to?

"Rarely. I am perfectly content to spend my time with my books and my cat. Books speak to me. They speak to me in a way that no human could ever speak. A book asks for nothing more than to be read, to have its pages turned. Best of all, it doesn't talk back to me; it doesn't want me to go here or there or live somewhere else. Books are more alive and more interesting than any person I have ever met. And if something I am reading annoys me, I close the cover and it shuts up. My son wants me to move in with him, his wife, and their crew of teenage head bangers. He told me that I would have my own space, but there isn't a space big enough to make me want to leave my own house. Besides that, he won't let me take my books with me."

"So, leave the books behind. You are fortunate that you have family that wants to take you in. I don't have any family. But if I did I would jump at the chance to be able to live with people who know and love me. It seems to me that leaving a few books behind is a small price to pay for having the opportunity to live with your loved ones. I would really think about it if I were you."

"Ollie was beginning to mutter "oh, stuff it you old geezer" when the doctor entered the room. He recognized her from the emergency room the previous evening. She picked up the chart from the end of his bed and flipped through the pages. "Well Mr. Tremlow, how are you feeling this morning?"

"I would be doing a lot better if I was in my own bed and I had something on this tray that even remotely resembled food. When are you going to cut me loose from this joint?"

"As soon as I speak with your son about your living situation I think we can discharge you. You cannot be by yourself until you put some weight on that leg. That is going to take about a week or so. It wouldn't be safe for you to be by yourself with that cast on and using a cane. Your son tells me that your house is too cluttered to use a wheelchair, so you will either have to go to a rehabilitation facility or, if you have family that could care for you that would be fine too. We will do whatever you prefer as long as you have someone to attend to you while you recover"

Ollie's face turned the color of a stop sign. If it hadn't been for the cast on his leg he might have flown off of the bed. "Now you listen to me, Missy. I have been an attorney for more than forty years. You can't keep me here against my will nor can you tell me where I have to live. Keep trying to feed my that crap and there will be any one of ten judges I know ready to issue a court order. And for the record, if it weren't for the fact that you are a women and me being a gentleman, I would be telling you just where to go. I am not incompetent, and I can take care of myself; I have been doing it for years without help from anyone else. I'd rather be pushing up daisies than to set my skinny ass in a wheelchair. So you better rethink your plan and get me some discharge papers to sign. Right now."

With one swing of his arm, he swept everything off of the tray next to his bed. Food from his cold breakfast sailed across the room splattering the walls as well as the doctor. Ollie sat up and attempted to swing his legs over the edge of the bed but was stopped by the side rails. He felt like a caged animal and began to bang and shake the bed rails. The commotion was loud enough to be heard at the nurse's station down the hall, which sent a nurse running in the direction of Ollie's room to see what all the racket was about, when the young doctor stuck her head out of the door and yelled, "get me 4mg of Lorazipam immediately." In less than a minute, the nurse arrived with the syringe. Ollie was still hollering at the top of his lungs when the sedative was injected into his IV line. The siege was over as the sedative began to take effect. Quiet had returned to the room, at least until the medication wore off. After that, all bets were off.

Chapter IV

Ranch style houses are a rarity in Massachusetts, the majority being of the salt box or triple decker variety. The single level home owned by Nick had been custom built on land owned by Ollie's family for over a century and deeded to Nick when he married. Another piece of property adjoining Nick's house had been given to his sister, Jenna when she married. Jenna's house was more traditional in nature; a colonial in styling with spacious rooms and modern amenities. Nick and Jenna were sitting at her kitchen table, coffee pot resting on a trivet, discussing the events of the past few days. Their father's recent injury and subsequent meltdown at the hospital had shaken the entire family.

"I really don't know what has gotten into him, said Nick looking at Jenna as he passed a hand through his hair. All of a sudden, he has become extremely irrational. Dad just can't get around like he used to, but he won't listen to reason. When I mention moving him to my house all he does is start screaming about his damn books. You know how many there are in that old place? It is nothing short of the Library of Congress over there; we don't have room for one-tenth of them at our house, but he refuses to go anywhere without them. It would be a complete waste of time trying to have him declared incompetent, which he clearly isn't. If I attempted to do that he would have every old fogey judge east of Worcester lining up to spring him. On top of that, he would never speak to me again, making it just a touch difficult having him living with us. I really have no idea what I should do."

Jenna got up and went to the refrigerator to get more cream for her coffee. Closing the door, she paused a moment as if a thought born of a distant memory was germinating. She nodded to herself, placed the cream on the table and sat down.

"I might have an idea as to why Dad is being so adamant about not moving in with you. Do you remember when we were young and Dad would read to us before we went to bed?"

"Yeah, I remember, replied Nick, stretching and interlacing his fingers behind his head. He used to read that book about gargoyles to us every night for what seemed like months because you loved that gargoyle shop on Newbury Street."

"And do you remember when he got sick one night from food poisoning? He was throwing up and we were so upset that we thought he was dying? Of course, we didn't know any better. Do you recall what he said to us to get us to calm down?

"Christ Jenna, that was decades ago. I really don't have a clue what he said. I don't even remember him getting food poisoning and us thinking he was going to croak."

"Well, I remember. He told us that as long as he had a book to read, he would never die. I was a child, and I believed him because it sounded as good a reason to me as any. He would say that from time to time, and of course, eventually, I thought it was a joke; just one of those corny things he was always saying. But maybe not; maybe he believes that if you move him out and he leaves all of those thousands of books behind that he will die. Those books are his security blanket, his insurance policy, his shield. If you take them away from him, what does he have left?

"Jenna, you are beginning to sound almost as delusional as he does. Do you mean to tell me that an educated man like Pops believes in a talisman; or in this case a couple thousand talismans? No. I don't buy it, he is just being stubborn. You know how he is; it's either his way or the highway. If I didn't know better I would believe that he was fighting us all just for the sake of being obstinate and just to show us that he is still in charge.. And you will be enabling him if you give credence to that nonsense that he needs his books to stay alive. To stay alive he needs to be safe and not tumbling down the stairs because stacks of books are blocking the bannister. He has to move out of that firetrap and either sell or donate all of those books. There is not enough room at my house for him to bring them with him"

She got up from the table and started slowly pacing. "Just think about it for a moment. While you don't agree, I know that I am right. Dad used to love that Twilight's Zone episode with the old guy and the grandfather's clock. Do you remember the episode about the guy always had to keep the clock running? If the clock stopped running the old man thought that he would die. What was the name of that episode? It was also the name of an old song or ditty. I remember it now. It was called, Ninety Years without Slumbering. We used to watch it with Dad and he would always use it as a simile for his books and dying. We both know that it is not real I but will bet that is what Dad believes. Then again, it doesn't really matter what we think. It is real to him."

"So what if he believes it. Doesn't the clock stop running and the old guy doesn't die? Or is Dad just leaving out that part?"

"Intellectually Dad knows there is no correlation between his books and him dying, but he is obviously

104

petrified to leave his books behind. We have got to figure out a way to get him to leave the house and move in with you without giving up his books."

"Yeah, I'll just build another house to give his books a place to live. When he is up to it he can just take a stroll and visit them. Wait, it just hit me, there is already a place like that. It is called the library."

"I believe that you may have stumbled on to something, Nick. I have an idea how we can save his library without it becoming part of your house. I am going to make a few calls and see what I can work out.

A number of weeks passed since Ollie's temper tantrum at the hospital. When he awakened from his chemically induced nap, his personal physician was by his bedside to explain why Ollie needed some supervision until his leg healed. After careful consideration, the realization hit him how much he disliked hospitals and did not want to make a trip there again anytime soon. Maybe a short stint at a rehab hospital would not be so bad after all. He was still determined that after the cast was off of his leg that he was going to return to his house. But that would be after the Christmas holidays that he always spent with his children. Better to fight that fight after the first of the year. He was still going to do it his way even if everyone thought they were in charge.

Much to his surprise, and concealed disappointment, the rehab hospital was not as bad as Ollie had feared. He was busy doing exercises every day. The food wasn't terrible, and he struck up some conversations with some of the patients. And the physical therapists were pretty cute too. Oh to be about fifty years younger and I would really give them a run for their money he chuckled to himself.

Nick and Jenna came by to visit every day. They would bring him a stack of books to read, so he was fairly content. Once one stack was complete, it would be changed out for another one. They also brought him his laptop computer, telling them he needed it to order some more Christmas presents since he had not gotten around to buying yet. Being unable to go shopping increased his reliance on online gift buying. That is what Ollie told them anyway. They should have known that their Dad had ulterior motives. Consequently, Ollie kept himself amused by ordering books online and having them sent to Nick's house. He knew that this would drive Nick to distraction. Contrary to what Ollie thought, Nick was a good sport about it, and brought the new stack to Ollie. It had always amazed Nick that his father never duplicated a purchase of a book, and that in the thousands of books purchased over the years there was never more than one copy of a particular title on the shelves. On Friday night, Nick would smuggle in a bottle of Pops' favorite single malt, continuing the tradition of their weekend drink. Although strictly against the rules, the staff chose to look the other way. Of course, Ollie didn't care which way that they looked because he was going to have his scotch whether the staff approved or not.

Soon enough, it was time for Ollie to leave the rehab hospital and head to family for the holidays. He needed his cane to get around, but that was nothing new; he had been using one years. Maybe a change had overtaken him; he didn't feel as grumpy as he frequently had in the past. Those emotions were replaced by a combination of resignation and sadness. Being combative was too much work, especially when he had to gin up being angry. While

Christmas always had a positive effect on him, there was the realization that settled firmly upon him that things were not going to be the same once the holidays were over. He wasn't even going to bother issuing his normal annoying commands from the armchair when he got to Nick's house. Why bother when nobody was listening anyway,

It was decided that it would be better if Jenna picked Ollie up from the rehab hospital rather than Nick. Jenna had a way of interacting with him that reduced the possibility of confrontation. It wasn't that Nick and his Dad fought all the time; it was just that Ollie tended to jab at Nick more than he did his other children. Jenna shared her father's love of reading; she just did not share her father's obsession of keeping books after she read them. This was a bone of contention between them to be sure, but not one that he usually fought about with her.

His belongings were packed away and stowed in the back of Jenna's SUV. Ollie said goodbye to staff and the acquaintances he had made during his stay. Jenna helped Ollie into the front seat and made sure his seat belt was buckled. Had she not done so he would have ridden without it secured, another one of his symbolic protests against authority.

"How are you doing, Dad? Are you ready to help with the holiday cooking and tree decorating? We wanted to wait until you got home to do some of the holiday stuff; didn't want you to miss out."

"Are the kids too lazy to help you, or too busy texting friends, or with sneaking out to see girlfriends or boyfriends to give you a hand?"

They both laughed because there was some truth in what Ollie had asked. All of the grandchildren were in their teens, and were more interested in avoiding the adults as much as possible, and getting the loot on Christmas morning than they were in the old family traditions.

Jenna stopped at a drive-through coffee shop to get them some coffee and then they continued on their way home. Traffic slowed as they entered the main street of the small town where Jenna lived. Street lights had come on, and the shops were lit up with holiday lights illuminating the windows. Many of the stores had pine boughs framing their doorways. A light coating of snow covered the sidewalks, enough to give the town a holiday glow, but not enough to make driving difficult. This was truly a New England town at Christmas; the kind of place found on the cover of holiday cards purchased all over the country. Ollie cracked open the car window just a bit so that he could hear the holiday bustle; his mind creating the pine scent he believed he could smell from the decorated artificial trees placed on each street corner.

"Nothing beats the town at Christmas, does it Dad? I remember you and Mom taking me down here to shop. Back then, the trees were real."

"Yeah, the place still does it up grand. You kids would go nuts looking in the store windows at all the toys, fighting with each other over who was going to get what. Same with your brood now, isn't it? You take them down here to check out the stores, don't you?"

"We do, but it is not quite the same. The stores don't carry the electronic gadgets that they want. You have to go the malls or the big box stores to get those items. They find most of the stuff they want on the Internet, and we order a lot of gifts online. I make it a point to get them down here at least a couple of times during the season, but it bores them, she laughed." Suddenly Jenna turned somber. "You know Dad; I spoke to some of the store owners not long ago. Online shopping has really cut into their business. Some sell online, but most don't have the ability to be price competitive with the large Internet sellers. If things don't change they may go out of business before too long. This place won't be the same if that happens. But nothing stays the same forever, does it Dad?"

Ollie made no reply and drove on in silence for a few minutes. That was all it took for them to pass through the main street and out of the town. Ollie wanted to talk to Jenna about what was going to happen after the holidays. Where was he going to be once the lights were put away and the holiday cookies were all consumed? He felt as if he were rushing to the edge of a cliff at high speed with no way to stop himself from plummeting over the side. It was the proverbial eight hundred pound gorilla sitting in the corner that nobody wanted to talk about. Sooner or later it was going to have to be addressed. Ollie decided that he was not going to wait.

"Jenna, I know that everyone is busy and it is not the most pleasant subject, but what is going to happen to me when the holidays are over? I want to go back to my house. I am comfortable there and I can't see being anywhere else. You and Nick, and anybody else for that matter, can check on me anytime they like. It's not that I don't love Nick and his family; and I am very touched that they want me to live with them, but I have been on my own for so many years I wouldn't know what to do with myself. I never wanted to be the troublesome parent that was hung around the necks of my children like an anchor when I got old. I know that I would really be happier and more contented at my own place."

"Dad, I wish that you could go back to your house. But it really is not safe. The stairs are rickety and there is so much paper in every room. If there were a fire, you would never get out in time. We know that you love the place and that you love your books, but the time has come for you to be with family. We want to take care of you just the way you have taken care of us all of these years. You deserve a little pampering."

"I don't need to be pampered; I'm not a senile old coot that is going shatter like a porcelain doll." After a couple of minutes riding in silence, Ollie continued, "But I won't be able to take my books with me. I can't live without my books. What will happen to them?"

"First of all, Dad, you will have books, just not thousands of them. Nick is building you a couple of bookcases for you to take some of them with you. Second, books are not people, they don't have lives. So don't worry about something happening to them. Finally, you can live without all of the books. You are not going to die without them. It's not like the clock; the old man didn't die when it stopped ticking. Another fall down the stairs because you tripped over the pile of books might kill you though. Imagine dying because the books caused it? Wouldn't that be ironic?"

"Well, what if I wanted to get a broad, get naked and play hide the salami on the couch. I can do that if I am at my house, but not if I live at Nick's. You kids are going to kill off my sex life, you know that?"

"Since when do you go around your house naked? In all the time I have known you I have never even seen you in a pair of boxer shorts."

"That's because I go, what do the kids call it now, commando."

110

"How do I put this nicely, Dad? You are full of it," she laughed.

"I am too old and too tired to argue with you and Nick anymore. I know what I know. This is not the way a wrinkled old fart should be treated. I could stop you, you know I could? I could go to court and stop you. But why bother, Ollie sighed resignedly. The holidays are here, and I don't want to be a bother."

"Everything will be fine, Dad. You will be fine. And you are not being a bother. Even if you were, I wouldn't want you any other way. Now let's go in and have a great Christmas." They pulled into the driveway and into the garage. Before Ollie could open the car door, Jenna's husband and her children were at the car to help him into the house. There were hugs, kisses, and back slaps to go around. Let the holidays begin!

Chapter V

The holidays were over. Presents had been open and the wrapping paper cleared away. Dinners consisted of the leftovers from the holiday meal. And everyone would have been happier with a pizza rather than the various iterations of turkey that had been served over the past few days. There is a natural let-down once Christmas Day passes. So much energy is expended on shopping, decorating, cooking and entertaining that a collective depression seems only natural. For Ollie, the end of the festive days of the season only added to his sadness. Today, he would begin living permanently with his son and daughter-in-law and their children.

Nick had spent the morning at Ollie's house picking up some of his father's personal belongings and clothing. The house would be put on the market for sale. Before that could occur, the house would need some work. Nick hoped that by bringing some of his father's possessions to his new home that he would make his Dad as comfortable as he could; he wasn't sure what Pops would want to take with him or how much would fit in his house. Attempting to make that decision for Ollie was a difficult matter, and Nick felt as if it wouldn't be right regardless of the choices that he made. The last thing Nick put in his car was the cage containing Micawber the cat. Nick hoped that the cat would get along with their dog, however, if the cat had the same personality as his father, there was going to be quite a bit of fur flying, and he doubted that it would be the dog's.

"Well Pops, I have you all set up at your new digs. Time for us to saddle up," Nick said. Ollie had been spending the day at Jenna's so that he wouldn't be underfoot while Nick was running back and forth moving his father's things around.

"Terrific," Ollie snorted. Jenna had already implored Ollie not to make this any more difficult than it already was going to be. He promised that he would be on his best behavior, which only amounted to moderate irritability. And that was on his good days, of which today surely not one.

Jenna decided that she would go along for the short trip to Nick's to get Ollie settled. At least for the moment, Ollie was not overly pissed off at her. She hoped that her presence might be calming; and if that did not work she could block Ollie from taking a swing at Nick with his cane should the urge arise.

The three of them got into the car and Ollie settled into the back seat. He wasn't paying much attention to the scenery passing by the window being deep in thought about the twists and turns his life had taken over the past month. Having to give up his house was one thing; but he conceded that it was something that he would have had to consider it sooner rather than later. However, the thought had never crossed his mind that he would have to give up his books. That was akin to mourning for a dear old friend who had passed away. There were times when he would spend hours just looking at each book as he slowly passed by the shelves; remembering where he purchased it or the person who had given it to him as a gift. He wouldn't be able to do that anymore. Where would they all go, he wondered? He could almost feel the beat of his heart slowing as he thought of the destruction of all he had collected over the decades. Could he have been right all along; were his books the key to his mortality? A spouse who is heartbroken over the loss of their partner frequently passes away within a short time after the first one goes. Would his remaining time be dictated by his loss?

His train of thought was broken by the sensation of speed as the car accelerated onto the highway. This isn't the way to Nick's place; where in God's name were they going, he thought?

"What the hell are you doing on 95, you dumbass? You forget the way home? Maybe you should have dropped some crumbs to help you along."

"No Pops, I didn't forget where my house is. I have to run a quick errand in the city and I thought you might enjoy the ride."

"Well, I might have if you had given me a little bit of notice. I have had enough surprises in the last month to last me for quite some time. Just make sure that we stop at Mike's while we are there if it's not too much of a bother. Maybe they have a cherry crumb pie or something. If nothing else I can bring back some cannoli that your kids like. It'll be a bribe to keep them from playing music at ear-splitting volume

"Sounds like a good idea, Pops. You seem to be mellowing all of a sudden."

"Just don't push your luck, Sonny. There's little chance of that happening anytime soon."

A trip into the city wouldn't be a bad thing, he thought. It wasn't a long ride and would keep his mind off of things for a while. He hadn't been to the city for quite some time. After his wife died, he considered moving to the city, but everything was just so expensive that he decided to stay close to the kids. Even after all this time, it was still a thrill to go back to the city where went to law school. So many memories flooded back to him; going to Fenway Park, rides on the Swan Boats with the kids, the city when it snowed. Even at his advanced age, he missed the excitement and the vitality of Boston. Outside of his family, and his books, the city was what he loved the most.

Everyone made small talk during the ride into the city. Mid-day traffic was fairly light, so they made good time. They passed the Public Gardens and a number of other familiar places when, finally, Nick eased into a parking space near the Theatre District. Ollie was surprised that they had stopped right across the street from the law school he had attended more than forty years ago. Why was Nick stopping here?

"Come on, Pops. I want to show you something."

Ollie shrugged and followed Nick across the street and into the lobby of the school. He had not been back in a number of years; however, he had gone there from time to time for some ceremony or the like. Certainly, there had been many changes since he had first set foot in the building. Everywhere you looked there were banks of computers. Even the students looked different; gone were the shirts and ties of his generation. Now everyone wore tee shirts with designer logos or the name of the manufacturer. "These are the lawyers of tomorrow," he muttered under his breath. Times sure had changed.

Nick motioned toward the elevator and they rode it down to the basement. When the doors opened, there were a large number of students and many of the faculty members standing in the doorway to a large room that used to be the student book store. Over the top of the doorway there was something covered with purple cloth with a string attacked to the corner. As soon as Ollie stepped off,

115

everyone began clapping. The noise startled Ollie, and he looked around to see who the applause was for,

"What is going on here, Ollie asked, thoroughly confused? I hope that I am not disturbing anyone."

A slender man in a blue pinstriped suit walked up to Ollie and held out his hand to him. "Good afternoon Mr. Tremlow. My name is Lawrence Hogarth, the Dean of the law school. I want to thank you for coming today for the celebration."

"Well, I am certainly not dressed for any celebration, said Ollie, looking down at his well-worn corduroy slacks and old sweater. I thought I was going to Mike's in the North End to get a cherry crumb pie."

Everyone laughed. Once the chuckling quieted down, the Dean stepped beside Ollie, Nick and Jenna and said, "it doesn't matter much what you are wearing Mr. Tremlow. We are here today to celebrate your generosity; your kindness. With the help of your family, friends, students, and the faculty of the law school, we have all come together to do this."

With that, a student pulled on the string attached to the material over the doorway. Lights over the doorway revealed a sign in raised brass letters bearing the words "Oliver Tremlow Library Collection."

"Mr. Tremlow, Dean Hogarth began, your son and daughter contacted us not long after your accident. They made us aware of your situation and that it was no longer an option for you to live in your home. We recognized your love of books and wanted to insure that your prized and very valuable collection is given the care you would require and that it deserves.

As you now doubt are aware, many of the manuscripts that have been treasured over the years are now only artifacts; they exists only as part of rare book collections in libraries or are no longer available in paper. It has become more convenient to read via electronic means than it is to hold open a book and savor its contents. That is why, in my opinion, that books should be treasured and collections be kept in a place of security.

"All of your books are here, Mr. Tremlow; all 8,344 of them. We are making them available to our students and alumni as research tools and for their reading pleasure. These books have been catalogued and shelved in the usual library manner. So that you can view your collection at any time, we have placed the entire catalog on our school website. And of course, you are more than welcome to come here and visit your collection at any time. You have given us and future students a great gift, Mr. Tremlow.

To say that Ollie was stunned would have been an understatement of the highest magnitude. For one of the few times in the recent memory of his family, he could not find any words. Of course, his being speechless did not last very long.

"You and Jenna did this? I thought that my books would have ended up in a dumpster or in a used book store. Do they still really belong to me?"

"Yes, they are still yours, Pops, Nick replied. The law school is just looking after them for you. By the way, we have another gift for you." Nick handed Ollie a box the size of a hard cover book. "Looks and feels like a book. You seeding the start of my new collection," Ollie quipped looking over the top of his glasses at Nick with a sly grin. "I do have a few years left in me to buy a thousand or so books before I am gone."

"You could say that I am helping you start a new collection, but without the storage issues. That is an e-reader, Pops. You can download almost as many books as you want on that. I know that it is not the same as holding open the paper ones, but you can always buy the real thing once in a while. I want to emphasize the "once in a while" part."

Everyone laughed. There was a reception in the Oliver Tremlow Library and everyone went inside to have refreshments. Ollie took his time and looked around the stacks. He plucked one off a shelf and opened it to the inside page. There was the book stamp he had marked in the book years ago to show when it had been purchased. He had to admit that it was a handsome library and that the law school had done a marvelous job putting it all together. Shaking hands along the way, he walked to where everyone was gathering around coffee and cake. The clock was still ticking, Ollie mused. It would seem as if he still some time left after all. He turned toward Nick and said, "C'mon dude, let's get out of here and go home before traffic gets bad."

"Which home are you talking about, Pops?

"There is only one place I know of, knucklehead. It's the place with no character and no books in it. Let's haul ass, Nick. I want to get there and see how this contraption works. Maybe you can throw some fake logs into that fake fireplace of yours to set the mood while I read, said Ollie with a grin on his face"

"I'll see what I can do, Pops. I'll see what I can do."

Justice at Christmas

Chapter I

What do you do when your world begins to spiral out of control? At first, the downward slide is slow, almost imperceptible. Just a few things feel off, unreal, unclear. Maybe it is something as simple as the inflection of the voice at the other end of a telephone call. Or it could be something that just doesn't look right on a report; a number you thought was different, a cut in a pie chart that was red instead of blue; something that you just cannot put your finger on.

Then the spiral begins to tighten, compress. The speed of the descent accelerates and becomes uncontrollable. Now you can see it; you can feel it. You whip around the bends barely able to see outside as the gravitational forces pull you into the vortex. People talk, however, you can no longer hear them. You view your life outside of yourself, as if you are watching your clone at a distance. No matter what you try to do, you feel helpless. You are helpless. You stay that way until the spiral spits you out from its tail and you go crashing to the bottom. And there is no way to stop unless somebody steps in to help; unless there is someone who will slow it all down. If you are fortunate enough someone may intervene. Should that not occur, you are finished

Grant Savage had no clue on that bright Monday morning that anything was out of the ordinary. He sat behind his desk in his 1,000 square foot office looking out the window overlooking the Baltimore harbor. Things could not be going any better for him right now. His business of selling overpriced consumer electronics to people who neither needed them nor could afford them was going gangbusters. His office held only some of the many expensive objects his money could afford. The shelves contained sculptor and statues, the value of which was many times more than the furnishings of a typical home. On the walls of his office was hung expensive artwork. Gold plated nautical instruments sat on his desk and on end tables even though Grant didn't own a boat and had no interest in sailing. His office contained leather chairs, a couch and a conference table. Behind his desk was a door that led to his private bathroom complete with a marble shower. Also on his desk was a computer that Grant used to track his company's sales in real time. The computer also contained software that he used to listen to the telephone calls his executives made and received. He could use his computer to intercept their emails without their knowledge. One of the reasons that he kept the French doors to his office locked was so that he could make sure nobody came in while he was watching employees or listening to their conversations. Grant trusted nobody, and wanted to make sure he could get rid of any employee he perceived to be disloyal. Some of his executives joked about the spying that they suspected Grant was engaging in, but they couldn't know for sure. Most would not be shocked were they to discover that it was true.

Grant had made millions of dollars many times over; basically by being a prick. He had found early on that there was a lot of money to be made on the misery and misfortune of others. His company, Rapid Response Electronics was not the first company he had owned or controlled. The plan he had devised acquiring wealth was simple, purchase a company, exploit a particular demographic until he had drained it dry and then sell the company for millions more than he had bought it. Upper level management would be sucked in to his bogus promise of big seven figure payouts when the company sold. Unfortunately, most would be fired or leave in disgust well before the company changed hands. That worked out just as well for Grant; it meant more green in his pocket.

How you were treated by Grant depended on where you were on the Rapid food chain. The hourly workers were as disposable as Post-It Notes. He would frequently change their work schedules without regard for child care needs; he would offer sales bonuses and then rescind them, or terminate an hourly worker on a whim just as they approached the number of sales needed for the bonus. The company claim to workers that they could earn a six-figure income was farcical, as none of the call center workers in the history of the company had ever came close to earning that much. Nobody ever would, Grant would make sure of that.

He didn't treat middle level management much better, but they were usually spared the threat of their employment being terminated on the spur of the moment. For the privilege of being employed by Grant, they would have to endure verbal belittlement and promises of raises that never materialized. In a way, they had more to fear as they had more to lose because they were earning a living wage while call center employees did not. Consequently, these managers would come to work a nervous wreck every day and wondering to themselves why they didn't just look for better employment.

The executives would be treated the best because they were Grant's playthings. They would be wined and dined at the most expensive restaurants in town. Grant would invite them to ball games and concerts. They would receive holiday bonuses and regular raises. If they were required to travel for business, they would always travel first class and stay at the finest hotels; eat at the finest restaurants. Grant did this because he did not have anyone to go home to and he would become lonely. He needed something to amuse himself with, so the executives became his toys. Like most toys, unfortunately, once the owner became bored with the toys, he discards them.

At one time, Grant was married, but that was years ago. He did have a son and a daughter who he saw rarely. When they did come for a visit, he would shower them with expensive things to make up for the time he didn't spend with them. Grant's parents had passed away not long ago. Occasionally, he would think of his mother, which was the closest he came to missing her. His father, on the other hand, he thought of often, and not in a good way. He despised Marc, who had been a civil rights attorney. Dad was always critical of Grant for putting money ahead of people. Grant hated his father for not caring enough about money. Marc had been brilliant lawyer who could have made baskets of cash if he had not been such a bleeding heart liberal, Grant thought. His father's lack of monetary success meant that they lived in a working class neighborhood, in a modest house not befitting the family. Or so Grant believed. Of his three siblings, two brothers and a sister, two became lawyers and continued his father's civil rights practice. His other brother was a high school history teacher. All three of them, in his estimation, had worthless careers and were abject failures. He would see them at family events, rarely, if he had the time or the inclination, but he did not go out of his way to initiate contact with them. Mostly he would ignore his family as much as possible, making sure that he was too involved with some business venture to make an appearance. Grant had missed graduations, his son's baseball games, his daughter's soccer games, family reunions and funerals. He was too busy for anything that did not add to his own portfolio or to his own enjoyment, and, in Grant's estimation, his family did not add to either.

None of that mattered; particularly to Grant. Anything he wanted he had more than enough money to buy. His youngest brother, Ted went to Grant's office a couple of years back in an attempt to get Grant to become more involved with the family. Grant ridiculed Ted and told him that he was spineless. In Grant's estimation, he already did enough for the family, telling Ted that they should all be grateful for the times he did show up. In reality, Grant did virtually nothing for the family, ignored then at all costs, and only showed up for family events when it benefitted him. Of course, Grant could care less what they thought, and let Ted know in no uncertain terms that he was infringing upon Grant's time. Grant was no more upset by the conversation than he would be by stepping on a bug.

Happily for Grant it was the week before Christmas. Experience had shown that sales at Rapid Response would soar this week as people made their last minute purchases to arrive before Christmas morning. He knew all too well that his slick marketing would drive thousands to contact his call centers in the U.S., as well as in India and Pakistan, to place an order for over priced items. When an offer seems too good to be true it was amazing how many would make the grab for it and lose what little money they did have. Rapid's scheme was to get the customer to agree to have their checking account debited weekly, and should the customer miss one payment they wouldn't see their merchandize until the entire purchase price was paid. If a customer canceled, their accounts would still be debited due to a no cancelation policy written in type so small that it would have been difficult to be seen with an electron microscope. Trying to get someone on the phone in the corporate office so the customer could lodge a complaint was a maze of confusion. A disemboweled voice would direct the complainant to a voice mail box that was emptied every day without a human being having listened to a single call. Paper correspondence went to the Rapid Response version of the U.S. Post Office's Dead Letter Office; they were opened and promptly shredded without being read, eliminating all trace of complaints.

Yes, it should be a great week, Grant thought. He brought his computer out of its sleep mode to look at overnight sales. Blinking on the bottom of the screen was a red tab, alerting him that there was some important appointment on his calendar. It was only a little past 7:30 in the morning and he usually didn't schedule any appointments until mid-morning. Strange, he thought. He clicked on the tab and the calendar page opened. Flashing in bright red were the two words "Jury Duty." That can't be, he thought. I have never had jury duty before. In fact, he could not even remember having gotten a notice.

Grant rose from his chair and walked out to his outer office to see if his secretary had arrived for the day. Not seeing her- it was early even for her to be in- he went back to his desk and began rifling through piles of mail. Finally, near the bottom of ignored mail, he found the notice. Dumb ass General Counsel he muttered, he should have taken care of this for me. He picked up the phone and demanded that Rick, his in house lawyer, who was always at work before Grant, come to his office.

Rick walked in, and before he could say a word Grant bellowed, "Why didn't you handle this?"

Rick Palmer was used to this early morning barrage from Grant. At just short of one year's employment, he had lasted longer than the last three lawyers had. Grant chewed up and spit out General Counsel like a dog would devour a bone. Rick was fed up with all the nonsense, but he didn't fancy the idea of unemployment with Christmas right around the corner. His resume had already been updated and he was ready to begin his search for a new position after the first of the year.

"Handle what?"

"Handle this," said Grant flipping the notice like a Frisbee at Rick.

Rick bent down and picked up the post card notice. He could see that it was a jury duty notice requiring Grant to report to the court house this morning at 9:00 a.m. Flipping the card over a couple of times, Rick considered his response. He knew that Grant was going to lose his mind; it was just a matter of how loud he was going to be. "Not that it really matters to you very much, but this is the first time that I have seen this notice. What exactly is it that I didn't handle?"

"All legal correspondence goes to you after I have reviewed it, shouted Grant. Why didn't you tell me about it? Why didn't you get me out of it? I do not have the time for jury duty and I can't go at this time of the year. You are going to have to fix this."

Rick decided to refrain from telling his boss why he did not tell him about something that Grant had already looked at. Rick had never laid eyes upon the jury duty notice and he had no doubt Grant had just tossed it into a pile along with other correspondence. Regardless, Rick was not going to allow himself to be on the hook for Grant attempting to weasel out of his own civic duty.

"There wasn't anything I could have done about it, even if I had seen the notice. I can't call for you to get out of jury service; that you have to do yourself. And you cannot ignore the jury summons. If you do not appear you

126

will be cited with contempt of court and a bench warrant will be issued. The next time you and your Lexus are stopped for speeding the deputy will slip silver bracelets on you." Rick walked over and placed the notice on Grant's desk. "You are either going to have to go down to the county courthouse, or you are going to have to call the Clerk of the Court and see if you can be excused. Given the late hour, I wouldn't bet on that happening. Sorry Chief, this one's all yours." Before Grant could get one word out of his stunned mouth, Rick turned, walked out of the office and closed the door behind him. He almost was doubled over laughing as he went outside to call his wife to tell her the whole story. No doubt that Grant was going to lay into him later in the day, but he would cherish the moment while he could. Grant didn't make a fool of himself often; he generally shifted the blame to somebody else. Fortunately, there was nobody he could realistically blame but himself. That was what Rick found so delicious.

Regaining what little was left of his composure, Grant considered his options. Under normal circumstances he would have told Rick to clean out his office and to hit the road. As edifying as that may have been, the jury summons was more time sensitive. Besides, he could always shit can that worm of a general counsel after he took care of this jury duty nonsense. Hell, there were many more slime ball lawyers where he came from. He was tired of Rick always warning him that he was violating one statute or was about violate another. Rick never played ball like the others. Just for spite, maybe he'd wait to fire Rick until the last work day before the Christmas holiday. Merry Christmas to you sucker.

Grant picked up the card and began to punch out the phone number of the Court Clerk. Somebody had to be at the Clerk's office early to handle questions about jury duty.

On this call, he would be the sweet, solicitous, charming Grant Savage who could schmooze anyone. No doubt that in less than five minutes he would talk the Clerk into dismissing him.

"Clerk's office, Ms. Twigg speaking, how may I help you?

"Good morning Ms. Twigg, I am Grant Savage, Chairman and CEO of Rapid Response Electronics, and I have sort of a problem. You see, I received a Jury Summons a while ago and I gave it to someone in my company to take care of. Unfortunately, that person didn't get me excused and I just found out this morning that I am supposed to appear for jury duty today, and well, as you can no doubt imagine, being the head of a large company it is really not convenient for me to serve on a jury. I know that you understand and will remove me from the roll."

"You said that your name is Savage? Grant Savage?"

"Yes. That is correct."

"Alright, hold on a moment."

Perfect, Grant thought. She is going to find the notice and she'll cross my name out. After what seemed like a long time with no response from the clerk, Grant was beginning to become annoyed. Incompetent clowns these government workers. She probably went out for a smoke just forgot all about me? He looked at the clock as it was getting closer to 8 a.m. Not very much time to get down to the courthouse if there is a snafu. To his relief, he could hear the clerk's voice in the hubbub of the Clerk's office and she was back on the phone a few seconds later.

"Sorry it took so long. The lists had already gone down to chambers; had to track them down."

"Not a problem Ms. Twigg, thank you so much for your help."

"So you say your name is Savage, right? Let me see here. Yup, found it right here; report to the commissioner in the first courtroom on the first floor."

"You don't understand Ms. Twigg. I cannot do jury duty. I am too busy. I run a very large company and I cannot take the time to be away, especially this time of the year."

Oh, I understand, Mr. Savage. You're like all the other folks who are busy around the holidays and do not have the time to take time off from work and come down here for jury duty especially this time of the year. Only difference is those folks don't own a large company. See the jury commissioner in the first courtroom on the first floor. If you get in your car right now you might just get here in time and not receive a fine for being late."

"Listen, Ms. Twigg. I am Grant Savage; I am person friends with the Mayor and a number of people on the city counsel. You go in and see the judge. Tell him that Grant Savage is on the phone about jury duty, and you do it right now!"

"Oh, you are THE GRANT SAVAGE? Why didn't you tell me?

"I didn't think that it would be necessary."

"You are quite right, it isn't necessary. I am not going to the judge to tell him anything. I don't care who

129

you are and I doubt that the judge cares either. But you are more than welcome to go tell him yourself when you get here. He might, however, care that you are fussing as much as you are about one day of jury duty. And since you are THE Grant Savage go see the commissioner in the Ceremonial Courtroom on the third floor instead of the commissioner on the first floor. That is where they hold the real juicy trials; the ones that last a couple days or more. Hustle on down here before you are late. Bye now, "THE Grant Savage."

Grant looked at the receiver before slamming it down. "I'll fix her ass when I get down there, he thought. How dare she speak to me like that?" Time was ticking off the clock as he grabbed his overcoat and hurried out of his office. He could make it courthouse in about ten minutes, and there would be hell to pay when he got there. Or, so he thought.

Chapter II

Swearing all the way to court, Grant cursed anyone and everyone he could think of for not getting him out of this mess. That it was his responsibility alone for filing the requisite papers to get out of jury duty was completely lost on him. He paid a lot of money- in his mind- for an attorney to take care of corporate legal matters. For most people personal jury service would not rise to the level of a corporate legal matter, but as Grant kept telling himself, he was not an ordinary soul. He had an expectation of those he hired, and his worthless general counsel had failed him miserably. That moronic fool was going to feel his wrath when he returned to the office.

His mad dash into the courthouse was interrupted by having to empty is pockets, take off his Rolex and his belt, and pass through courthouse security. Did these overpaid, flunky court officers really believe that Grant would carry a weapon into the courthouse? Being made to stand in line with the flotsam of society was another just one more humiliation as far as he was concerned. And he was particularly incensed by the attorneys flashing their bar cards which allowed them to bypass the metal detector. He was going to say something to one of the guards but thought the better of it. Should he be admonished for being a couple of minutes late, he would blame it on this particular inconvenience. Dashing up the stairs, he paused at the door of the Ceremonial Courtroom on the third floor to catch his breath. He swung open the massive wooden door and entered.

A number of years ago, the Ceremonial Courtroom had been restored to its original state. Built in the early 1800s and in disrepair, meticulous work was done the bring it back to reflect its former opulence. Rich mahogany bench and counsel tables gleamed, reflecting the light of the magnificent crystal chandelier. Brass rails ringed the jury box, which contained twelve burgundy leather chairs. Green shaded lamps were on each counsel's table, and the rug had the state seal emblazoned upon it. Chairs for the spectators went back in twenty rows from just behind the courtroom floor, giving the room a theatre-like quality. Now only used for special occasions such as swearing in elected officials or very high profile cases, the magnificence of the courtroom inspired awe in those who were called there.

Grant however, was not impressed. He stood at the top of the steps and could see there was not a soul in the place, save for one old man placing files on the two counsels tables. His "hey buddy" was met with a "Shhhhhh" by the old gentleman who looked up from his work and gestured for Grant to come down. He walked down the center aisle and thrust the jury summons at the old man, and before he could speak the old man said, "You are in the right place, Mr. Savage. Have a seat at this table and the judge will be out shortly."

That's more like it, Grant thought, sitting down at the table. The judge must realize how important I am and is going to come out and dismiss me personally. I'll have to make sure to speak to him about that insolent Clerk, Ms. Twigg, for her making me come all the way down here and wasting my time, he thought. She'll be bagging toys at Toys R Us by the time I finish telling the judge what a witch she is. More and more people were quietly coming in, most taking seats in the gallery. Two bailiffs placed documents on the judge's bench. They were followed shortly thereafter by the judge's clerk, who took her place at the bench, next to where the judge sits.

Grant was drumming his fingers impatiently on the table wondering when the judge was going to come out of chambers. This is such a waste of his time, he thought. By the time he got through with this nonsense half of the morning would be over. Looking at the room filling up, he began to get an uneasy feeling. The people in the gallery, the bailiffs, even the man who sat down at the table next to him looked vaguely familiar. He was unable to put his finger on exactly where he might have seen this man before, however, the feeling of discomfort would not leave him. Maybe it would be a good idea to step out for a moment and splash some cold water on his face. Unfortunately for him just as he was rising to go to the restroom, as if reading Grant's mind, the judge emerged from his chambers and strode to the bench.

Clerk: "All rise. Persons having business before the Honorable Judge Harvey and this honorable Court, this Court is now in session."

Grant stayed standing and was just about to begin his rehearsed lines attempting to get out of jury duty when he felt a hand on his shoulder. He turned to see the hand connected to one of the bailiffs. "Sit down until you are called, Sir," the bailiff said. Feeling sufficiently intimidated, Grant complied.

Judge: Our case today is People vs. Grant Savage. One count of Extreme Narcissism; one count of Extreme Disregard and Callousness toward Family, and one count of Taking Advantage of the Poor and Less Fortunate. How do you plead Mr. Savage?"

It took Grant a few seconds for the judge's words to sink in, then, the chair he was sitting in flew backwards as Grant scrambled to his feet. "Wait just one minute. I came here because of a jury summons I wanted to have dismissed and to complain about an obnoxious court clerk. Now you are telling me that I am charged with some farcical stuff that are not real charges. This better be some kind of joke, and if it is one, it is not a very good joke at that. And on top of it, I expect an apology"

"I can assure you Mr. Savage, that this is no joke and that the charges in this court are legitimate. You might wish to moderate your tone toward the court or I will hold you in contempt. As far as an apology is concerned, if anybody is going to do any apologizing it will be you. Now sir, I will ask you again, how do you wish to plead?

Nuts to this, he thought. Grant turned and took a few steps to walk up the stairs. Looking over his shoulder with a look of disdain he said, "I do not recognize any of these so-called charges, and am not hanging around for this crap." This little diatribe was nipped from going any further by both bailiffs taking Grant by the arms and unceremoniously depositing him back in the chair behind the defendant's desk.

"Mr. Savage, I suggest that you show a little more respect in this courtroom, said the judge. Should there be any more outbursts from you, your holidays will be spent in the county lockup. Given that you appear to disagree with the proceedings taking place, I will save you the trouble of deciding how you wish to plead and enter a plea of not guilty. Does the Plaintiff wish to make an opening statement?"

Seated at the table next to Grant was an elderly gentleman. He was a short man wearing a baggy, worn suit and sporting a bow tie. A snowy white fringe of hair ringed his partially bald pate, and he had a bushy white mustache that gave him the appearance of an extremely short walrus. His face showed its age, lines, crevices and wrinkles etching the landscape, and he required the use of a brass-headed cane to rise from his seat.

"Yes, yes your Honor, I do have a few words that I would like to say before I call my first witness. Mr. Savage over there does not know me, but I do know him. Maybe not personally, but I do know all about him. Known about him since was a child trying to sell broken toys to even younger children. He grew up to be a fine looking man that Mr. Savage. But as they say, you can't judge a book by its cover. No, no, you cannot do that. He's got some money too, does Mr. Savage. Quite a bit of money, truth to be told. You can see it by his fancy suit and those custom made shoes. Yes sir, Mr. Savage is quite the dandy, isn't he?

Now this fella might be good looking and have all this money, but he isn't really a very nice man. He makes his money selling stuff to people who can't afford it, doesn't deliver on his promises to his customers, and then sues them even though those poor people never get their goods. I suppose that in the grand scheme of things he is no different than quite a few people out there in the business world who do the same sort of thing. No doubt he doesn't see anything wrong with what he is doing. No. No. I doubt that he loses one wink of sleep over his many customers that will not be able to give their children anything for Christmas because they fell for his slick advertisements and his fast talking call center employees.

Maybe the saddest thing of all regarding this young, rich fella over there is the way that he treats his own family. They aren't the type to go around asking Mr. Savage for money. Nope, they haven't once done that. All they ask of this fine gentleman is that he joins with them at times of celebrations and be part of the family. They would love it for him to come around every now and then and join them for dinner.

But he is too busy for that. He is too busy to visit for Thanksgiving or on Christmas. He has too much to do to accept an invitation to celebrate an anniversary or a birthday. Never been to a family reunion; never been to a graduation; never been to a christening. Doesn't have the time for it; doesn't have the time for any them. And even though he has insulted his brothers and sister; made fun of them for the professions that they have chosen, they are always ready to welcome Mr. Savage into their home and into their hearts.

Yes, your Honor, it is certainly a sad state of affairs when one becomes too important, too self-absorbed, too self-centered to be part of his own family. Especially when you family nurtured you in your youth, paid for your college education, and helped you start out in the world of business. It's called narcissism, and it is a foul thing when you begin to believe that you are more important than the world around you. Well, that is exactly what Mr. Savage believes, and that is exactly the reason that Mr. Savage is here today. Thank you, your Honor.

The old attorney turned and with some difficulty went back to his seat. For a moment, the court room was silent and there was anticipation about what was going to occur next. Seeing that there was a break in the proceedings, Grant rose from his seat and moved to the center of the room. He was about to speak when the Judge said, "What do you think you are doing?" Momentarily caught off guard, he looked around the room to see to whom the Judge was speaking. Realizing it could only be him, he said, "I am going to respond to the nonsense that old man just spewed about me. I have the right to my own opening statement."

"Sit down and keep your yap shut. You are not an attorney so you don't have a clue what you have a right to. I'll let you know when you can say your piece. Mr. Potter, you can call your first witness."

Suppressing the wish to express his outrage at the miscarriage of justice, Grant turned and made a show of exaggerated slowness returning to his seat. He drummed his fingers loudly on the table, only stopping when coming under the withering glare from the bench. I am going to just sit and wait out this farce, he thought. The less I say, the sooner I can get out of her and back to the office.

Time ticked on as a parade of people took the stand to testify against Grant. Even though he tried to ignore what they were saying, it was impossible. Some were former employees who relayed stories about how Grant treated them; firing them for the slightest infraction, and how he seemed to take enormous pleasure out of doing so. One customer, a soft spoken elderly woman told of how she contacted the company to purchase gifts for her grandchildren for Christmas. She had no credit and was on a fixed income and was so joyful when she found out she could buy all the gifts she wanted through Grant's company, only to later find that Rapid Response emptied her bank account. Since he account was overdrawn without her knowledge, she defaulted on the weekly payments. Consequently, no merchandise would be sent and she would have no gifts for her grandchildren. Her complaints fell on deaf ears as she was told to read the agreement she had signed; one payment had been missed so she was not eligible for early shipment and no refund if she canceled her order. Through all of this, Grant sat at the Defendant's table, no longer stifling his yawns of boredom.

"Your Honor, I have one last witness I would like to call. I would like to call Marc Savage to the stand."

Grant shook the cobwebs of inattention out of his head and stared in disbelief as an elderly gentleman walked to the witness stand. His father, Marc Savage was going to testify against his own son? "Hold on just a minute now. This man cannot testify against me."

"Why is that," the judge inquired?"

"Because he is dead. My father has been dead and buried for over ten years. I don't know who that man is, but he is not Marc Savage. My old man is now nothing more than bones and dust."

"He looks alive to me," the judge responded. "How about you take your seat and keep quiet. You may learn a thing or two." Grant shrunk back in his chair, scratching his head in disbelief.

"Mr. Savage, Potter began, who is that sitting at the Defendant's table over there?"

"That is my son Grant."

"He seems to believe that you are deceased?"

"He is correct, Counselor. I have been dead for the past ten years. However, I have been keeping an eye on him from, ah, up above, as the saying goes."

"Really, continued Potter? Would you kindly tell the Court what you have witnessed?"

"Well, I would like to go back a little further some to when I was alive. You see, I was a lawyer as my occupation. When I first began, well before Grant or the other children were born, I worked for a large law firm. The firm represented rich people and large corporations.

Quite a bit of money can be made doing that, and I do not fault them for doing it, nor do I believe that there is anything wrong working for a large law firm. Just wasn't my cup of tea, as the saying goes. After a few years, I realized that it wasn't the kind of work I wanted to do; it was not why I went to law school, which was to help people. So I went out on my own and started a small law firm; just a few lawyers and myself. It was definitely a struggle for the first few years. We didn't make the kind of money that a large corporate firm did but, eventually, it was a good living. The best thing about it was that I could represent the types of people who really needed help. I took on unpopular cases; some people did not like that too much. Don't get me wrong, I was no Atticus Finch by any means. Those times were difficult for my family I admit. Kid took some guff at school for that. They were tough though; they could take it and they did.

We didn't live the life of kings, mind you. We didn't live in a one room shack either. Our life was comfortable. The kids didn't want for the necessities. Maybe they didn't always get the most expensive clothes, or the each have a television in their room. But they got what they needed with a little whipped cream thrown on top from time to time. Everyone went to college on my dime; it didn't cost them one red cent. My wife and I taught them that your life shouldn't be judged by what you owned, but by the good works you did for others. Hell, we weren't a religious family; I hadn't been in a church for years until they rolled me into one in a box. I wanted our kids to understand that your place in the world is determined by how you occupy it. You are repaid many times your kindness. Most of the time the repayment is not in money or material things, but in knowing that you made someone's existence just a little bit better. My kids got that. Well, most of them got it. Grant was always a little different.

From a fairly early age, Grant was obsessed by money and social standing. He began by doing odd jobs, and then had a paper route, just like a lot of other kids. He tried to sell his broken toys to other kids. I put a stop to that pretty quickly. He gave me lip about that; told me if the kids were stupid enough to buy busted toys that was their lookout. When he was old enough he bought a riding mower and cut grass around the neighborhood. He would only spend money when he absolutely had to, or when spending would enhance his ability to make more money. One time his sister asked if she could borrow a few dollars from him so she could get her mother something for her birthday. Grant refused and told her if she wanted money badly enough that she should get a job to earn it. Eventually, he had enough customers so he could hire kids to cut grass. He hired neighborhood kids to do the work while he managed schedules and looked for more business. Their pay was as little as Grant could get away with, but they needed the work and really did not know any better. When I told him that he should pay them more, he told me that if they didn't like the money they were making that they could just go find another job.

Grant took some heat at school about our social standing, or what he perceived to be the lack of it. The schools Grant went to were populated with lower-middle class kids. My wife and I certainly could have put all of our children in private schools. It was important to us that they did not have a sense of entitlement just because I was an attorney, and we wanted them to understand that most folks had to work hard and struggle to make ends meet. Grant always felt superior to his classmates, even though we were of modest means. He had a vast dislike for the kids who received free lunches, or those whose family was receiving government assistance of any sort. And he had an even greater dislike for those who might come forward and help someone who needed it. In his mind they were chumps. To this day, I cannot understand why Grant feels this way about people.

Grant and I clashed quite a bit, especially after he graduated college. There is no question that he is a very good businessman. He could take a company and turn it into a money maker in very little time. However, his business models were not always the most ethical, and he would skirt the line between good business practice and unlawful ones at almost every business he owned. It was as if he took immense joy at separating people who had very little money from it. One time, before he married he came home one night regaling everyone around the dinner table on how his business had caused a number of his customers to go bankrupt and lose their homes. I asked him how he could make money by having his customers file for bankruptcy, and he said there was a world full of stupid people who would gladly purchase things they didn't need and that he could scoop up handfuls of them all the time.

Not only did he treat his customers like dirt, he treated his employees even worse, if that is possible. He'd fire people on a whim, and particularly seemed to enjoy terminating people's employment close to holidays. He spied on people, listened to their phone calls, intimidated and berated top management, especially in front of other managers. Top executives would receive telephone calls from him late at night, on weekends, and when they were on vacation. Nothing was too trivial for him to bother people about. He made all business decisions, even though he hired very smart people to make decisions to benefit the companies he owned. Grant would tell these executives that if they stayed the course with him, then they would reap the benefits when the business was sold. Before that could happen, he made sure that he badgered these good people and made their lives so miserable that, if he didn't fire them, they would quit on their own accord before he had the chance to get rid of them.

It is one thing to disagree with me over how he conducted his business. At the end of the day, he has to live with himself about whether the money that he's made is honest money or not. I know that Grant didn't have much regard for me because of my criticism of him. And he always blamed me, at least in his vision, for not providing the kind of life and the material things he thought he deserved when he was a child. My way of doing things made me an idiot in his eyes. I can live with that, if you'll pardon the pun. Now, he has more money than he could spend in multiple lifetimes. Why, the house he lives in now would swallow up our old house three times over. He doesn't want for anything, at least in the material sense.

Yes, he believed that I was a silly old fool. I made my decisions as how to live as I saw fit, a quality it would appear that Grant and I share, I suppose. That is alright by me. I love my son, always have. The thing that does stick in my craw though, is the way that he treats his brothers, sister, and their children."

"How's that," the old lawyer asked?

To Grant, his family is not worth the cow crap in a manure factory. He acts as if his siblings somewhere along the line did him the same type of wrong that Grant perceives that I did to him. Grant was the youngest, and his siblings protected him. There was nothing his brothers and sister would not do for him. They doted upon him; took the blame for him when he did something wrong. They would take the punishment.

Yet, even today, Grant would wish to be anywhere other than to be around his siblings and their families. Whatever the occasion, he does his best to find any excuse not to attend. On the rare times that he does show up at a family event, he would disrupt it by getting into an argument with one or all of his siblings. It was at a Thanksgiving dinner not long ago that he told his brother Ted, who is a teacher that he was a loser and a sucker. Teaching is, in Grant's opinion, for sissies or for those who could not find anything else to do with their life Grant told Ted that he makes Ted's yearly salary in one month, as if it was the money that drives Ted to be the great teacher that he is. His other two siblings? They are just a carbon copy of their stupid father so far as Grant is concerned. They took over my practice when I, ahem, made other living arrangements. They are continuing the public service work I began, and Grant believes them to be idiots for doing so.

It has been so difficult for me is to watch Grant increasingly ignore his family. I always believed that, up until the time Grant left for college, we were a close knit family. We spent holidays and special occasions together. My kids prefer the company of family more than that of friends. As terribly as Grant has treated them, they have sincerely wanted him to be a part of each special event; to celebrate the birth of niece and nephew; to be at graduations and birthdays. They are truly pained, not at what Grant says to them, but that he won't even answer a phone call or acknowledge an invitation. He is always too busy; the family occasions are too asinine or trivial to be bothered with. Grant's family is an enemy that has never done anything to deserve the neglect and enmity the he heaps upon them. They just hope that someday he will realize just how important family is. I am not so sure that after all the abuse Grant has heaped upon them if they would be there for him anymore should something happen to him. After all, just how much horse crap is a family supposed to take? How much belittling are they supposed to endure from someone who acts as if you are not even alive. I fear that one day that Grant will need his family but he has pushed them so far away that they no longer will extend their hands to him."

The old grey haired attorney walked back to his seat and turned to look at Mr. Grant seated at the other table. "Is there anything that you wish to say to your father?" Grant pushed his chair back and stood. As far as he was concerned, this charade had gone on long enough. But he wasn't going to leave without a parting shot, carefully aimed and potent enough to inflict maximum damage.

"I don't know who this apparition is, nor do I particularly care. But he can go to hell and pass this message on to dear old Dad. Did I despise my father? You bet I did. Did I believe that he shirked his responsibilities by not providing for us to the maximum extent he could have? There is no question about it. Do I think that my siblings are dolts, idiots, cretins and fools? Absolutely. Would I ever do anything to help them if they were in need? Not on your life. I came down to this Court this morning because I was supposed to have jury duty. Instead, I get hauled before some mystical court and get slapped with some absurd charges having to do with taking advantage of the poor and extreme narcissism or some such nonsense. Now, I have had enough of this crap and have had an entire morning wasted being subjected to this comedy of fools. So, if you will kindly excuse me, I am going to take my leave of this absurdity and get back to my office before the clowns that I employ find a way to drive me out of business. Thank you."

"Stay right where you are Mr. Savage, said the Judge, banging his gavel for quiet. This won't take very long. I have listened to everything that has transpired, and you are quite the specimen, Savage. It is quite clear that you are self-centered, ego maniacal, stingy, and I am sure quite a few other adjectives that I wouldn't use in this courtroom, or want on the record. The way you treat people is abominable; the way you treat your family is unconscionable.

What you have been charged with Mr. Savage are not crimes; that is true. But they are unacceptable practices for people to engage in and live in a decent society. You act as if you are the only person on the planet, yet you couldn't function and have your wealth without people producing for you and buying from you. You despise the very people on whose back you make your fortune. This may seem as if this is all a joke to you; but it was not for your benefit alone. The people who are sitting here today are very interested in how you reacted and whether or not you had any introspection into your actions. You obviously have no insight into yourself, sir, and have no repentance at all. The saying that you reap what you have sown is of particular applicability to you. The whirlwind aimed in your direction will be one that you will regret for many a year to come.

Having said my piece, I find that you are guilty as charged on all counts. Your penalty is the time that you spent away from your job this morning. No doubt, the inconvenience of your time here is worse than anything anyone has said to you in this courtroom. Let me say this to you in closing. Take heed of what you have heard. This joke and charade, as you have called it, is predictive of your behavior going forward, I fear. Defecating on your fellow man and your family will be tolerated for only so long before you stumble and fall into the same pile you have been pushing others into. Your turn is coming sooner than you think, and this may only be Act I of the drama. We are adjourned."

Chapter III

Without stopping to say anything to anybody, Grant bounded up the steps and out of the courthouse. It took less than five minutes for him to get in his car and race out of the municipal parking lot. Looking at his watch, he could see that it a little past one o'clock. Crap, he thought, half of the day had already been taken up with the buffoonery at the Court. He hated wasting time, especially when there was so much to do before Christmas. Media placements had to be made for maximum exposure. Call center coverage would have to be expanded to handle the increase of volume generated by the new commercials hitting television and radio. This was not the time to have half of his day taken up by the antics of this morning.

Grant grabbed his cell phone and dialed the number of his general counsel. He waited but after a few rings the call went into voice mail. Next, he dialed the main number and that went into voice mail. Nobody was answering the phones, and Grant was beginning to get progressively angrier and angrier. It was expected that the phones were to be answered by the second ring; he had fired a receptionist just a week ago for not following that edict. Well, this one wasn't going to make it until Christmas, as the first thing Grant planned to do when he arrived at the office was to ax this incompetent new receptionist. It couldn't happen soon enough for Grant, waiting at the last stop light before the driveway to his company.

His steps were purposeful, one might even say frenetic, as he walked toward the front door of the building that housed his company. The elevator took him to the second floor. He stepped out, turned to the right toward the double glass doors of Rapid Response. Reaching out he grabbed the handle of the glass doors and pulled. The door would have snapped off its hinges had the door opened, as hard has he pulled on the handle. But it didn't; and it would not open no matter how hard Grant pulled on the handle. "You can yank on that handle until you are blue in the face, a voice from behind Grant said, but you can't get in there."

Grant swung around to the sound of the voice and saw his general counsel leaning against the wall about ten feet from him. So focused on getting to his office, Grant never noticed that he was standing there. "We had some visitors while you were away doing your civic duty today. They really wanted to have a chat with you, but they understood that you had jury duty. They'll catch up with you soon enough. Actually, it probably all worked out for the best that you weren't here. I would imagine that you will want your personal attorney with you when they do get around to speaking with you."

"What the hell are you talking about? Why are these doors locked and why can't I get to my office? "

"Do you remember we had a conversation about six months ago about your No Refund policy? I told you that you can't keep customer funds and not send out merchandize. There was also the issue of complaints not being resolved. Remember I told you that you couldn't make a statement that their good payment record would be reported to credit rating agencies to build up their credit score if you never had any intention of making the reports? I recall saying to you that eventually someone was going to get really pissed that Rapid was taking advantage of people and scamming them? If my memory serves me correctly, and it always does, do you also remember me telling you that a big pile of crap was going to tumble down on top of you and take you and your shell game out? Well, guess what? Consider yourself taken out."

"Why don't you give me a straight answer? Grant yelled. Because I do not have the faintest idea what is going on."

"Of course you don't have any idea. Probably because you believe that you can get away with anything. So I will make it very simple for you. The Feds came here this morning and closed you down." Rapid Response has been put into receivership. All assets have been seized. Since you are named personally in the suit, all of your assets have been frozen as well. That means credit cards, bank accounts, property, anything in your name. You cannot touch anything until this comes to court." Rick handed the legal papers to Grant, whose hands were visibly shaking as he took them.

"They can't do that! Rapid is a limited liability corporation, they cannot seize my personal assets, only those of the corporation! Why didn't you stop them? How did they get all of this information," Grant said in rapid fire fashion as he scanned the papers.

"Let's go through this one at a time, shall we? They can shut you down pursuant to the provisions of a number of banking and consumer credit and protection statutes that they have alleged that you violated. The Feds usually give you some warning and let you clean up your mess, but they believed your mess was too big to clean up. They wanted to make sure that they protected the corporation assets so that when they liquidate them there is enough to pay the people that you shanked. For some reason, they seem to believe that you have a history of screwing people out of their money. Being that you didn't learn much from your last business exploding and your stockholders left holding the

149

bag, they were not going to give you any more time to bilk any additional people out of their money. As for your contention that they cannot seize your personal assets, well, you are dead wrong. They maintain that the company is just an alter ego of you. In other words, you are the corporation and since you and the corporation are one and the same, they can seize your assets as well as those of the corporation.

Second, there was nothing I could do to stop them. The closing and the asset seizure is completely lawful. I did try to get through to you when the Marshalls arrived to let you know what was going on, but you were in court. You never called me back. Then again, I didn't expect you would, seeing that you never return my calls or emails.

Finally, over the past month or so, I have received several calls from investigators who work for a couple of states Attorneys' General. They told me that they were preparing to file suit against Rapid sometime in the next couple of months. You and I discussed this. The AGs had some pretty good information, and they passed it on to the Fed. I made a few phone calls to the Fed myself to help them fill in the blanks, especially as it pertained to fraud. Inducing people to give you money in exchange for helping their credit rating, when you have no intention of doing so isn't very nice. It is also unlawful. The actual legal term is fraud in the inducement. But being nice or doing things within the letter of the law has never been particularly important to you."

Grant's face turned pale as he listened to his General Counsel continued speaking. This is not, could not be happening. He must be dreaming. Everything that occurred since this morning was not real. All he had to do was open his eyes or click his heels three times to make

Rick and everything vanishes. Unfortunately, all was as it appeared to be. Grant was not dreaming.

"Wait a minute, you told the Feds about what was going on here. That was privileged information. You're not allowed to talk about anything that goes on here with anyone. First I am going to fire you. Then I am going to sue you and have you disbarred. I'll have your license to practice law. You will never get another job as an attorney as long as you live."

Rick chuckled. "Well, it seems the Fed took care of the termination of my job, not to mention the termination of everyone else who was working here. They beat you too it because everyone here was put out of work when they shut the joint down. As for filing suit to have me disbarred, go have at it. You see, confidentiality and privilege do not extend to when a client is going to commit a crime or the crime is ongoing. The fraud I spoke to you about continued after I advised you to stop. That being the case, I was required by operation of statute to let the authorities know that you were breaking the law. I'll be happy to send you the section of the statute if you like, but if you want to sue me, go right ahead. It would be my pleasure to get up on the witness stand and let everyone know what a crooked, heartless bastard you are. Besides, as a whistleblower I get a cut of the assets the Feds have seized, so I expect that I will be receiving a sizable severance courtesy of the government. Hell, I am going to be the first and no doubt last person to get one of those "big" payouts you are always bloviating about. You go have yourself one big Merry Christmas, Chief." Rick turned and began whistling Deck the Halls, as he walked down the hall and pushed the elevator button. As he stepped in he gave a smile and a wave to Grant. The President and Chief Executive Officer of a company that no longer had any assets was left standing in the hallway with a sheaf of legal papers in his hand. With nothing left to do, he too walked to the elevator and went down in the next car.

Gray skies and a cold wind greeted him as he left the building. How did he miss all of this? Why hadn't he seen this coming? The truth was that arrogance and greed had created the tunnel vision through which he viewed the world. He did not understand that money, power, and control did not motivate everyone. In the past, he prided himself in his ability to hire executives who believed as he did. And should they show even the slightest hint of humanity toward customers, he fired them before they could cause any trouble. The flaws of others were always the problem; Grant never viewed anything that went wrong as his own doing. Rick had shown signs of disloyalty in the past, speaking out when customers were treated like crap. His general counsel frequently gave Grant legal opinions which displeased him. He would storm into Rick's office ranting about how Rick was an idiot; that he should go back to private practice. After arguing back and forth, Rick would always back down. How then did Rick manage to fool him so completely?

Grant had gotten into his car and was only a few minutes from his home as he continued to run the events of the last couple of hours through his head. Pulling into the driveway of his very large home, he mentally was ticking off a list of things he needed to do once inside. He would have to call his personal lawyers right away; that was the most important thing. There had to be something they could do to get the doors of Rapid open again before Christmas rolled around. Then he was going to find a way to completely ruin his spineless, former General Counsel who was inconveniencing his life. A malicious grin grew on Grant's face at the thought of the hell he was going to bring down on Rick. He has a wife, four children, college tuition, mortgage payment; everything would go up in smoke when Grant got done with him. Grant began punching numbers into the security lock at his front door thinking how much fun this was going to be. He finished entering the numbers and pushed the "Enter" key on the keypad and turned the door handle.

The door did not open. That is odd, he thought. He was sure he entered the correct code. Oh well, just have to try again. The door still would not open. It wasn't until he tried the number a few more times and was unsuccessful that he noticed a piece of paper taped on the wall to the left of the door. The grin disappeared as he read the content of the paper. Just as his business had been seized, so too had his house. The security code had been deactivated, the windows barred, and any other entry padlocked. It was painfully obvious that he could not enter his million dollar home.

A few minutes passed with Grant standing numbly at the front door, when he heard footsteps crunching on the frozen grass coming toward him. Maybe it was a federal agent coming to speak with him. Grant mused to himself that if it was someone in authority he could get them to at least let him into his house. After all, it was the middle of the winter and getting pretty cold. Grant walked out from the portico of his house and turned toward the sound. He swore when he saw the man now standing on the grass by the walkway. It was the old man he saw in the courtroom this morning. Grant thought that he must be going mad.

"Not having the best of days, are you son?"

"Who went to bed last night and dreamt up this nightmare? You again? How'd you get here from the courthouse, float through the clouds?

"It really is not important how I arrived here. And to answer your first question, this is a nightmare of your own making."

"Is that so? You are telling me that I deserve all of this?"

"That is a question you have to answer for yourself."

"Now I get it. This is some modern day Christmas Carol where I am going to see the errors of my way. I am going to find redemption, save Tiny Tim, but him the prize turkey, and give money to the poor. Fat chance of that sort of thing happening. You can go back to where you came from or Ghost of whatever Christmas you came from because none of it scares me."

"I will be on my way soon enough, son. My purpose here is not to frighten you or to redeem you. That is the point; you are past redemption. This is a hole that you have dug with your own shovel. Call it karma; call it anything you like, but you are reaping the seeds of misery you have sown. You have treated people like dirt for so many years, beginning with your own family. You never had time for them. You have scorned them, mistreated them, and ignored them all because they did not follow your path and believe that the world was made in your image. Our family has always had empathy for those who are less fortunate. You, on the other hand, have spent your days trying to find ways to separate those unfortunates from the few dollars that they have left, all for your personal gain. And you succeeded, by preying upon the simple dreams the poor have of providing a computer or a television for a child.

What has all of your money gotten for you now? Do you think that your brothers and sister are going to come to your rescue now, especially after that display in Court today? After all of the Christmas' that you were too busy to attend, do you believe that you are going to be a welcome presence in their homes this Christmas season? Are they going to extend a helping hand to you when you never extended one to them? Yes, I have taught them to be loving, kind and generous, and charitable, so I am sure that you will see them as vengeful when they turn their backs on you in your time of need. I am frankly surprised that you would think of asking them for charity when you have no clue as to the definition of the word. Maybe someday they will visit some kindness in your direction. For the time being, you are going to suffer in the same manner that you have made others suffer. You will see how small you are in this world; that you don't really matter much in the grand scheme of things. You will be the same insignificant being that you have accused your siblings of being."

Grant took a step toward his father, disdain written across his face. "Do you really think I need you, or anyone else to get by? Even if all that has gone on today is not the product of a bad dream, I have enough money that I never have to work again. Take away my house, I'll buy another one. Close down my business, I'll just start another business and make millions on that. So go away old man, you are nothing but a tiring joke."

"Maybe you have some money to keep you going for a couple of months or so. That is not really the point. More ratchet jawing won't get you to understand and I can see that I am just wasting my time. So I will get going. See you around one of these days, son." The old man gently patted Grant on the shoulder and turned away and began walking before Grant could react. He started back toward his front door, stopped, and looked over his shoulder in the direction of his father. He saw nothing. Grant tried one more time to open the front door to his house but was again unsuccessful. Believing that any further attempts would be a waste of time, he walked to his car, got in and drove away. Not every Christmas story has a happy ending. Grant Savage was neither seen nor heard from again.

Nightlights on Christmas

Chapter I

I used to love Christmas; always did. My thoughts of that wonderful holiday would begin way before the traditional start of the season. I could not wait for the holiday movies; after all, who doesn't love It's a Wonderful Life or Miracle on 34th Street? You might even have found me at midnight Mass on Christmas Eve, the one time of year that I would go to church. Toss in the decorations, the cookies, Christmas tree, holiday parties, Christmas carols, and it was the most exciting, beautiful, wonderful season of the entire year. Not for me anymore. Not for the last few years though. There had been nothing but loneliness, sadness, and bitterness come the 25th of December and the days leading up to it. No family or Christmas Day dinner; no joyful opening of presents surrounded by loved ones and the beautifully decorated tree. Each holiday season over the last five years has been a little more depressing than the one before it. I can guarantee, however, that this Christmas will be very different than the last. That is because tonight, the first Sunday of Advent, I intend to end my life.

The one tradition I will keep, and one which has nothing at all to do with Christmas is the one of writing a note to tell of the reasons why I believe ending my life is necessary. I am not seeking sympathy; I am not built that way. To most, my decision could only be considered to be idiotic, stupid, absurd, or a combination of all three. That is a completely reasonable conclusion, if you will pardon the pun. Ending your own life is certainly a drastic step to take just because you're a little sad at the holidays. I totally agree. I am trading in the possibility of my life changing for the better somewhere down the road for the nothingness of death. Death is irrevocable, at least as far as I know. And if there is anything on the "other side," I doubt that I will endear myself to whoever runs the post-mortem establishment by arriving early. I will, however, take my chances.

For the purpose of identification, my name is William Monaghan, but I go by Billy. I am fifty-seven years old and live in a small town outside Chicago, Illinois. Born in the Bronx, New York, I have lived in New Jersey, California, Maryland, Massachusetts, and Illinois. Over my fifty seven years, I have been to every state in the nation at least once, and to forty seven other countries around the world. Travelling was part of my job for quite a long time, and I enjoyed every minute.

Until about five years ago, and for the last almost forty years, I have been a musician. Nope, I have never been famous, and I doubt that you have ever heard of me, unless you really love to read liner notes. During that time, I have been playing guitar and doing back-up vocals for some very well-known rock and roll bands when they go on tour. I have also been a studio guitarist. It has been a great life, and, as the saying goes, it was one long run of "Drugs, Sex, and Rock and Roll. That was my life until five years ago, when my health began to decline sharply.

The first thing to happen was that my voice started to go. Decades of smoking and screaming at the top of my lungs every night began to take their toll. I really began to notice it in my late forties when I didn't have the breath to hold notes as long as I had been able to in the past. Over the next year or so, my voice began to get scratchy and hoarse, and to break up on higher notes. I saw a number of doctors; all chalked it up years of smoking. They told me that I wouldn't get it back even if I quit, so what the hell, no reason to stop smoking, was there? Fortunately, I didn't need my voice to rip it up on the guitar, so while I didn't do much concert work, I was still in demand for studio musician work. Then the other shoe fell.

I was in my apartment just hanging out one day. It was between gigs, and I was catching up on watching some football. There were some beer, chips and various other munchies on a table to my left. I reached over to pick up my beer from the table and I noticed that my hand was shaking. That was definitely weird. I set the beer down and attempted to pick it up again. More hand shaking. To matters worse, my fingers started to get really stiff for no reason. Over the next few weeks, the shaking became more pronounced, as did the stiffness. I couldn't play the guitar because my left hand was the one I used to play the chords or to slide up and down the neck of the guitar to do solo riffs. Again I went to see my physician who sent me to a specialist. Upon completing some scans, I received the bad news. It was Parkinson's disease. My playing days were over.

Maybe it wouldn't be quite as bad if I had some family around to help get me over the emotional shock of my career being flushed down the crapper. Travelling from state to state and never having put down any roots, until recently, does not make for a stable family life. Sure, I met a lot of women in my years of traveling. I fell in love with some of them, too. But going from city to city was a little like being in a new candy store every day. There was always a new flavor to taste. Being a part of the band meant parties with celebrities and groupies, and I was never far away from the next beautiful girl. Seeing guys in the bands that had been divorced multiple times made it much easier for me not to get too connected to anyone. The next day there was always another town, making it much simpler to stay on my own. No emotional entanglements for me.

All my relatives are either dead or I have lost track of them a long time ago. My parents and grandparents are all deceased, and have been for many years. I don't stay in touch with any uncles or cousins. I didn't see eye to eye with a few of them on certain things. I lost touch with others because it was too difficult for them to keep track of where I was crashing. Moving around so often, it was hard for anyone to know where I was at any one time. Never did have much in common with my siblings, so it's been years since I have seen them. For the life of me, I couldn't tell you where they even live these days. And the friends you make when you are on the road are only your friends when you are on the road. The band, the roadies, and the groupies all vanish once the tour is over. Being that I was not a "member" of any of the bands I toured with and just a hired hand, my connection to them was only for as long as we were on the road. Fame is a very fleeting thing for most of these guys, and I was just a rental. It is not the glamorous life that many people think. Whatever glamour there was on the road ended forever the moment the tremors in my hand began.

Things got progressively worse as time went on. The tremors continued and then I developed an unsteady, shuffling gait. For someone as independent as me, it was sheer torture. Sure, I was prescribed medications and they helped to a certain extent. Unfortunately, there was not going to be any silver bullet. Medication made my head feel fuzzy and disconnected to the world around me. Taking walks, another activity that I loved to do was a waste of time; I couldn't really go anywhere of any distance. And the old love life shriveled up pretty quickly too. Not too many women are interested in a long haired, fifty-seven year old dude with Parkinson's. I really can't say that I blame them much.

I was always good with my money, so that has nothing to do with deciding to take a ride on the Stygian ferry. Put away enough from all those years on the road so that I would be pretty set for years to come. Money does not have much significance when you are all alone and your health is the shits. What am I going to do, spend it on a big house and fill it with expensive doodads and gee-gaws? That is really not my style. Sitting around reading, listening to music and smoking the occasional bone is my speed. And it is a much too slow speed when you realize that it is never going to get any faster.

The Christmas holidays coming up in about three weeks or so just makes things all the more difficult to deal with. Over the past five years, my acquaintances from the music scene have stopped coming over or inviting me to their places for Christmas. Who wants to have someone over for Christmas dinner that looks like a drunk fixing to bust up the good china? Nobody has reached out the past two years, so I have spent the past couple of years alone in this apartment. There hasn't been a Christmas tree in here for years, neither have I bothered to put up any decorations. What's the point? It's not like a crowd is going to be visiting and see them. Besides, what do I have to celebrate anyway?

So, maybe I am being a wuss for deciding to check out. Facing another Christmas alone just doesn't do it for me. Watching the joy of others on the streets or in the stores holds absolutely no interest for me either. Oh, I could cook a fancy holiday dinner for myself, but it loses its cache when you're the only one that you are cooking for. None of it is worth the effort, so why pretend that it is? Any regrets that I have, well, it is really too late to do much about them. The only thing that bothers me a little is that I will not leave behind anything of value. I do not mean money or material things; any of that stuff will be disposed of in my will. Yes, I do have one. What I mean is that I left no mark on the world. People are neither better nor worse off for my having lived. Absolutely a zero sum game as far as I am concerned. Playing in a few bands and having my name in some liner notes is not much of a legacy. No time left to go back and make good on broken promises or mend the people that I have hurt along the way. I was a very good musician, a good back-up singer and I had fun doing it. That, unfortunately, is going to have to be enough. But, having read this note, you all know that it isn't.

Well, I am about at the end of this short tome. I have just taken a fist full of sleeping pills and a few other pharmaceuticals and washed them down with a glass of exceedingly good twelve year old single malt. Indulgence is not necessarily a bad thing, one that I believe that is well deserved as I shuffle off the mortal coil. In a few minutes I will begin to become drowsy and unable to write coherently. Before that occurs, I will take my leave and go to my bed to lie down. Falling off of this chair, hitting the floor, and possibly foaming at the mouth is something I would prefer to avoid. After all, I would like to keep my dignity intact as much as possible. Thank you to the person who finds me and who reads this letter, and I will apologize in advance for the one who does wind up with that unpleasant task. Look at it this way; it beats the mess of a gunshot to the head or hanging oneself, doesn't it? One hates to leave questions unanswered, and I suspect there will be a few once you find me. I may not have answered everything, but I have, at the very least, given you an idea as to why I believe that this was necessary. Goodbye all! It has definitely been a blast.

Chapter II

It didn't work out quite the way Billy had planned. He had not expected to wake up with an IV in his arm and both arms tethered to the bed rails. He didn't expect to wake up at all. Obviously, someone must have found him and called for an ambulance to take him to the hospital before the pills and booze could finish him off. His memory was pretty fuzzy, so he didn't remember anything from the time he drained off his glass of scotch to awakening a couple minutes ago. How long had he been here? Was it hours or was it days? The scratchiness in his throat led him to believe that at some point he had had a breathing tube inserted down his throat. Must have been pretty serious, he concluded, for him to have been on a respirator, if that is what had occurred. One thing was certain, he was not going anywhere for at least a little while.

During Billy's short conversation with himself, a nurse had poked her head into the room. She saw that his eyes were open and figuring that he was might have a question or two, she went to find the physician who was in charge of Billy's care. By the time that Dr. Crane entered the room, Bill had cleared the majority of cobwebs from his head. He was in his mid-to late 30s, about average height with a receding hair line. Dr. Crane did not wear the ubiquitous white coat or a tie; he was in corduroy slacks and an Oxford shirt open at the neck. Unless you knew that he was a physician, he looked like an everyman employed in an everyman type of job.

Dr. Crane pulled up a chair next to Billy's bed, sat down and smiled at him. It was a nice, friendly smile; the type that immediately would put his patients at ease. That was unless the patient happened to be named Billy Monaghan. "So, William, how are you feeling? My name is Dr. Crane. It's good to see that you are finally awake. You had a few rough days there, so I imagine that you are still a little groggy."

"The name's Billy. I can pretty much figure out where I am, and the reason that I am here. When do you figure that I can get these restraints off of my arms? I don't particularly care to be tied down like a rodeo bull. The other question that I have for you, is when can I get out of here? I don't much like hospitals either."

"Well, first off, I think that we can remove these restraints now, Dr. Crane said. We only put them on to protect you as you were thrashing quite a bit for a while, and we didn't want you to tear out the IV line. You appear to be pretty calm now, and there isn't anything in this room that you can hurt yourself with." Dr. Crane got up from the chair and began to remove the restraints that pinned Billy's arms to the bed rails. "As for your being discharged, well, that's probably going to take a couple of days. I want to have a chance to talk to you and see why you felt the need to try to kill yourself. I also want to see how you interact with the patients here so I can get a feel for how you will do once you are discharged. And, of course, we are going to want to get you started on some antidepressants and see how you tolerate them before we discharge you"

"So, I assume that I am in a locked psych unit? Terrific. Just what I need, spending time with Nurse Ratchet and a bunch bat shit crazy people. And I am not real keen on taking any more medication than I already am, Doc."

Dr. Crane chuckled, "I believe that you have the wrong impression of what a psychiatric unit is like these days. Most of the people here are high-functioning individuals just like you. Some have attempted suicide and are trying to work through the reasons that brought them here. Others are dealing with deep depression and anxiety. There are a few that hear voices, but they don't bother anyone. If you saw these people on the street, you wouldn't think there was anything wrong with them. They do take medications, as you will, but they are not zoned out zombies. There is nothing here that you should worry about other than trying to get well. As to taking antidepressants, well, you are going to have to take them for at least a little while to see if we can get your mood stabilized. Sometimes all I may have to do is to adjust the dosage of the meds you are already on. Let's have an open mind about this and see if we can get you out of here in a few days, okay?"

Billy saw a white box that was clipped onto the sheet of his bed. He knew that it controlled the head and foot of the bed, as well as serving as a remote control for the television that was bolted to the wall. Pressing one of the buttons, he raised the head of the bed so he could more comfortably see the doctor. The only way out of the hospital would be for him to play the game and make the staff believe that he was not going to hurt himself once he was released. He could do that. Once he got home, however, he was going to find a way to off himself that left nothing to chance. "Okay Doc, let's get started. The quicker I get out of this bed the quicker I start working on getting out of here."

"Whoa sport, let's take things one step at a time. What's the rush? You were unconscious for a few days, so I want to make sure that there is nothing medical lingering with you before you are transferred to the unit. We are going to watch you for a few hours, get you something to eat, and have you take a shower. If all goes well, we will get you situated on the unit a shortly after dinner. Does that work for you?"

Dr. Crane got up and pushed the chair back to its original spot, and stuck out his hand. "I'll see you after dinner to make sure that you have gotten settled in, okay?" shaking Billy's hand. "We'll let you get a good night's sleep and start fresh in the morning. See you later, Billy. He walked out the door, leaving Billy to ponder his situation.

*B*illy showered after dinner and shortly thereafter was led through the hospital to the locked psychiatric wing. Prior to leaving, he was allowed to get rid of the hospital gown and was given the clothes that he arrived at the hospital. He could wear those on the psych unit, and he was grateful for losing the air conditioning from the open gown that froze his backside off. After showering and putting on his own clothes, he was beginning to feel somewhat human again.

There was nothing remarkable about the psych wing; it could be mistaken for any other floor of the hospital, except that a nurse or orderly had to unlock a door for anyone to enter or exit. He was told that he would be observed for about twenty-four hours, and assuming there were no problems, he would be able to cross over and to the unlocked unit. There he would be able to move around more freely; take walks around the hospital grounds and go to the cafeteria or the gift shop with a pass. From there, he would be discharged. When that would happen depended on how Billy progressed. As soon as it was determined by Dr. Crane that Billy was no longer a danger to himself or to others, he would be released. As long as he showed none of those behaviors, the maximum time he could be held involuntarily was 72 hours.

He had no doubt that one of the first things that would occur was that Dr. Crane was going to prescribe some kind of antidepressant for him. Nuts to that, Billy thought. He had no intention of taking medication any longer that he absolutely had to, which was odd given that he had gulped down a fistful of pills a few days before. He was going to be the perfect patient and get out as soon as he could. So if that included taking anti-nutso pills for a day or two, so be it. Just because his first attempt to end his life was unsuccessful did not mean that he wasn't going to try again. He just wasn't going to tell anybody that little gem. All of the crap that led up to his first attempt was still there. A couple of pills and a few days of speaking with a shrink were not going to suddenly have him seeing life in a new, rosy way. He could bullshit with the best of them, and, although he did not relish the idea of being in a psych unit, he could definitely play the game well enough to fool the staff. He made a promise to himself that he would not be coming here again. Not because he abandoned his plan for suicide, but because this time he'd make sure that he didn't fail.

Most of the patients were in the television room, so he walked in and found an empty seat and sat down. Outside of Dr. Crane, who stopped by to tell Billy that he would see him for an extended chat tomorrow morning, he didn't speak with anyone else. He didn't plan on his being in the loony bin long enough to be making any friends. It was not that Billy was unfriendly by nature; he just did not want to hear anyone's sob stories. In addition, having only regained consciousness less than twelve hours ago, he was still kind of sleepy. Hopefully, he could take his leave of the television room soon and go to his room to get some shut eye. He wanted to be fresh so he could speak with Dr. Crane and begin the process of getting himself discharged.

At 10:00 p.m. there was an announcement that evening medications were being distributed. People began to get out of their chairs and head for a window at the back of the room. They formed a line, were given their medications, and a nurse watched to make sure that each patient swallowed the meds. Billy remained where he was watching the line move along. He wasn't sure that any medication was prescribed for him, so when there was nobody left in line he got up from his seat and began to make his way to his room.

"Mr. Monaghan, please come to the nurse's station. Mr. Monaghan, please come to the nurse's station."

Guess there are some magic bullets for me after all, he mused. He showed the nurse his hospital bracelet and she scanned the bar code. He also had to spell his last name and give her his date of birth. She came back to the window with a small medicine cup containing two capsules, each one a different size and color. "The red one is for sleep, and the other is an antidepressant," the nurse said. For an instant, Billy was going to tell her that he didn't need an antidepressant, but thought better of it. He realized that if he complained it might complicate things, and even may delay his release. "Not worth it," he thought. Swallowing both medications, he walked away and towards his room. It was a single room, which suited him just fine; he didn't want a roommate. Less than ten minutes later, he had undressed and climbed into the bed. Shortly thereafter, he had fallen into a deep sleep.

Billy awakened in much better shape than he had been in the night before. His mind was clear and without the grogginess he had been experiencing. This didn't change his determination to get released from the hospital and complete his plan for suicide. Hopefully he could convince the doctor than he had made a mistake and that any thoughts of suicide had disappeared. He acted cheerful at breakfast, interacting for the first time with some of the other patients. It was all an act. In reality, he had no interest in these folks at all. Their petty problems could not hold a candle to the things that he was going through. Some of the younger ones fell all over themselves when he told them the names of some of the groups he toured with. It was probable a mistake to have done that because after breakfast he went to the day room to read a newspaper, and he couldn't get through one story without being interrupted and asked about his music career. But he kept his cool, put down the paper and politely answered all their questions, even if he had answered the same ones at the breakfast table not fifteen minutes earlier.

It wasn't until after the morning group session than Billy was called to the nurse's station to see Dr. Crane. They walked together down a hallway and the doctor used a key to open one of the private office doors. It was softly lit and comfortable; the type of environment that was designed to put a psychologically ill patient at ease.

Billy sat down on a leather sofa across from the doctor. He smiled; waiting for the interrogation that he knew was soon to begin. Dr. Crane flipped through Billy's chart for a moment or two, made a few notes on a separate pad then put the chart down on the end table beside him.

"Well Billy, I have read through your chart, which includes your rather extensive suicide note, so I have an idea of some of the issues that you have going on. Do you want to tell me about it now that you a few days removed from the events?"

"You see doctor, there isn't really much to tell. I made a really stupid mistake. Yeah, I have been pretty down about the physical stuff I have going on, but the pills and the booze are not the way to take care of them. I overacted to the holidays coming up and was thinking what a bummer it would be to chill by myself on Christmas"

"Many people spend the holidays alone, some by choice and others because they have no other option. I believe that there is more to it than what you are telling me. Had you not passed out on your way to the bed and not made all the noise that you did, your neighbor would not have called the police. If you had gotten here about five minutes later than you did, we wouldn't be sitting here having this conversation. I mean that you would have been quite dead and there wouldn't have been anything that anyone could have done to save you. You are quite fortunate; extremely lucky I would say."

"I am very lucky doc, I know that. Don't know what I was thinking when I acted so foolishly. I do not intend to act that way again, I can assure you of that."

"Billy, I have seen a lot of patients over my career, so don't try to sell me any crap. Very few people write out as detailed a suicide note as you did. Most people who are successful at killing themselves don't even bother to leave a note, or if they do, their note is only a few lines long. I can tell by the way you express yourself and from your musical career that you are not someone who gives up easily. So cut the horseshit and let's have a meaningful conversation or you will wind up enjoying the psych unit's brand of hospitality for much more than a couple of days."

Billy was taken aback by Dr. Crane's bluntness. He was sure that he could hoodwink him, particularly after he had surveyed the intellectual makeup of the inmates he had already observed on the unit. Maybe this was going to take a little more inventiveness than he had figured. Crane appeared to be much more of a hard ass than Billy thought, mistaking his mild manners and soft appearance as being someone Billy could push over easily.

For the next hour, Billy gave a short history of his life to the doctor. Dr. Crane listened, would make a few notes on his pad, but generally had no response to what Billy was telling him. He told the psychiatrist about the Parkinson's and how it precluded him from playing the guitar at the level necessary to secure employment as a studio musician. As the hour was coming to a close, the doctor put his notebook on the table and brought the session to an end.

"Alright Billy, we have to wrap it up here for today. I want you to think about a few things before we meet again tomorrow. You have told me that your health and it's impact on your career are the reason you decided to end your life. I want you to think about why that is. Why is suicide the only answer you could come up with? Is there any other way that you can use your talents that will be fulfilling to you? Can you do something else, even if it is not music that will be rewarding? I will see you again tomorrow at about the same time and we'll talk about that. In the meantime, I will think about some suggestions I can pass along to you that could help you transition from where you are now to where you want to be"

Returning to the unit, Billy was confused. Didn't he already tell the doctor why he wanted to end his life? Wasn't the fact that he couldn't play anymore or sing anymore reason enough? "I can't just sit around for the next however many years of my natural life and twiddle my thumbs. Oh wait, I won't physically be able to twiddle my thumbs eventually," he mumbled to himself. He was further put off by the way this doctor was able to elicit stuff from Billy that he didn't want to be talking about. He said too much for his own good at times, instead of keeping his trap shut. If he wanted to get out of this place sooner rather than later, he was going to have to be quite a bit smarter and measure what information he was going to divulge to Crane. Unless he wanted to be spending quite a bit of time in the hospital, he had to convince the doctor that he was a safe bet not to attempt suicide again.

The next day Billy was moved to the unlocked unit. For the most part, it was a carbon copy of the locked unit, differing only in that patients received passes that permitted them to go to the cafeteria, gift shop, or to take a walk in the hospital's tranquility garden. Being in the open unit was a step in the direction of being discharged. How a patient handled this modicum of freedom was only part of the decision making process that determined whether or not he or she could handle being back in the general public. It usually took a few days for someone to make the adjustments necessary to be discharged after arriving on the open unit.

Billy continued to see Dr. Crane for the next two days after leaving the locked side. He was anxious to get out of the hospital. There was no doubt in his mind that he still was going to commit suicide once he was released. Nothing that had happened while an inpatient, nothing Dr. Crane said in therapy, not the group therapy, and not the medications had changed his mind one iota. The holidays were quickly approaching, and he did not want to be around for them. So he kept a pleasant demeanor on the outside while he seethed on the inside. As long as he did not reveal his true feelings and intentions to Crane, and as long as he did not explode at one of the pathetic inmates (as he called them), he should be discharged in a day or so, as the he had already been in the Nut House past, the seventy-two hour hold. But no matter how soon they cut him loose, it couldn't come soon enough for him.

Billy sat in Dr. Crane's office for the fourth time since he had been admitted. These sessions were a waste of his time as far as he was concerned, but it was part of the drill that he had to go through. Hopefully, this would be the last time he would have to see this clown, Billy mused, waiting for the session to begin.

"There is something that I wanted to ask you, Billy. You feel pretty sorry for yourself, don't you; like someone dealt you a pretty crappy hand of cards, right?"

Billy was stunned at the question. The few questions that Dr. Crane had asked over the last couple of sessions were generally to clarify something Billy had said. Billy was caught off-guard and was not prepared about anything particularly in depth. "I do not have the faintest idea what you are talking about, Doctor. Why would you think that I am feeling sorry for myself?"

"I am very familiar with the game that you are attempting to play. You come in here after damn near killing yourself and you pretend that you are miraculously cured. Acting as if you are cheerful and happy, ready to resume your life as if nothing happened once you are discharged doesn't fool me for a second. Your goal is to leave hear and try again, only this time I bet that you'll be successful. What will it be this time, Billy, a gun? Are you going to give hanging a whirl? Of course, you are only thinking of yourself just as you have always only thought of yourself. You have never put down any roots because the only thing you have ever had any interest in was having a good time. Screw responsibilities, right? The stage lights were never going to dim and the groupies would be falling through your door forever, weren't they? Well guess what, your body tossed a wrench into your plans. Your body failed you, just as everyone's eventually fails them. Some break down sooner and some break down later. It sucks, doesn't it? The only difference is that when it happens, most of us don't turn to suicide as the answer. People get up every day and struggle through their pain and their misery; they fight for one more day of the life you so blithely decided to end. And if you think you can bullshit me into believing your line of crap, than you better think again carefully."

Bile was rising up in Billy's throat. No way was this Bozo going to talk to him like that. Unfortunately, he could not just walk out of the room. No, that would derail everything. How far could he go without upsetting all of his plans? The more he thought about it, the more anger took over his emotions. "No, I am not feeling sorry for myself. My physical condition is real and I cannot do the things that I used to do. I am finished in my profession. Done. Music has been the only thing I've known for forty years. What am I supposed to do now?

"Do you really believe that you are the only one on the planet that has been dealt a raw deal, Dr. Crane responded. Nobody could possibly have it worse than you, could they? There isn't anyone other than you who have ever come down with a debilitating illness that has ended a career? We're sitting in a hospital, man. Why do you think that all of these people are here? Do you think it is their warped idea of Club Med? Of course they aren't. But you think; I'm Billy Monaghan, rock guitarist and music God. How dare something happen to me. Nobody has it worse than you, do they?

"Of course there are people who have horrible diseases. I have never said or implied otherwise. The difference is that their problems don't affect me. Whether they get better or worse is not my concern because it doesn't matter to me what happens to them. I am the one who cannot play music anymore. I am the one who cannot sing and go out on tour anymore. I'll bet those people have someone to look after them. They have families; they are not alone. They don't have to suffer all by themselves like I do. They don't spend Christmas looking at the four walls of their apartment knowing that nobody is going to come over for a holiday dinner. I've done enough of that and I don't want to do one more Christmas that way."

Dr. Crane set forward in his chair and put his notebook down. He hesitated for a moment before he spoke. "All of this is quite a revelation, Billy. How narrow your world must be if you believe that everyone goes through their pain with a crowd of people by their side; that nobody is lonely and miserable but you. At Christmas, everyone has their family around; there is always holiday cheer and the Norman Rockwell dad carving the turkey. For someone who has seen as much of the world as you have, your view of it is mighty narrow."

"So, what are you going to do Doc? You cannot keep me here forever. At some point you are going to realize that I am going to be cut loose from this place and you will have no control over what happens to me. I haven't said anything to you about killing myself while I have been here. All I plan to do when I am released is to go home, sit around and watch television and maybe have a couple of beers now and then while I watch the Bears lose another game. Maybe I'll watch some of those Christmas specials, have a little egg nog, and decorate an artificial tree. No reason for you to worry about me, I'll be just fine."

The psychiatrist sat back and twirled a pencil between his fingers. Billy was right. The hospital could not hold him forever. In fact, insurance wouldn't pay for more than another day for Billy based upon the clinical notes. Sure, Billy was a narcissist, and he was combative. Unquestionably there was a moderate level of depression at work too. There was also little doubt in his mind that once Billy was released that he would make another suicide attempt. The second attempt tends to be successful. Unfortunately, he was not outwardly suicidal, and he was no threat to the public. There must be some way to keep Billy safe without him being hospitalized.

Dr. Crane pondered on a few possibilities. He looked down at his notes, considering a couple of things he had written down. Then it came to him; something that might get to Billy and make him look outside of himself for a change. The down side was that it could drive Billy deeper into his depression. However, it just might give him the opportunity to see that some people had problems greater than his own Dr. Crane was going to make the pitch and see how it went. "You know what Billy; I am going to sign your discharge. But I am going to attach a condition or two. There is a hospice center affiliated with the hospital just down the road. There is a group of people who volunteer there, a very special group of people. They go into the hospice center and sit with those who are at the end of their life. Some of these residents in hospice have no family to be with them. The volunteers stay with these folks so that they will not die alone. As a component of your outpatient therapy, which I will require as a condition of your discharge, I want you to volunteer to be part of this group. You will go there every day, if you don't show up, I will have the police visit you at your apartment to check and make sure that you are safe. It's your choice. You can do this, or I can keep you here until I believe that you are emotionally ready for discharge. Call it medical extortion if you like because I cannot require you to volunteer. Why don't we call it a suggestion, or if you are into the movies, look at it as an offer you can't refuse"

Isn't that a great choice, Billy thought to himself. I can either stay here with the loons, or I can go and hang around with a bunch of end-timers waiting to kick the bucket. The prospect of being around a bunch of wheezy geezers didn't thrill him. And the thought that someone might come checking up on him pretty much sucked. On the other hand, being stuck in the psych unit didn't get his motor running either. All things considered, freedom was much better than his present accommodations. "Hey doc, I have just a couple of questions for you. How long do I have to "volunteer" at this hospice place? And what will I be doing when I am there?"

"I think that you should count on volunteering at least through the holidays. As for what is expected of you, well, you will have to participate in some simple training before you go over to hospice. After that, you will be expected to be there each day and sit with a patient and keep him or her company. Sometimes all you have to do is listen to them. At other times you will be with another volunteer comforting the resident during their final hour. Make no mistake, this is not an easy thing to do, but I think that you may be the kind of individual who will get some benefit from volunteering."

"Sounds pretty grotesque," Billy thought. Sitting around, holding someone's hand while they croak wasn't his idea of a fun way to spend the holidays. Since he had no plans anyway, and it was going to get him out of here, why not? "Alright doc, I'll do it. Now, when do I get out of here?"

"I'll have to make a few calls. Then the nursing and volunteer coordinator of the hospice center will come over to speak with you. If I can get everybody on the same page, I don't see any reason why you cannot be discharged and begin training tomorrow."

"Sounds like a plan, doc. Let's get this show on the road."

Chapter III

From the outside, the hospice center looked like any other outpatient hospital building. It was a single story square building of non-descript architecture, similar to elementary school buildings built back in the 1960s. There was an outdoor area that could be accessed from each of the four corridors where patients and their families could sit when the weather was pleasant. Only upon entering the hospice could one see that this space was entirely different from the main hospital building.

Once inside, any resemblance to a medical setting was nonexistent. The combination reception and visiting area was a large room with a fireplace and leather sofas and chairs. Since Christmas was only a couple of weeks away, in the corner opposite the fireplace was a fully decorated, large Christmas tree. There were tasteful, Victorian style candles upon the mantle, and evergreen roping around the inside doorway. Christmas music was playing softly in the background, coming through speakers in the ceiling. The décor of the hospice was soothing, with soft pastel paint on the walls and muted lighting. Everything was meant to be soothing, even the halls were very quiet. There were only two beds per corridor, and all were large private bedrooms; much larger than those private rooms found at the main hospital. All were exquisitely decorated and if you removed the heart monitors and the IV poles there would be no discernible difference in accommodations between the hospice and a fashionable hotel.

There was a nurse's station on each corridor, which blended in so well with the other rooms, one might never notice it was there unless you were looking for it. Two nurses manned each station, so there was a one-to-one ratio of nurses to patients. The other thing that was noticeable was the one thing you didn't notice at all. The typical medicinal smell so closely associated with hospitals was not present. Each room and public space contained wall scent dispensers, giving the hospice a floral elegance rather than an alcohol and disinfectant aroma.

Make no mistake, this was not a hotel; this was a place where people came to die. The residents (they were not called patients) had one type of end-stage disease or another for which there was no cure. Instead of passing away in a cold, sterile hospital room, or because they required too much care for their families to administer at home, they came here to pass their final few days in relative comfort. A family member would usually spend the final few hours of the resident's life holding their hand or mopping their forehead so that they would not pass on alone. Unfortunately, that was not always the case. At any given time, there may be one or more residents that have no immediate family. Since, in many instances, these individuals are elderly; this was not particularly surprising as much of their family had passed along before them. The nurses on duty try to be with them when their time comes, but that is not always possible. The volunteers supplement the nursing staff and sit in with the resident, not only when the resident is passing on, but also during the last few days so that the terminally ill person is not alone.

Billy opened the door and entered the hospice a couple of days after his discharge from the hospital. He returned to the hospital the day after he was discharged to attend an orientation on volunteering at the hospice center and what was expected of him. And at least every eight hours since he had left the hospital, someone from the psych unit called him to check in and make sure he was complying with the terms of his discharge. There was no question that Dr. Crane intended that Billy was going to be on a tight leash.

At first glance, Billy was startled by the look of the facility. Having never been in a hospice before, he really did not know what to expect, his couple of hours of training notwithstanding. "This joint looks nothing like a hospital," he thought to himself. "Looks more like a fancy mansion. Maybe I could get used to hanging around here for a bit." Taking a few steps down the corridor, he stopped and poked his head into a small cutout in the wall where a young women dressed in a sweater and jeans was working on a computer. "Hi there, he said. I'm Billy Monaghan, the new volunteer. Can you tell me where I can find Ms. Burns?"

"You found her. I'm Natalie Burns. Please call me Natalie. It is so good of you to come, Billy. Follow me into the conference room and we can chat for a couple of minutes. Would you like some coffee or some water?

He accepted some coffee and went into the conference room and took a seat at the oval table. From what he could tell, Natalie was probably in her early to mid-forties, with dark hair and blue eyes. She seemed to be the type of person who didn't fluster easily and who had a soothing voice that was upbeat, but not obnoxiously so. Hopefully he would get to work with her while he was doing his volunteer work; she wasn't bad looking.

"Billy, I have looked over your chart and some of the other paperwork that Dr. Bob sent over...."

"Who is Dr. Bob? I don't know anybody by that name."

"Oh, I am sorry, I mean Dr. Crane, Natalie chuckled. Everyone around here calls him Dr. Bob.

Anyway, we are very happy to have you here. As I am sure you can imagine the holidays are a very difficult time of the year at hospice. Not only is it difficult for the residents, but it is very difficult for the staff and the volunteers. When you are supposed to be happy and joyful and enjoying Christmas, it can be very difficult to do that when you are watching people die. I believe that it takes a special type of person to volunteer here throughout the year. So I do understand if some of our volunteers would rather be home with their families at Christmas."

"I don't have any family, Natalie, so being here over the holidays is not an issue for me. There isn't much for me to do, so I might as well be here. I do admit that I am somewhat nervous. I mean, I have never done this kind of thing before. Been a musician all my life, but I can't do that anymore. So you will have to excuse me if I ask a lot of questions."

"That's not a problem, Billy. I'll explain how things work around here. There is really no way to train somebody for this type of work. Some people cannot handle it; their emotions overcome their good intentions. Others thrive on it, with each resident they help; you can see their compassion and charity grow. It is an amazing thing to watch.

Okay, to make it easier to understand, let's break this down into two parts. There is the volunteer and then there is the resident. Those are the only two components that you will have to concern yourself with; everything else you leave to me.

First, let me start with the residents. Here, we call them residents not patients, the reason being that patients are in the hospital undergoing some form of medical treatment, such as chemotherapy or radiation. Our residents are not being treated for anything; they receive palliative care only, meaning that they are being made comfortable in their last days. This hospice has eight beds, and it is rare for us not be at capacity. The usual length of stay averages about ten days, although some residents have been here as long as a month or more. The majority of time they do not leave their beds, but they can if they have the strength to do so. There are no set visiting hours; friends and relatives may visit anytime they wish; twenty-four hours a day. The staff is here for the family as well as for the resident. We try to comfort them as much as possible, and we are with them, if they wish, when the final hour has arrived.

Each of the rooms has a sitting area, a flat screen television, a full size bed. We try to the extent that we can, limit the medical equipment in each room so that the residents have the feel of being in a room in their own home. Generally, the only piece of equipment you will see is a telemetry machine to monitor heart rate, respirations and blood pressure, all of which is also monitored at each nurse's station.

The reason that we have volunteers is because there are generally two to three residents here at any one time that has no family. They tend to be older than the general resident population, but that is not always the case. Volunteers are encouraged to spend as much time with a resident as either he or she can. The expectation is that the volunteer will be at the resident's bedside when they pass away; the idea being that the resident will not have to die alone. Of course, you are not expected to be here continuously around the clock, however, there are a few beds that a volunteer can bunk down on if that is what one chooses to do. Most of the volunteers work in teams of two. This way they can switch off so that somebody will be at the resident's side continuously. Some volunteers do prefer to work alone. They tend to be those individuals who have been volunteering for a long time. Until you become comfortable, you will team up with another volunteer. It will be less nerve wracking for you that way. I will introduce you to your partner as soon as we have finished chatting.

How you handle the time you spend with a resident is up to you as long as they do not become upset. If they are up to it, you can take them to the great room, or you can take them outside. Most residents handle their passing without much of a problem. For the most part they have been ill for quite some time; many have been battling their disease for years. They have accepted their prognosis. And they do not mind talking about what they are facing; in fact, they usually want to share with the volunteer what they have been through and what is in front of them. Of course, there are a few who decide that they are going to fight the inevitable with whatever little strength that they have left. Those patients are too difficult to be handled by volunteers; the nurses will deal with those residents. Now, I am sure that you have many questions. Most of them can be addressed by your partner. Her name is Melanie, but everyone calls her Mel."

They got up and walked from the conference room out of the nurse's station, down the hall and into a cafeteria. "This is our dining room, Natalie said. Most of our residents take their meals, if they are eating at all, in their rooms. The dining room is used primarily by the staff and by the resident's guests. It is open twenty-four hours a day for light snacks, coffee and the like, and serves full meals from 6 a.m. to 8 p.m. You can come here to catch a break, grab a snack or a meal and unwind a little. One other thing I forgot to mention, there's a chapel down the next corridor should you want to pray or you just need a little solitude. There is a chaplain on call who is happy to come down and speak with you any time you wish. We try to make the hospice as quiet and peaceful as we can. Everyone who works or volunteers here needs a quiet place to spend a few minutes for reflection. You can choose to do whatever works for you.

Melanie sat at a table in the back of the cafeteria doing some paperwork. Form where Billy was standing, she looked to be in her mid-30s, long reddish hair and slender build. She smiled as they approached the table and extended her hand. "Hi there Billy, my name is Melanie but people call me Mel. Glad to be working with you. Have a seat and we can get started. Would you like some coffee, water or something else?" Billy shook his head and sat down across the table from Mel. "Okay then, said Natalie. I'll let you guys get to it. When you are finished for the day just come up to the nurse's station and sign out. If you decide that you are going to stay over, which I wouldn't suggest the first night, just let one of the night nurses know. They will take care of everything."

It finally struck Billy as to how uncomfortable he was with this whole thing, and this was before he had even met any of the "residents." Swirling in his mind was visions of old shriveled up geriatrics, oozing rank bodily fluid from sores and wounds. The thought sent a chill through him that was visible enough for Mel to notice. "The whole hospice volunteer thing just a little much for you, isn't it? Bet you think that you have bitten off more than you can chew, huh? I was creeped out when I first got here and it all seemed so overwhelming. They are just like us, only older, and dying much more quickly than we are. Once you meet your resident you will be surprised how attached you become. Let's talk about our guy for a couple of minutes before you meet him. Got ahead, get yourself some coffee or something to eat."

Mel's reassurances did little to ease his feelings. What was he going to say to this person that was going to have any impact? Whoever the dude is, he's got one foot in the grave and the other on a banana peel. Does it really make any difference to the guy if Billy holds his hand as he drifted away to never-never land? Well, he committed himself to giving this a shot. And it was either do the volunteering gig or go back to the nut farm. With that final thought in mind, he took his coffee and went back to the table.

"Okay, our guy is Ben, and he is in Room 7 in the hall parallel to where we are sitting. The rooms are pretty easy to find, they go in numerical order around the building. He is a sixty-eight white male, suffering from terminal pancreatic cancer. That means that the cancer has spread throughout his body to his lungs, brain, and other organs. Ben came here two days ago and he is still pretty lucid. He can still get out of bed with minimal assistance but that will end fairly soon. At most, he has about ten days left, but a week would be more likely. What you will find is that the residents will seem to be doing fairly well, but they reach a point of no return and slide downward fairly quickly. He is on light pain medication that will be increased as his pain increases, and he has also been prescribed tranquilizers to keep him calm. This is pretty much the extent of treatment for all the residents, because it keeps them pretty much pain free and lessens any anxiety they may be experiencing.

Ben has no family. His wife passed away about ten years ago and they never had any children. He is the youngest of five children, all of whom has passed on, all from cancer. There are no parents or other blood relations left. Ben was a production manager for a national newspaper where he worked his way up from a paper

187

handler to his management position. He retired from the newspaper just two years ago.

He appears to be a really sweet man, with a great sense of humor, particularly about his circumstances. He spends most of his day reading, and has told me that what disturbs him the most about his situation is that soon he will no longer be able to hold a book or to see the pages. You will find that most residents try to keep their mind active until the very end. They do not have much time left, and they want to use every minute that they do have. Ben likes to talk to people and have them around when he is not reading. He doesn't watch much television, and the only times that I have seen him upset is when watching the nightly news. Oh, and he also cusses up a storm when his favorite sports teams do not win. Do not ask him about the Cubs. Ever."

Mel looked at her watch and said, "The nurses should have finished up getting Ben settled for the day. Let's go have you meet him and you two can get to know each other. By the way, I'll take the night and overnight shift tonight, you can do it tomorrow if you are comfortable enough tackling it. Like most of our residents, Ben doesn't want to be alone at night. Frequently, a resident will wake up at night frightened and it is reassuring for them to have someone there to comfort them and talk to them. Overnight can, in some ways, be busier that the rest of the day."

They left the dining room and headed towards Ben's room. Even with all the information that Mel had given him, this whole thing was not particularly reassuring. "What do I say to this guy, Billy asked? I don't know this guy from Adam, and I don't want to say the wrong thing to him and get him upset."

"Just be yourself. There really isn't any right or wrong. The most important thing is just for someone to be there."

The door to Ben's room was open, so after tapping lightly on the frame, they both entered. It was a fairly large room, with a sitting area, small galley style kitchen, and a bathroom with a shower. The room was large enough to have room for a fully decorated Christmas tree in one corner of the room, artificial of course to comply with fire safety laws. Blinking lights and ornaments lent coziness to the room, leaving it appearing less antiseptic than it might otherwise have looked. There was a window behind Ben's bed and the curtains were open, permitting a view of the inner courtyard and for sunlight to stream through. Being that it was winter and the days were short, the brightened room was appreciated any time the sun wished to poke head through the clouds. Today was one such day. "How are you doing today, Ben? You are looking pretty chipper. Be glad that you are not outside, it is a really cold and windy one out there, Mel said."

Ben was in the sitting area of his room wearing fresh pajamas and a robe. He looked up from his book, smiled and said, "Hello Mel, glad that you're back. I see that you brought a friend along. What's your name, fella?"

Billy walked up and stuck out his hand and then introduced himself. "Hi Ben, my name is Billy, it's great to meet you." Mel pulled up another chair so that there was a third seat. "Billy is a new volunteer; he is going to team up with me to hang around with you. Having an Billy around will help me so that I can get home once in a while or else my husband won't know who I am anymore. Of course, this is completely up to you. If you would rather not have both of us, then you let me know and I'll take care of it."

"Well, he is pretty scruffy looking and all with that long hair and beard. What are you, some kind of hippie? You ought to get Ethel in here with her scissors and razor. She could have quite the time getting that mop and beard under control. Why, she could stuff a pillow with all the hair she could get off of you"

Billy looked at Ben, then at Mel, and again at Ben, not quite knowing what to say in response. "Ah, you see, I ah, hmmm, I don't know, just wait a minute. Listen Buster, I have been wearing my hair long and wearing a beard for forty some years. I'm not going to get it cut for you or anyone…."

"Lighten up, will ya Billy? Can't a guy on his last legs have a little fun around here? It's not as if I can run around here chasing nurses anymore. I was just playing with you."

Mel had her hand to her mouth trying not to giggle. "That was the sense of humor I was telling you about. Ben likes to take pot-shots at people. Remember Billy, I did warn you."

Billy's face turned the shade of a ripe Macintosh Apple when he realized he had been gotten. "I'm sorry for getting so bent out of shape, Billy said. I'm not used to this whole volunteering thing yet and I let my nerves get the better of me. I apologize for being thin-skinned."

"Hell Billy, no need to apologize. Look at it this way, in a week or so I won't be around to get mad at, and you won't have to worry about being thin-skinned, will ya?" Ben looked over the rims of his glasses and waited a moment to see if anyone was going to respond. Waving his hand before anyone had the chance, he told them that it was a joke, and not to be upset with his allusion to his future, or more precisely, his lack of future. "Hey Mel, Ben said. Why don't you get your skinny fanny up and make us some tea. Then I am going to toss you out so Billy and I can get to know each other better. If I am going to be holding hands with this fella when the lights are go out, I want to know where that hand has been."

Billy and Ben talked together that day and at length every day over the next week. There were few subjects that they did not discuss. It was of no consequence what the hour was when they would begin chatting; only ending when Ben would drift off to sleep. They would talk about Ben's life and about Billy's life. They would talk about the mistakes that they both made along the way. Stories about Billy's escapades on the road would leave Ben in stitches, and he would want to know what it was like being a musician. Ben would speak about his wife and how much he missed her. He hoped that there was a Heaven so that he could be with her again soon. They talked about their own illnesses, and how each felt about the calamity to their health that had befallen them. Billy spoke about his suicide attempt, and how he had come to that moment where he believed that taking his own life was preferable to living a life where he would be unable to perform music anymore.

It became apparent after the eighth day that the end was coming quickly to meet Ben. The inexorable slide had come and was now close to the bottom. Almost imperceptible at first, Ben continued to decline from the third day forward. The cancer that his body had been fighting finally had broken through his body's weakened defenses and was marching on to win. In the beginning, Ben took to his bed more and was sitting in the sitting room less and less. He had no appetite, and the thought of eating interested him not at all. Finally, he spent most of his time sleeping, awakening abruptly and looking afraid, especially at night. Back to sleep he would fall, comforted by the sight of either Mel or Billy sitting by the side of the bed. He was also comforted by the nightlights that Billy placed in every electrical socket in his room, providing a glow not unlike that of the candles at a church. All of this, along with anti-anxiety medications kept Ben on an even keel throughout the night, the time of day when panic was most likely to occur.

On the ninth day, about one week before Christmas, it was apparent that Ben's passing was only hours away. The monitors that measured Ben's heart rate and respiration were removed from his room. There would be no flat line to watch or sound to be extinguished when Ben's heart ceased to beat. All one had to do was to look at Ben for a minute or two and see his erratic breathing to understand why such monitors were unnecessary. When the life forces in Ben's human form ended, it would be as peacefully as any terminally ill person would have wished.

Both Mel and Billy were in Ben's room for the final moments. They held his hands and told him that it was okay to let go. It is not uncommon, at the end of one's life that the person seems to require permission to take leave of their body and cease their existence. Ben did not verbally reply but seemed to understand, his breathing slowing a little more in seeming response. Ben had told both Ben and Mel that wanted to hold out for one more Christmas, but it was not to be.

Individuals in these situations choose their own time of death. There is no empirical proof of this, but it that is the way it seems to be. Many pass away at night, when the systems of the body slow during sleep. In the case of the terminally ill patient, it may occur at night when the hospice has fewer staff on duty, so as not to be the burden they believe they would be should they pass during the day. During the day when the hospice is busier dying would bring on unwanted attention. Ben preferred to slip away with as little fanfare as possible, so he chose the middle of the night to end his earthly journey.

Mel crossed Ben's hands when he expired. It was painful for both of them, but Mel knew it would be different for Billy; this was his first time befriending a resident of hospice. For many volunteers, the first passing was the last one for them, and they never volunteered again. She wondered if that would be true of Billy. Outwardly, there was no indication what his emotions were, but he did not rush out of the room. That was a good sign.

The hospice nurse was notified of Ben's passing. The two volunteers could now leave at any time of their choosing, but they waited in the room until the body was moved to the morgue a couple of hours later. Few words were spoken between Billy and Mel, for what could they say to each other? Mel was a little surprised when Billy did not leave the room after he was told that he could do so. But neither of them wanted Ben to be alone. Mel smiled to herself; maybe Billy was going to be a keeper after all.

Two days later, there was a memorial service for Ben in the hospice chapel. Most of the staff including a number of volunteers attended. Billy and Mel were there. After the service, the body was going to be interred next to his wife. Billy decided to go along to the cemetery. Burial would be the last time he would be with Ben. He really couldn't even understand why he felt the need for closure; he only knew Ben for less than two weeks. Billy took one of his guitars with him and quietly played a song that Ben would have enjoyed. Then he left. Saying goodbye was an important thing for him to do, even if nobody knew it but Billy.

Chapter IV

It has been just about seven years since I first volunteered at the hospice center and that Ben passed away. Obviously, I am still alive and did not commit suicide as I was so intent upon doing that year. Now, I am the Volunteer Coordinator at hospice, and have been for the past couple of years. Things have become a little more difficult physically for me, but I no longer contemplate suicide. So many people have to go through much worse than me, and they do it with such dignity and grace that I would have been a coward to take the easy way out.

I never expected that volunteering seven years ago would have taken me down this path. Ben had quite a bit to do with that. I'll tell you about that in more detail in a moment. Christmas fell not long after Ben was laid to rest. I figured that Christmas would be a great day to end it all for myself. Fortunately, Mel invited me to spend Christmas day with her and her family. I went back and forth in my own mind about what I should do. Finally I decided that I could put off my plans for one more day. I also figured that if I declined the invitation that I would be spending the yuletide with Dr. Bob back on the psych unit.

What a wonderful family Mel has. They are so supportive of the work that she does, never complaining about all the hours that she spends at hospice. Mel and I talked quite a bit about what was going on with me that Christmas day. Of course, she already knew about my hospitalization and the reasons behind it. In the beginning, she was skeptical about whether or not it was appropriate for me to be volunteering at all. But Ben and I hit it off so well that soon her apprehension evaporated. I never realized how much volunteering meant to the residents who had no family to be with them. Then again, I had not been thinking much about anyone but myself up to that point. As we chatted that day, I realized that Mel was doing some volunteer work at home by having me to her house for Christmas. I had to admit that there was something to not being alone at Christmas. It was the first time in years that I had spent Christmas Day with anyone other than Jack Daniels and a bag of chips.

Once the Christmas holidays passed, I had plenty of time to sit back and reevaluate where I stood. I thought back to conversations that I had with Ben, and some of the things he told me about his life. He had fought in the Vietnam War and had seen innocent civilians killed by both sides. It was particularly difficult for him when his platoon went into a village after it had been bombed with napalm. The bombs did not kill any of the enemy, but it did do a number on the residents of the village. Collateral damage it was called. The sight of women and children burned to a crisp never left him. He told me that he had nightmares for years about what he had seen there. He said that he felt responsible because he did not protest against the war and went willingly when he was drafted. I cannot imagine the toll it must have taken on him over the years having witnessed all that destruction and death and feeling that he had a hand in it.

When he came home from the war, he got into drugs and began drinking heavily. I had read that quite a few veterans went down that road. Ben bounced around from odd job to odd job for a number of years, trying to forget the war and to find himself. No matter how far he ran, the terror stayed with him. Finally, he landed in a small town in Illinois, not far from Chicago where he found a job in a printing plant that published a major city newspaper. He would stay at that job for the next thirty some odd years. He met his wife at the printing plant, and they were married a few of years later.

Ben and his wife lived a good life together. They were too in love with each other to share with anyone else; that is why they never had children. Or so he said. I really didn't believe that story because he seemed to have enough kindness and love to spare. I figured that he had something going on with a fertility issue and that he blamed himself. He talked a lot about Agent Orange, so maybe that had something to do with there being no children.

Hard times would occasionally visit the couple, as they do with everyone. During the course of their life, they both lost parents, siblings, grandparents, aunts and uncles. All of Ben's siblings died of some form of cancer. He figured that the disease would eventually come and get him too. Cancer, he thought, would not give him the longevity we all hope for. When he was diagnosed with pancreatic cancer shortly after his wife passed away, he was neither surprised nor upset. Knowing what to expect from watching his siblings succumb to the disease, he used his time wisely and lived each day as best he could until he was too sick to do it anymore. That is when he entered hospice. I remember him telling me that it made no sense to be upset about the things he wasn't going to see and do, but to cherish the things that he did do. He understood that he could not change either.

Ben also wanted to know all about me. We talked about the cities I had seen, the places I had been to. In the beginning of our friendship, I wanted to keep my medical condition and my thoughts of suicide to myself. Frankly, I was ashamed to speak about them. Here was this man, lying in a bed at the end of his life, and I was going to tell him that I was planning to take my own life? That would have been quite the bummer, don't you think? But I finally manned up and told him everything. You would have thought that I had insulted the Chicago Cubs the way he got pissed at me. He wanted to know how I could even remotely consider taking my own life when there were eight people who were dying in this hospice. They had no choices left to them. The only way that they were going to leave hospice was in a box, and that the only place they were going when they left here was either the funeral home or the crematoria. Did I really believe that death was preferable to the relatively minor problems that I was experiencing? I had options, he told me, that he and the others did not have. "Like what," I asked him. "You can teach, you can write music, you can be a producer, you can use your musical talents in so many ways." When I left him that afternoon, he seemed genuinely hurt and upset with my stubbornness and my resistance. I didn't want to listen to him because I knew that what he said to me had more than a kernel of truth to it.

The first words out of his mouth when I saw him the next day were, "You're a selfish prick." I was dumbfounded at the outburst, but I knew what he meant. To be honest, at the time I didn't really care. I tried explaining to him that I was fifty-seven years old, and that you couldn't teach a really old dog a new trick. He was having none of it. "Do you think that just because I have accepted that I am going to die in a few days that I wouldn't rather live? Let me tell you something Pal, I would trade my cancer for your Parkinson's in a New York minute. Just because you are one of the few people who would even consider doing volunteer work here, that doesn't give you license to think you are worse off than the inmates. Listen, you don't have to be all by yourself; that is a choice that you are making. Okay, you are not the rock and roll celebrity you once were. You are young and have years, probably a least a couple of decades ahead of you.

Instead, you come in here feeling all sorry for yourself. It's a good thing that I can't get out of my bed or I'd rear up and shove my cane up your ass. Leave your dark apartment and find out just how precious life is, and I will bet you will find someone to share life with. I have no intention of having you hang around my deathbed if are just treading water until your head cracker believes you are sane enough to be left alone. Reach down and grab your balls Sonny, be a man and decide what you are going to do. But if your decision is to turn on the gas and stick your head in the oven alongside the holiday turkey, then get your scrawny ass out of my room right now and do not come back.

I didn't have the stones to just walk away on Ben, and leave the mess for Mel to clean up. The truth was that I spent so much time over the past few years wallowing in my own misery; I couldn't or wouldn't look forward to see that there was a life beyond being on the road. I knew Parkinson's was not a death sentence, although I was acting as if it were. Even if I had been in good health, at some point the road was going to become too exhausting; the truth was that it was taking more and more out of me each year before I became ill. Looking back I realized that Ben was pointing out another road for me to take. He was the Google Earth to help me find my way, now that I had reached the proverbial fork in the road.

Following Ben's advice wasn't easy, and it didn't happen overnight, but I eventually did move forward and left the idea of suicide behind. I continued to volunteer at the hospice center. Volunteer work gave me things that I could not have received anywhere else. No longer did I look at life as some commodity that only has worth if I was the one placing my own value upon it. Being alive is much more than respirations and blood circulating through one's veins and arteries. Sharing with others, especially sharing with the residents has been such a blessing. I always believe that I receive more from them than they do from me. That is one of the reasons that I always want to be with a resident around the Christmas holidays. I am not a religious man, but there seems something very special about making sure that someone is not alone during that time of the year.

Taking more of Ben's advice, a couple of months after he Ben passed, I created my own website to advertise giving music lessons. Eventually, after some little bit of time, I began to get some students. Over the years, my hands became stiffer due to the Parkinson's, but I can still do enough with them to teach. The teaching supplements my salary as the Volunteer Coordinator, so life is comfortable; I don't earn as much as I did when on the road, but I have settled into one place and eventually purchased a small house, leaving that small apartment behind.

Doing more meant getting out more, and I eventually I met a person that has added so much dimension to my life. Never did I believe that I would be able to settle down with one woman. To tell you the truth, I was not even looking for someone when Donna popped into my life. I met her one day as I was browsing through some gear at Guitar Center. Just a chance encounter, but she thought that I looked familiar to her. Come to find out that she had seen me at a concert years ago. Talk about feeling ancient. One thing led to another and I asked her out for coffee. Things progressed slowly at first; I was not used to being with any one person for an extended period of time. The thing that was, and still is so special about Donna is that we can just sit down and talk for hours about anything and everything. When I told her about my suicide attempt, I was afraid that she would run out the door, but that didn't happen. She said something to me that has stuck with me all of these years. It was "Sometimes it takes a light a long time to warm up before it glows, but when it finally does, it glows forever." Without question, I could not let go of someone like that. We have been married for four years now, and it is as good today as it was when we first met.

Without Ben, I would not be here to tell you this story. There needed to be a Ben or the path I was traveling would never have taken the marvelous turn that it did. Without him, there would have been no Mel, no Donna, no music students, and probably, no more me. There had to be a Ben, and I had to meet him for things to be as they are now. Nothing miraculous and magical would have come my way without meeting Ben and my holding his hand when he passed on. I wouldn't have written about my experience, and you wouldn't be read it. Hopefully you will take a few minutes to think about those who are alone on the holidays, and during the entire year. Maybe you can do something that will change a life or two. I doesn't have to be an earth shattering change because most of the times the smallest kindness means the most. When you change someone's life, you change your own too. Merry Christmas.

A Conversation with my Ghost

Chapter I

"These are great seats, aren't they?

"They couldn't be better," said his friend.

"Can't wait to hear what they have to say about you."

Jeff and Bob were sitting on wooden beams about thirty feet above the floor of the church. They didn't have to worry about anyone sitting in the pews below either seeing them, or hearing the content of their conversation. That was because they were both dead. Bob was newly deceased; the people below were attending his funeral. His physical presence was in the casket close to the altar. His friend Jeff, who passed away five years ago, came to his friend's funeral. After all, it was the least that he could do, since Bob had attended Jeff's funeral. Besides, in the mortal world they had been best friends, having known each other for more than fifty years.

"You actually look pretty good down there. Nice suit too; did they have to buy it or did you have it lying around?

"Thank you Dr. J. I haven't looked that good in years. And it's an old suit. I've had it for a long time. I am sure that they had to split it down the back so that it would fit; gained quite a bit of weight the last few years, you know? Nice touch with the rosary beads, don't you think? I wonder where they got them from. For the life of me, I cannot remember ever owning rosary beads."

"The priest is doing a nice job down there, said Jeff. Any idea who is going to do the eulogy?"

"I think that it is going to be one of the kids. They probably had to draw lots to see who got stuck with it. I really would rather that nobody said anything at all. When I did your eulogy I could hardly keep it together. The priest should just sprinkle me with some holy water and be done with it. All of the crying is really a bummer."

"You said some really nice things about me at my funeral. It's too bad that I couldn't be around to do yours. You know, you have to give those folks a time to grieve. That's what these things are all about."

"But funerals are so sad. People feel crappy because they should have been nice to you when you were around. All of a sudden you are gone and they are beside themselves now that and they realize it's too late." Bob looked down at the people as the service continued. Not a great crowd, he thought. But why worry about that? The number of people who come to see you off isn't important, is it? "Hey, I bet that those people down there would crap their pants if they knew we were up here watching them? Can we play a practical joke on them? Something like knocking some dust off of these beams and watching them trying to figure out where it came from?

"No we aren't allowed to do stuff like that. It isn't permitted; I'll give you The Handbook later and you can thumb through it when you have the time."

Soon enough, the service was over and the bereaved walked out of the church. They waited on the front steps for the casket to be placed in the hearse and they walked to their cars to drive to the cemetery for the interment. "So, what's next," Bob asked.

"We can go to the cemetery for the burial if you like."

"No, I don't think so. The idea of being potted in the ground like a turnip and waiting for the worms to use me for lunch has never appealed to me. Is there some place we are supposed to go, or some place that we have to be? Or do we just drift around forever? I am kind of new at this you know, but if I had my druthers I would love to spend eternity playing practical jokes on people. I am just that sort of guy. Hey, why don't we sneak around and find some naked women? Either that or go somewhere and get a drink?"

"You really are going to have to sit down and read that Handbook. There's a bunch of stuff we can do that would have been really difficult while we were alive. Unfortunately, there is also quite a few things that we are not allowed to do now that we are dead. It's confusing, but you'll get the hang of it pretty quickly."

"So, what do I get to do with all of this time on my hands? I sure do have a lot of questions. Like, how long are you going to hang with me? Where do I go when it's time to go home? I would assume that I can't go back to where I used to live when I was alive. Every once in a while I would love to sit down and read a book. Will I be able to do that? If I want to go somewhere, do I just float there, or do I have to walk or catch a bus or something? "

Yeah, it is a little confusing, I know. You see, it works something like this: you are a spirit, just like the stories about spirits you have heard in the past. We get to float around and see what's going on. Or, if want to go somewhere we can hop on a bus or a train. If you'd rather float there, that is fine too. Or you can just appear. Just remember that you are not a superhero; you are not faster than a speeding bullet, or leaping tall buildings with single bound; you know the rest.

You have no home, so to speak. There is no need to sleep or eat because you don't have any parts that require rest or nourishment. You will never feel tired or hungry. People that have passed on before you are here too, so you can go visit with them whenever you like. Some pretty famous people up here to ratchet jaw with. It makes for some pretty interesting conversations. And now, this is the really cool thing, you can talk to the people that you have left behind. They can hear you, but not in the way that you are used to people hearing you. You can't tell them to do bad stuff because they won't be able to hear those sorts of things. And they won't answer you back, so don't expect a response. Sometimes, you can help them through some rough spots that they are going through. The communication part is a little complicated but you will learn how do it with some practice.

As for me, I am going to hang with you for a bit. When you first get here, it is kind of strange. You can feel a little helpless and alone. The one thing about the system that is a little awkward is that there is no transition. Once you were there and now you are here. Everything happens very suddenly. You were alive, now you are dead. Everyone is assigned a "minder" when they first arrive. That is so they don't freak out when they first get here. In time, you will probably go off on your own and do your own thing. Believe me, there is quite a bit you can get done when you do not have time hanging over your head."

They both decided to sit down on a park bench in Central Park in the heart of New York City. Bob didn't know how they arrived there, but he had the feeling that stuff like this was going to become a common occurrence. Night had fallen and it was snowing lightly. It took him a moment to realize that he was not cold, which he would have been if he were alive, given that he was only wearing a pair of jeans and a tee shirt. Not far from where they were sitting he could see the ice skaters on the frozen pond enjoying the snow and the cold. What was today's date, he wondered? Was there a calendar up here that corresponded to what was going on down there? There had to be; it couldn't be June when it was snowing in New York. That wouldn't make any sense.

"Hey Dr. J, what is the date today?"

"Hmm, Jeff pondered. I usually don't keep track of that sort of thing anymore. There's not really any need. Hold on a second and I'll find out. Ah, it's December 22nd, why do you ask?"

"I figured that it was winter. The snow is a big tip-off. And I can what looks like Christmas decorations on some of the buildings around Central Park. So I was wondering if it is before or after Christmas."

"That's right; you were in a coma for a couple of days before they pulled the plug on you. Guess you weren't exactly keeping track of the days, were you?

"There was a fairly large blank spot there. One moment I was farting around on the guitar and the next I was up in the church rafters with you. It was certainly a little disconcerting at first. This whole thing is still a little weird, if you ask me. I guess that you get used to it after a bit though, right?

"Yeah, you do. It helps if you keep moving from place to place. If you do that, you don't dwell as much on the fact that you are dead."

"You know, the one thing that bums me out is that I won't be around for Christmas, Bob sighed. It has always been my favorite time of the year, you know?"

"I know. The being bummed part passes too. But it isn't really as bad as you might think. Up here, time really doesn't have any meaning. You can visit your past holidays anytime you like. You can also visit future ones, you know, see how the family is doing? There are also little ways that you can help out; make things better. Don't misunderstand me, you can't make presents appear or disappear. You can't put presents under the tree from Dad. That's not permitted; remember the Handbook. Sometimes just being there has a good effect on people. Did you know that people can feel when you are around? Not the ones who didn't know who you were when you were alive, but family and friends. It's not like "Holy shit, Bob just put his hand on my shoulder." The feeling of a presence is much more subtle than that; none of that Clarence helping out George Bailey stuff. And you can help out people who you've never met; they just don't feel you hanging around. Makes the holidays more fun and it beats just hanging and watching people having a blast. It can actually become almost a full time job if that is your inclination."

"Wow. It does sound better than spending eternity window shopping. I'll tell you what; let me dig into that Handbook and we'll meet up again and get started. Is that okay with you?"

"Sounds like a plan."

"I just have one question, Jeff. How do I find you when I am done? I suppose that there is no text messaging here?"

"All you have to do just call me back. You know, something like Hey Jeff, I'm finished with the book, or something like that. It's really quite a bit simpler that you imagine. See you in a bit."

Chapter II

Bob sat down to read the Handbook at a coffeehouse located on Boylston Street in Boston. He figured that if he could go anywhere he liked, he might as well spend as much time as he liked in his favorite city. The Handbook was the approximate size of the Manhattan White Pages. It was going to take him forever to read through this thing. But then again, he did have forever.

There was a fair amount of snow on the ground, which he liked. It was always a bummer to live in a place where there was no snow for Christmas. Living in Maryland for almost twenty years had been crushingly boring; there was never any place to go or much to do there. He swore that once his youngest had graduated and gone off to college that he was going to move the family to either Massachusetts or Maine. Unfortunately, having a stroke put the kibosh on that plan. The ability to go anywhere in the world he wanted now was pretty cool, but it seemed to him that it wouldn't be as much fun without his family along.

Man, he wished that he could have a cappuccino and a scone. Unfortunately, there really was no practical way to purchase one. He wasn't hungry; it was just that they looked so good. First, he didn't have any money, which made sense because he didn't need any. Second, even if he had money, he couldn't ask for a barista for the cappuccino because she could neither see him nor hear him. And finally, although it would be great for laughs, a coffee and a scone floating across the coffee shop with no body attached to it would scare the crap out of the customers. Bob was sure that stuff like that was prohibited somewhere in the Handbook. He would also have to keep an eye out that someone didn't decide to take the seat he was using and sit on him. The person wouldn't feel anything, but Bob would be pinned underneath until the customer got up and left. He was quickly coming to the realization that he still had to be careful and aware of people, even if he was dead. That's why there is the Handbook. The Handbook, the Handbook, the Handbook. There was no instruction manual when I was alive; now that I am worm food I have to read directions on how to be dead? Maybe going through some sections that appeared more important than others would help get the hang of some basic things. I can start with the simple stuff first, Bob thought, and read up on the subtleties as I go along.

Bob went and sat on a big wall clock over the barista's work area where he figured that he would be out of the way. For the next several hours he stayed on the clock reading. The first couple of hours, the minute hand knocked him off the clock because his feet were dangling over the edge. After the second time being pitched off the clock and into a mop bucket on the floor directly below, he decided to move his feet and lie across the top of the clock. He definitely preferred the dusty ledge to dirty mop water.

He kept on reading for what seemed like hours. Time was such an odd concept now; he wasn't sure how long he had been up on the ledge, especially since the minute hand of the wall clock was no longer sweeping him to the floor. Was it minutes, hours, days? Looking up from his reading he did notice that all the store lights were out and there were no people in the store. How am I going to get out of here now that the store is closed and locked, he wondered? "You are still floundering around, aren't you, Jeff said. Situations such as this are covered in the book in Chapter 95. That section is called "Overstaying Your Welcome."

"Jesus Jeff, you'll be the death of me."

"Too late."

"I mean you scared the crap out of me. How'd you get here?"

"Pretty much the same way that you got here did. Do you remember how you arrived?

"Let me see. I was sitting in Central Park with you and then you left. Next thing I remember is sitting at that chair over there watching the snow falling. After that I seem to have bumbled around for a bit until I figured out it would be best to sit up here out of everyone's way. Then poof, here you are."

"Moving around is pretty simple, once you get the hang of it. You think about where you want to be, and then, there you are. If you think about someone who is up here, then they are here and you can hang with them, if they are not busy. Pretty much, it is all up to you. Any time of your life you can call up and you go back to it. You can't change any of the stuff in your past, but you can affect the present and the lives of those who have not ascended to your present status, if you know what I mean."

"But you see, I don't know how I can change stuff for people. The Handbook says that you can't do things like move stuff around so someone doesn't get hurt, or get them a job, or give them a car. If you aren't allowed to help them out in those ways, what can I help them with?"

"You didn't read far enough to get to that part yet. It's in Chapter 144: You Didn't Really Hear Me Say That. That chapter explains how to speak with the living without them knowing that you are there. You get inside their head, figuratively of course, and suggest to them the best

212

course for them to take. Now, you cannot tell someone to do something they wouldn't normally do, like robbing a bank or stealing a car. Most of their life is predetermined, so you can't prevent an accident where they would suffer a fatal injury, or stop someone from getting married. But you can show them the right path to take, or how to they might be happier. It's a cool thing, really."

Bob sat on the ledge thinking about everything that Jeff was telling him. To say that he was confused was the understatement of what, the month, year, forever? Time did not appear to have much meaning in whatever place that he was since he was no longer mortal. Wasn't heaven supposed to be a happy place? There had been no "pearly gates," no St. Peter standing guard. Hell, he hadn't even met God yet. On second thought, he had only been dead a little while and God probably had more important people who had died that he had to take a meeting with. It's probably more like a private audience with the Pope, where there about five hundred people in the room. Or maybe you have to take a number; something like he would have to do at the deli department at Wegman's.

But what if this isn't heaven? What if this is the other place way past the basement? That could be possible, couldn't it? The Circles of Hell multiplied by a factor of ten; maybe even more? Sure. Individualized punishment, one that is specialized just for you, not one size fits all? Christ that would really suck. Banging around all over the place not having a clue what you were doing or not knowing what was going on for eternity could be a real ass-kicker. That would be enough to make you think about suicide if you were not already suicide proof. I wonder what I did that pissed off someone upstairs to deserve that. Nah, the whole thing didn't make sense; he had been a pretty good dude when he was alive. Giving to charities

and doing lots of pro bono work. This must be Heaven.
It's just an adjustment, that's all.

But, why is it that I don't feel happier? I don't have
to go to work anymore. No more bills to pay; no aching
back or aching knees to slow me down. No more fear of
flying; what do I care if the plane I hitch a ride on crashes?
All the stuff I wanted to do but couldn't I can do whenever
I want. There are only few restrictions on being able to do
anything. Given all of this, I should be much happier than I
am right now.

"Bob, nobody up here is happy all the time. You
were never happy all the time when you were alive, were
you? Eventually you will get used to the idea that you are
free of your body, but you are not free of your mind. We
can call it your soul if it makes you feel better. The things
that made you sad before will still make you sad now.
Sure, there are some trade-offs being up here. On the plus
side, you can visit and talk to your dead relatives,
something you couldn't do after they passed away. The
flip side of that coin is that you can't have any back and
forth kind of conversations you used to have with the
people who you left behind. For me, I didn't care much for
most of my relatives when they were alive, so I spend most
of my time with my friends. I was really happy when you
got here. Now we have all the time in the world to smoke
some bones and solve the problems of the world. Yes,
marijuana is legal up here. The jury is still out on whether
other drugs are going to be legalized; the Big Guy hasn't
made a decision on those yet."

"Thanks a lot, dude. Any word yet on
prostitution?"

"You know what I mean, man. It was not as if I
was sitting up here saying to myself, Man, I can't wait until

Bob snuffs it so I finally have something to do. I'd been boppin around doing my own thing when I found out that you were making the trip up here; made for a good day. So I volunteered to be your guide for as long as you need it to get acclimated.

Listen, I know that you are bummed about not being around your family anymore. It's a tough time of the year to undergo such a life altering change. A life ending change would be more precise, wouldn't it? For you, I know it is especially difficult the way you used to love Christmas and all. Remember that it is not going to be particularly easy for your family either. Every year about this time they are going to feel the pain of your passing. Christmas for them, at least for the next few years at least, is going to be a time when celebration is going to be more painful for them than it is for you. I can remember you telling Bernadette that it didn't matter to the kids much if you weren't around for Christmas. You have no idea how wrong you were. Do you know that they aren't even doing the Dickens Advent calendar anymore? That was a tradition that you never missed, until this year of course. They don't want to continue it because you are not there."

"They should continue reading A Christmas Carol, and doing all of the things we used to do, whether I am there or not, Bob satd. Where is that darn Handbook? It has to cover something like this situation, doesn't it? If it doesn't then I am going to have to speak to the head Honcho around here and get some things straight with him. Or is it her? I would imagine that equality is something that has made its way up here. I didn't ask, but the right wing evangelical bunch is not in charge here, are they?

"Not to worry, my liberal partner in crime. We can get this all worked out in plenty of time for Christmas. It's a busy time of the year, no doubt, especially with the big birthday party coming up soon. But I have a friend in Guilty Conscience Repair who can fix you right up and then we can go down and see what we can do. I just have one request though?

"What's that, Jeff?"

"After we hang with your family for Christmas, what say we go to Italy on the day after? We can relive, so to speak, our Latin class trip to Rome when we were fifteen."

"That'll be the shits, my man. Let's do it!"

Chapter III

The holidays at Bob's house this year was a real downer. Bob's wife pretty much forced the kids to go along with decorating the house in an attempt to have things be as close to normal as they could be. Everyone knew that was going to be next to impossible. They went through the motions just to keep themselves occupied. Bob was the driving force behind the Christmas holidays. He directed the decorating, setting up the Christmas village, and spent way too much money on gifts for his wife and the kids. Nobody wanted to celebrate without him there. Tragically, he was not going to be there for this Christmas, or for any other celebration. They would never get used to that, but they would have to adjust. As the old saying goes-Life goes on.

As the days ran down to Christmas the house began to look as if Bob had never left. The family was getting more and more into the season. Unfortunately, there was the underlying dread surrounding Christmas Eve. That was when Bob and his wife prepared and served their signature Christmas Eve dinner. Although they didn't follow the traditional Italian Christmas Eve dinner of the seven fish (they couldn't because his wife was allergic to sea food), they served up such specialties as antipasti, pasta carbonara (Italian bacon and eggs), bracciole, veal parmigiana, struffoli, and cannoli. Everything was made by hand, except the cannoli shells. No doubt that Mom could make all of it herself, but Bob was always in the kitchen with her, getting in the way and changing the recipes so that each dish was just a little different than it was the year before. All of the family would be there, the children, grandchildren, and the sons and daughters-in-law. They would sit around the table and all through the house telling stories, busting on one another, and just having fun. After the dinner and dessert had been consumed, everyone would trickle down to the basement where they would watch "Christmas Vacation" and "The Muppets Christmas Carol; both family favorites. Everyone had seen the movies so many times that they took turns calling out movie lines. With the tree lights on and the other lights down low, the younger children began to get sleepy, making it easier to get them to bed at a reasonable hour so those who needed to do some last minute wrapping of presents could do so.

As with every Christmas Eve, the family began trickling in sometime between mid-morning and mid-afternoon, depending upon distance and traffic. It was just after lunch when Bob and Jeff arrived. Popped in would probably be a better way to describe their arrival as one minute they were not there and the next minute they were. Everyone that was expected had already arrived, except Heather and her two children, who would be arriving soon.

People were sitting down drinking coffee and not saying a whole bunch of anything. It appeared as if everyone was just going through the motions, not really wanting to be there at all.

"What a solemn bunch of pineapples they are, Bob said, leaning against the kitchen entryway. They are moping around like a bunch of zombies."

"Did you really thing that they would be acting much differently? It hasn't been that long that you've been gone, you know.

Isn't there any way to cheer these folks up? I really don't want to hang around if they are going to be so maudlin."

Jeff walked over to Bob's son, Sean who was helping Bernadette putting together antipasti. He leaned over and whispered something into Sean's ear. He neither reacted nor showed any change of demeanor in response to what Jeff had whispered to her. Jeff came back to where Bob was standing, without saying anything to Bob.

"Whatever you said must have had a huge impact; he hasn't said anything or moved from the spot since you said whatever it was that you said to him."

"You're expecting instantaneous results, Bob. It takes a little bit of time for what I said to him to sink in. You have to remember, it is not as if he could hear what I was saying to him. This is more akin to giving someone nonverbal cues so that they can retrieve things from their long term memory. He is now going back and going through past remembrances, to find the "file card" he wants. Sometimes it takes a few seconds, and sometimes it takes hours for the help we have given them to rise to the surface."

Sean kept helping put Bernadette, rolling salami, cubing cheese, and placing cold cuts on a platter. After a few minutes, he took a break, getting some coffee and a small plate of cookies. He took a bite of a cookie and suddenly began laughing. "Hey Mom, do you remember the year that Dad baked all those Christmas cookies? "Yes, Bernadette began. He was studying for the bar exam. It was a couple years before Zach was born. You were two years old, Heather was ten and Nick was eight. He was watching you guys and when he took a break from studying he baked Christmas cookies. By the time he was done, he baked something like fifty two dozen cookies"

"Yeah, said Nick. Dad was so stressed out about the exam that he ate most of the cookies himself. I remember his telling me that he ate so many of them that he gained twenty pounds."

Everyone was crowding into the kitchen to see what all the laughter was about. "I could never figure out why your Dad was spending so much money on flour, sugar, oatmeal and chocolate morsels. He would tell me that he was baking cookies, but there were never any in the house. He couldn't bring himself to tell me that he was eating them as fast as he was making them," laughed Bernadette. Now everyone was laughing and telling funny stories about Bob. And there were quite a few that they could tell. The one thing that was missing was all the sad faces. They were having fun even though Bob was no longer with them.

"You see, that's how it works. It is not so difficult to distract them from missing your presence to enjoying themselves at the holidays. You are always going to be there for them, although you are never coming back. The trick is to keep it going, because it will only work for a short time, then they will realize that you won't be with them tonight at their dinner. You are going to have to find something else to keep them going."

"How about I suggest that they take out our old photo albums after they finish dinner so they can reminisce about past Christmases? Maybe I can plant that bug in someone's ear so it is their idea?"

"That's not a bad thought, replied Jeff. You just have to be sure that it is done in the right spirit. Pictures can elicit both good and bad memories. Make sure that when you plant the seed that the person concentrates on celebration of the holidays, and not what they have lost. It is definitely a tricky line to navigate."

Bob stood next to his oldest son, Nick. He amused himself for a couple of minutes by sticking a wet finger in his ear. Realizing that he wasn't going to get any response from his son by giving him a "Wet Willie," Bob began to whisper in his ear. "Hey Dude, why don't you suggest that after dinner that everyone gather together and look at the old family photo albums. Concentrate on the good memories and how great the holidays were together. Keep it light. Tell funny stories you remember."

Bob leaned back and watched Nick for a couple of minutes. Nothing. Nick continued to sip from a cup of egg nog as if nothing had happened. Bob looked back at Jeff and shrugged his shoulders as if to say, that worked well. Was there something he was supposed to do before he whispered stuff to the live folks? Could there be some Harry Potter-ish type of spell he had to use; Expecto-Petronum or some such nonsense? Ah, bet it was in that darn Handbook. Where did I leave that book, he wondered? He patted his pant pockets and then he opened a button in his shirt and pulled out the massive instruction manual. Flipping pages, he was dumbfounded to see that he had done everything correctly. He scratched head trying to figure out what went wrong.

"Psst, you told him to do it after dinner. It's not after dinner yet, they haven't even eaten dinner" Jeff hissed at him. Bob gave Jeff thumbs up to acknowledge that he had heard him. Now the question became what was he going to do until they all sat down and ate dinner. That was going to be more than four hours away. Jeff motioned Bob over to him, as if had read his mind. "Time doesn't work the same up here as it does down there. For the lack of a better way to explain it, we can fast forward to the time and place we want to be. You can see the results of suggestion and don't have to wait around in "real time" for them to happen. Think of it as a perk. Besides, it is in…"

"Yeah, I know. It's in the Handbook. Why didn't they put that thing on a disk or a flash drive, or something? Damn bulky thing weighs a ton. Wait a minute; don't tell me, the Big Man is not tech savvy?"

"Does it really make much difference, asked Jeff, a wry smile upon his face? Which would you prefer, lugging around a laptop or the Handbook? It's six of one or a half-dozen of the other, as they say."

Bob was about to reply when he saw everyone in the dining room having dinner. Man, that was quick, he thought. From what he could see, there was not a whole lot of conversation going on between the brothers and sister. Single word answers were the responses to the few questions asked. This went on from the appetizers, through the main course, to the desserts. Finally, as Heather and Mom were getting up to clear the dishes, Nick cleared his throat and said, "Hey Ma, why don't we get out the old photo albums after we clean up and look through them. We had some wild Christmas' with Pops and we can do a "Greatest Hits" type of thing."

Nobody said anything to Nick about his idea. He couldn't tell if everyone was angry at him for bringing up Pops, or if they just wanted to ignore the entire idea. "Are we going to all mope around every Christmas because Pops isn't here? It's sad; I get it, but there are grandkids here who don't want to see all the adults here acting miserable. They deserve a nice Christmas, just as Mom and Pops gave us great Christmas' every year. Pops would want that. So, I am going to get the albums out and go through them whether or not anyone else joins me. Then I am going downstairs and watch Christmas movies like we do every Christmas. You guys can do what you want."

Nick went to the closet in the living room, took down the photo albums and sat back down at the dining room table. As he began to flip through them, the family began to trickle in and look over his shoulder. First were the grandkids, his nieces and nephews, asking who certain people were in the photographs? Next was his Mom who sat down next to him. Finally, Sean, Zach, and Heather came to the table. It took less than five minutes before they were all pointing at the album and pointing out images of themselves twenty or thirty years past.

"Look at that picture of Sean when he was about five, laughed Heather. That was the year he got Buzz Lightyear. You would have thought that he scored the lottery."

"I remember that year, Mom said, I had about twenty people looking for that toy and not one store had it. Finally a friend in Canada bought it and sent it to me. Your Dad thought that I had lost my mind going to that much trouble, but you can see the results. Look at how happy Sean was."

"Do you remember the year that Dad tried to fool us into thinking that Santa and the reindeer had landed on the front lawn? We watched him from our bedroom window spraying the lawn with fake snow out of a can, and he used his boots to make footprints on the front steps so we would think that they were Santa's footprints? He thought we wouldn't figure it out, but there was no snow within miles and it was almost sixty degrees out on Christmas morning and the "snow" didn't melt," laughed Zach.

"How about the time that Mom wanted a three carat necklace for Christmas? On Christmas morning she opened a beautifully wrapped box from a high end jewelry store and Dad had made a necklace out of three carrots and a string," Sean added.

"Or the time when Pops bought me a carton of smokes and Crazy glued all the packs together? I had one huge pack of cigarettes made up of twenty packs. What a pain in the ass that was," Nick said.

"I think the best gag was the Playboy magazine," Sean was laughed so hard that it took him more than a few minutes to tell the complete story. "I think I was about sixteen years old. I looked in my Christmas stocking one Christmas Eve and saw a Playboy magazine in it. When I thought that nobody was watching, I snuck it upstairs to look at it. I flipped through it and couldn't find any pictures of naked women, only recipes. Dad and his friend Jeff took the front cover off a Playboy magazine and carefully glued it an issue of Bon Appetite, and then put it in my stocking. It was done so well that you would never know that it wasn't a real Playboy."

"I remember that," said Jeff. "You worked on that cover for hours, Bob added. That was a masterpiece; a work of art."

For the next hour or so, the family flipped through the albums and contributed stories about their Christmas memories. They were genuinely happy for that hour. Unfortunately, they could not carry it through for the entire evening. Fewer and fewer stories were being told until the silence that blanketed their dinner a couple of hours ago returned. Some decided to go downstairs to watch movies, as was their Christmas Eve tradition. A couple wandered off into the kitchen for a snack. Nick began to gather up the albums to put them away. "You know, he said to nobody in particular, there was so much more I wanted to say to him. I was always too busy; something always got in the way. Now it's too late." Everyone stopped and looked at Nick for a moment. Nobody knew what to say in response. Then, they all went on with whatever it was that they were going to do.

Chapter IV

After watching the Christmas movies, those who were still awake gathered up the children who had fallen asleep and brought them upstairs and tucked them into their beds to continue their slumber. The adults were not far behind them, hoping to capture a few hours of shut-eye before the little urchins awakened at an ungodly hour to begin opening their Christmas presents.

Nick carried his six year old niece to her bed and headed down the hall to his bedroom. The day had been difficult, with emotions rocketing back and forth like an out of control clock pendulum. He did not believe that he would get to sleep quickly, but the turmoil had sucked the energy completely out of him. Sleep came over him almost as soon as his head hit the pillow.

Nick was restless in his sleep, tossing and turning. Sometime during his nocturnal jousting he had knocked the blankets off the bed and now he was cold. Shivering, he reaches down and picked up the covers. As he was straightening them out he noticed something out of place at the end of the bed. Seeing that there was nothing there, he lay down on his back and then sat bolt upright. "Hey Nick, how are you doing?" Sitting on the foot board of the bed was his Dad, or at least that was who it appeared to be. The apparition was blue in color and he could see right through it to the opposite wall. I must be dreaming he thought.

"No, you are not dreaming, dude. I am the real deal."

"What are you doing here? You're dead.

"Never been deader, Bob laughed at his pun. I came back for a short visit. But keep your voice down, if you would. If someone came into the room and saw me it wouldn't be a good situation."

"What? You think it is a great situation for me? I must be dreaming; in a couple of seconds I'll wake up and I'll realize I had a nightmare."

"Actually, you have that backwards. In a couple of minutes you will be back sound asleep and never remember that I was here."

"So, to what do I owe this pleasure? Are you planning on taking me back to Christmas past or to Christmas future?

"Neither. Dickens has a copyright on those places, so we can't use them. I would get in quite a bit of trouble if I did. I was watching you before, and something that you said struck me and I wanted to talk to you about it for a couple of minutes."

"You are watching me, are you? Terrific. The thought of someone following me around from the grave delights me to no end."

"I would have thought that you would have been glad to see me, especially after seeing all of those long faces this afternoon and this evening. You can never figure people out. Anyway, you said that there were a number of things that you wanted to say to me that you never had the chance to say. That caused me think a little, so I thought that I would drop by and talk to you about it"

.   "A visit in the middle of the night that scared me half to death is the perfect time for us to have a little chat? What is it that you want me to do, sit here and think of everything I didn't say and say them to you now? You'll have to forgive me if the list is a little short at the moment. I hadn't planned on having any conversations with a ghost at this particular hour."

"That's another thing we are not allowed to do. You see, up here we have this big instruction manual called the Handbook. Covers all kinds of situations; in fact, there are so many regulations that you wouldn't believe how long it took to read through them all. Just astonishing. Anyway, we are not permitted to have someone go back and try to talk to us about things that they didn't do or, perhaps, that they wanted to do differently. You couldn't speak to me about them if you tried because I have turned that part of your mind off temporarily. Don't ask me how I did it because it is way too technical to explain it to you. Think of it as the Butterfly Effect

Okay, what you said made me think of something that I would say all of the time to you guys. I would always tell you to treat people, not just family; as if this were the last day you were ever going to see them. If you do that, then you wouldn't have any regrets if something happened to them or to you. You would all shake your heads and give me a whole lot of lip service that you were going to do that, but you were all full of crap. All of you, including your Mom, and including me, never took any of that to heart. Lord knows that there is a ton of stuff that I wish that I could of said to all of you. Look at where I am now. I never got to say it to you, or your brothers, or your sister, or to your mother. So I get to regret not doing it until you all get up here and I can talk to you freely again, which I don't want to happen anytime soon. And I suppose that you could really screw up and wind up down in the basement, but who knows."

"Let me get this straight, by seeing you tonight I am going to remember to live as if every day could be my last? I am going to remember something now that you are dead that I couldn't remember when you were alive? How is that supposed to work?"

"Well, I'll remind you."

"Great. I get to be haunted by you for the rest of my life. By the way, you don't happen to know when that'll be by chance/"

"Nope, that is classified information. Only a few people up here know about that kind of stuff. But I won't be haunting you; just giving you subtle reminders; like a cattle prod or a whoopee cushion or a joy buzzer."

"You are kidding Pops, aren't you?"

"Of course I am, son. You will just remember it at some point each day. It will be like me whispering in your ear, but you won't hear it. I will be passing it along to everyone else while they are sleeping. You got the first visit because you were the one who tried to make the holidays merrier for everyone. The other little piece of advice I will be passing along to everyone is for them not to be sad on Christmas. As the saying goes, I might not be there in body, but I am there in spirit. And I always will be here on Christmas, you can bet on that. There is no place I would rather be than with all of you on Christmas morning."

With that, Nick lay back down and went to sleep. He remembered nothing about the visit from his father that night or any other night. When everyone awoke the next morning, they opened their presents and laughed and had the grandest time that Christmas day. It was as if Bob had never left. Little did they know?

Warm ocean breezes and bright tropical sunshine drenched the beach. Beautiful women wearing low cut swimsuits played in the surf, or walked along the edge of the waves. The sweet aroma of meat cooking in an open pit made your mouth water; and it was only a short walk to the tiki bar where you could quench your thirst and kiss all of your troubles away.

Not too far from the bar under a palm tree sat two gentlemen on lounge chairs. They were both wearing shorts, colorful island print shirts, and had straw hats upon their heads to keep the sun from burning their round, balding pates. If you looked really hard, you couldn't see them. If you looked extremely hard, you still couldn't see them. All you could see was two empty lounge chairs.

"Great seats, Dr. J; you seem to have a knack for finding the perfect location. Too bad that we can't work on our tans, but I have to tell you, the view is outstanding." At just that moment, two beautifully tanned women wearing incredibly skimpy swim suits walked within inches of their chairs. "Oh man, what I could do with that. Sure would get my motor running if I had a motor to get running anymore. By the way, I thought that you wanted to go to Rome after the holidays, Bob continued. What made you change your mind?"

"When I thought back to that school trip, I remembered that the weather was rainy, chilly, and damp. Seemed to me that a little sun and some fine scenery would be a good way for us to spend a few days before the New Year rolls around, don't you think? We can go to Rome when it is warmer"

"You will get no argument from me, brother. After all of the crap that has been going on the past few weeks, it's nice to just sit back and relax."

Jeff adjusted his sun glasses and turned toward Bob. "You know Counselor that was quite a nice little deal you did with Nick. Visiting him Christmas Eve in his sleep was the perfect way to help make Christmas happy for your family. You are definitely a quick study."

"Thank you my man. I remember you saying something about not being allowed personal visits, so I went to the handy, dandy Handbook and looked to see if there was anything in there I could use to get through a little quicker. You see, us legal types know that there are always exceptions to every rule, so I figured that would be the case up here too. I did a little research and found a section called Waking Sleeping Beauty that said you can wake someone and keep them in a semi-hypnotic state for no more than five minutes in order to get a special message to them. I knew that would be enough time to get my message across to Nick. Worked like a charm."

"Glad it all worked out, said Jeff. Hey, I just remembered something. Springsteen is doing a concert in Madrid tonight. Do you want to go? After that we can hop off to the French Riviera and soak up some more sun tomorrow."

"Oh man, I haven't seen Springsteen in concert in a long time. Make you a deal; I'll go to the concert tonight if you'll go with me Friday night to see Journey in Las Vegas. What do you think? Is it a plan?"

"You and your Journey fixation; I'm not going to have to spend eternity going to Journey concerts, am I?

"Nope Dr. J, I was only kidding you. No Journey concerts for me for a while. Let's get going to Madrid, I don't want to miss the opening number. Man, this is going to be a blast."

The Fireplace

Chapter I

Christmas is a magical time of the year when one is seven years old. There is more snow on the ground, it is always colder, the lights in the shops are always more colorful and brighter, and the Christmas trees always smell fresher and are bigger. While in reality these visions are not necessarily so, children tend to remember Christmas that way. The Currier and Ives prints are how we remember Christmas. The wonder of the season never snuck up on you back then. Children were aware of the coming of Christmas as soon as they finished up their Thanksgiving dinner, knowing that the next day the stores would be decorated, and that all the new toys would be in the windows, just waiting for their names to be included in the letters to Santa. Yes, it truly was a wondrous and joyful time.

The year was 1962, and the place was the borough of the Bronx in New York City, six days before Christmas. Seven year old Dickey Stonebottom was out with his father, Humphrey, to find the family Christmas tree. Before we journey farther into this holiday tale, an introduction to Dickey is appropriate.

Dickey, outside of his somewhat unusual name, was a pretty typical little boy. He was a third grader at St. Simon Stock School on Valentine Avenue. Dickey attended church every Sunday (whether he wanted to or not), loved the Yankees and Mickey Mantle, and believed in God, Santa Claus, and President Kennedy. In the summer he played stickball with his friends in front to his apartment building on Tiebout Avenue. When the snows of winter came, he could be found building snow forts in the courtyard or sledding down the hill in front of his building while dodging cars. He loved to read and to build World War II model airplanes, tanks, and battleships. All in all, Dickey was a fairly typical child of the Bronx in the early 1960s.

On this 19th of December, Dickey was out with Dad helping to find the most perfect, the most wonderful Christmas tree in the entire world. This was a holiday ritual for the Stonebottom family for as long as Dickey could remember, which was not a particularly long time since he was only seven years old, and it was only the second time he had gone with Dad to select a Christmas tree. Prior to that, the tree would magically appear in the living room, fully decorated, after Dickey had awakened from a nap.

Dickey and his Dad were out early this morning; it was barely past 9:00 a.m. when they arrived at the Hunts Point rail yard not too far from Yankee Stadium to survey the trees. The morning was sunny yet very cold, with fires burning in fifty-five gallon drums spaced at intervals throughout the yard to provide a temporary respite from the cold. Evergreens were stacked on the sides of rail cars, and more were piled inside the open doors of the freight trains. Throughout the yard one could smell the sweet aroma of pine. Nothing brings the spirit of Christmas more to life than the scent of cut Christmas trees.

Dad, with Dickey trailing a few a few steps behind, examined the trees with the eye of a gourmet chef about to choose a side of beef. Yanking on tree branched to check the needles, pounding tree stumps on the ground, Dickey marveled at the practiced eye of his father. Dad was not a see one, grab one tree sort of guy. Only the best tree was good enough for the Stomebottom family. Even if it took looking at hundreds of trees or bringing Dickey home frozen solid from the cold, with his limbs snapped off from frostbite, Dad was going to find the right tree,

Unfortunately, regardless of how wonderful and beautiful the tree that Dad selected, whether large, small, short, tall, skinny or fat, the tree would never be quite good enough for Dickey's mom, Betty. It was the Law of Opposites; whatever tree was purchased, the opposite was the type preferred. Of course, Mom did not wish to go out in the cold and participate in the selection. She was happy to judge the tree after it was far too late to do anything about it.

"Humphrey, where did you get that God awful tree," Mom would bellow the instant the first tree limb made it past the apartment threshold.

"Betty, where have I been getting trees for the past five years," Dad replied, realizing far too late, making the mistake of answering Mom's question with a question of his own. This just momentarily postponed the inevitable by giving her time to think up a sharp retort.

"You haven't gotten a good tree at that rail yard yet. This year it is too damn (short, tall, large, small, skinny, fat), you (dolt, idiot, knucklehead, cretin). The first ball you hang form that tree will fall right off and smash on the floor.

"How about you come along next year to supervise," was Dad's usual rejoinder, refusing to back down in the annual battle of the Christmas tree.

Mom would then slam down whatever she had in her hand, or if she had nothing in her hand she would go find something, pick it up, and slam that something down. "You expect me to trudge around that train yard with a

236

bunch of kids in the (cold, mud, snow, blizzard, rain monsoon, tsunami)?" Then she would storm off muttering under breath something about Dad's brain being the size of a pine cone.

Back at Hunts Point, after going on more than an hour searching, Dad was narrowing the trees down to a number of finalists. He would shout, "Hey Johnny, what's this one cost." After Johnny told him, he'd shout out again, "So, what's my price?" Unknown to Johnny or to anyone else in the Bronx, there was a special Stonebottom price that was lower than the public ever received. Dad would continue yelling out to five or six different people, coincidentally all named Johnny, attempting to secure that lowest Stonebottom price until a buying decision was made. Dickey never could figure out how Dad knew everyone's name, until years later his Mom told him that Dad called everybody whose name he didn't know Johnny.

The tree was finally selected, the Stonebottom price paid, and Dad tied the tree to the top of the old Rambler station wagon. Dickey and Dad settled into the front car seat, alternately sipping from a cup of hot chocolate and slapping their hands together trying to get the circulation going. "What do think of the tree, Dickey?"

Dickey took a few seconds to answer, waiting for the car heater to melt the ice that had frozen his lips together. "I think it's great, Dad, the best tree ever. Can't wait to see it lit up with the tree lights and all. And it sure smells great. Mom is going to love it."

Dad snorted and put the car in gear for the short ride home. "Of course she's going to love it, just like she's loved every other tree I've ever brought home," he muttered to himself as they pulled out of the rail yard. The tree only fell off of the car once

Chapter II

The tree was wrestled up the stairs and into the apartment while Dickey had his lunch of chicken noodle soup, a grilled sandwich, and milk. Dad manhandled the conifer into the tree stand, leaving behind busted tree limbs, small piles of pine needles, and the contents of a couple of coffee tables in his wake. His ever trusty Craftsman drill was at the ready to sink guide wires (pronounced "guy wires" by Dad) into the wall to ensure that some seismic event did not topple the topiary. Mom continued to spout her opinion as to the sorry specimen Dad had lugged up the stairs, so it was only a matter of minutes before Dickey learned a few new words he had never heard before and was warned never to use. All in all, it was a fairly tame performance, if past years were any indication.

Dickey finished his lunch and put his dishes in the sink. He then ventured into the living room where the tree was undergoing branch surgery. "Need any help, Dad," he asked. "No thanks son. I just have to find a place in the wall that I haven't drilled a hole into yet. Humphrey had drilled so many holes into the wall and spackled them over that there probably wasn't a whole lot of wall left. That meant that each year the tree inched closer and closer to the hallway where there was virgin territory for his drill.

"Come on, Dickey," his Mom called out from the kitchen. "We have to go out and get some things for the Christmas party tonight. Go knock on Ms. Whatley's door; she's coming with us. We're going up to Arthur Avenue to get some of that cheese Dad likes that smells like feet."

Dickey groaned. He did not like Myrtle Whatley at all. She had a mustache, and bore a striking resemblance to

Fred Flintstone. Myrtle was a large woman with a ponderous bosom and legs akin to bridge supports. For a woman with all that bulk, she had a voice similar to that of a mynah bird whose neck got stuck in a car's fan belt. And she never stopped talking. If that weren't enough, she smelled like a package of Enzo's moth balls. But the saving grace, at least as far as Dickey was concerned, was that they were going to Arthur Avenue. Maybe he could talk Mom into buying him a slice of pizza at the Half Moon. "Okay Mom, I'll be go knock on her door.

Arthur Avenue was the Bronx version of Manhattan's Little Italy. Located off Fordham Avenue, it was a place of wondrous aromas that caught your attention blocks before you reached it. There was the Arthur Avenue Market that had fresh fish, cheeses, fruits, Italian breads and pastries, sausages, roasted peppers, and marinated mushrooms. Shops along the street sold jars, cans, bottles and sacks of stuff, all labeled in Italian. The language that was spoken in those shops was melodic but strange sounding to the ear, and the men standing on the street corners wearing large, gold pinky rings and smoking big fat cigars was stranger still.

Dickey loved Arthur Avenue, its food, and the little old Italian ladies with their two-wheeled shopping carts who always seemed to be shaking their fists or waving their arms at the shop vendors and speaking Italian one hundred miles per minute. Extremely gaudy Christmas lights were strung across the street attached to the telephone poles. Each stall at the market had either a plaster Virgin Mary or a crucifix nailed to a piece of wood to protect people who worked and shopped there. There were so many exotic looking people on the sidewalks and walking in the streets-no cars even attempted to pass down Arthur Avenue on a Saturday- and so many sights, smells, and sounds that no child could help but to be amazed.

"Maybe I can swipe a snail as we go past Mr. Sardini's," Dickey thought. Sardini's was one of the open fish stalls at the market that had bushel baskets of live snails alongside baskets of mussels, shrimp, clams, squid, cod and bronzini . When Sardini was distracted with a customer, Dickey liked to try and swipe a snail and put it into his pocket. The reality was that Sardini always knew when a kid pocketed a snail, but he usually made as if he too busy to bother. Unless the kid tried to grab a handful of them, then he would holler at the top of his lungs, "Ay, waddya tinka you doin? You putta dosa tings back or I breaka you fingas." That usually did the trick.

Dickey liked to watch the snail poke his head out of its shell and look around. Of course, snails didn't live very long, but he didn't mind. Once the snail died, Dickey wanted to give it a decent burial. Unfortunately, living in the city meant there was not an abundance of dirt in which to dig a hole, so Dickey did the next best thing. He kept the dead snails in a cigar box under his brother's bed. He figured that he could always blame his sibling, George should they be found, not realizing that George cruised around in a stroller and was far too short to have reached the basket of snails. Since Dickey had been swiping snails for quite some time, there were now about fifteen decaying snail carcasses in the cigar box. So far, Mom had not discovered Dickey's dead snail collection. Then again, George was not yet toilet trained.

Mom, on the other hand, did not much like Arthur Avenue. She disliked Italians in general and despised their cheese in particular. The aromas wafting from the stores that were ambrosia to other made her gag. For some odd reason, the thought always entered the back of her head that some Mafia goon was going to "whack her as she bought some mozzarella or a loaf of bread. When going to Arthur Avenue, she always made sure that she brought at least one

240

adult was with her, along with one or both of her kids, because mobsters don't take out children. This was her protection.

"How many people are you having over tonight, Myrtle screeched? A party is an awful lot of work so close to Christmas."

"Humphrey always wants to have a party around Christmas, even though all the work falls on me. Let me see, we invited about twenty people altogether, not including my family. I invited the Galfaloons, the Wilsons, the Sweedlepipes, the Monfaluccis, the Waffleneds, and a few others that I cannot remember at the moment. Everything is almost done. We'll have hors d'oeuvres, and drinks, and that horrible cheese that Humphrey likes so much. If I could handle putting up that miserable tree myself, Humphrey would be out here freezing his can off and dealing with these pasta fazoolis. One of these days he is going to make me come down here and one of those gangsters is going to stick a shiv in my back, I just know it."

Mom purchased the stinky cheese, some loaves of bread, a couple of bottles of wine, and a number of other things that Dickey couldn't recognize. After about an hour, the shopping complete, they began to walk home. As they made their way back, Myrtle was howling louder than the increasing wind. The sun was becoming more and more obscured by the clouds. Maybe it would snow tonight, Dickey thought. That would be fun. The one thing that was not going to be fun was having to be at the party tonight. No kids were going to be there except Dickey and his brother, George, and he was too young to be much fun. Mom would also make Dickey dress up like a little penguin- wearing a black suit, white shirt and a tie. Jeeze, wasn't it enough that he had to have his hair slicked down and wear a tie to go to St. Simon every day, but on the weekend too? And they wouldn't let him have much of the food either. Mom rarely let him near the good stuff that Dad liked namely the mozzarella and the sharp provolone. Oh well, he would just have to mooch it from some of the guests, or swipe it off of their unattended plates when they were not paying any attention.

Dickey entered the apartment, put down one of the bag of groceries, and then put his coat and hat in hall closet. He walked into the living room to see how the tree was coming along. Dad had all the lights on the tree and was starting to put the ornaments on the branches. "Wow Dad, that looks really good." "Thanks Dickey, I hope that Mom likes it," knowing that there would be a fat chance of that. "What do you think of the fireplace, Dickey?" He turned his head to look at what he had failed to notice when he first came into the room.

Between two chairs opposite from the Christmas tree was a red and white brick fireplace standing about three feet tall. It was made out of cardboard with red painted bricks and a brown painted cardboard mantle on top. There was a cut out where the fire would be. In that cut out were fake cardboard logs and a fake black fireplace grate. But the best part was found behind the fake logs. There was located a light socket which held a red light bulb. Around the bulb was a metal contraption with a sharp point on the end. A gold piece of metal resembling an open umbrella was balanced on the end of the point. This piece of metal was not particularly large, and was very thin. Heat from the lit bulb made the plate spin slowly on the point, and gave the illusion of fire dancing across the logs. The effect was primitive but sufficient. However, once you looked from across the room, one could see that the fireplace had a decided tilt to the right, no doubt a result of cheap mass production. Or the starboard list could also have been from a failure to carefully read directions, which Humphrey (and most men) was very good at. It didn't really matter though; Dickey could hardly believe his eyes. His Mom wouldn't be able to believe hers either.

"You're the best, Dad. I love it, I love it, I love it," Dickey said running up and throwing his arms around his father. Humphrey smiled. It was wonderful to see his son so happy. Unfortunately, the smiles only lasted a few seconds.

"What's all the hollering about," Mom said as she entering the living room. Catching sight of the fireplace, she stopped short as if slamming head first into the side of a building. Had she been wearing sneakers instead of her usual high heel shoes, there would have been the sound of the screeching of tires along with the acrid smell of burning rubber.

"WHAT THE HELL IS THAT THING AND WHAT IS IT DOING IN MY LIVING ROOM?" Mom thundered.

"Dad stood between the fireplace and the tree with a startled expression on his face. To him it was obvious what it was. "It's a fireplace, Betty. What does it look like to you?"

"No Humphrey, it is definitely not a fireplace. It is a cardboard box that is painted red, has a red light, and a piece of tin foil. So I will ask again; what is that monstrosity doing in my living room?"

Dickey began to get a funny feeling in the pit of his stomach. It was the type of feeling he would get when his mother planned on making calves liver and beets for dinner; sick to his stomach and ready to barf.

"Look, Betty, I thought that it would look great for the party. It was cheap and it almost looks like a real fireplace. Dickey loves it and I think it gives the apartment a real homey feel."

"It gives the place the look and feel of Amos McCoy's ramshackle dump on Tobacco Road, Humphrey."

Suddenly, the atmosphere is the house changed and it did not feel as much like the Christmas season as it did just a few moments ago. In the gathering darkness of the late afternoon, the red and green tree lights took on a devilish glow. The angel on the top of the tree, so beautiful a short time ago now appeared to leer down upon Dickey with a sinister grin. That funny feeling had transformed into a rising lump in his throat.

"You do this every year, Humphrey. You seem to be compelled to bring something hideous decoration home every Christmas. Last year you rented a bear rug to put in front of the tree. What a dead bear has to do with Christmas I will never know. Who rents a bear rug anyway? What possessed you to do that?"

"Funny Betty, you didn't seem to mind the Kodak's we took on that rug, remember dear? You seemed to enjoy playing The Mighty Hunter and the Helpless Animal, didn't you?"

"Never mind that. The year before you decided to spray paint the Christmas tree silver. SILVER! Did it ever occur to you that Christmas trees are called evergreens for a reason? Green! Not silver, or blue, or any color other than green. And this year you bring me a two-for-one special; a packing crate disguised as a fireplace, and a Puerto Rican angel tree topper with a flashing, multicolor halo. Where did you pick up that number, at the Spanish store on the corner of Webster Avenue?"

During this thunderous outburst by Dickey's Mom, Humphrey appeared to shrink in stature by the minute. He put his hands in his pockets and looked at the floor, totally deflated. Few people could suck the life out of a room faster than Betty could when she got up a head of steam. She was the all-time Champeen when it came to taking Humphrey down a few notches, and there was little that he could do to stem the tide of his wife's displeasure.

Dickey hated when his Mom belittled Dad that way. He could feel the tears welling up in his eyes. Crying would only make matters worse, he knew. Slowly, began to edge out of the room and remove himself from the field of battle.

"Maybe the fireplace wasn't the best idea, okay Betty? But the point is that it brings a little happiness to the kids. It is a symbol of what brings people together at the holidays. I know that is only cardboard and that the red bulb doesn't really look like a real fire. It isn't completely level and it does tilt a little bit. But can't you use your imagination and think of it as something that brings us all together to enjoy the lights and magic of Christmas?"

"Enough with the Charles Dickens metaphors, Humphrey. I have people coming over here for a party soon and our friends are going to take one look at that red and white thing and think that they have arrived at Bob Cratchit's hovel instead of the Stonebottom apartment. What's going to be next, Humphrey, you going to run out and buy Tiny Tim's crutch?

On that final note (for now), Betty turned and strode out of the living room. Humphrey heaved a sigh of resignation and glanced over at Dickey, who had almost managed a complete retreat from the living room. His Dad gave him a weak smile and gave him a thumb's up to let Dickey know that they fireplace was not going anywhere; at least not for the time being.

Dickey smiled back at his Dad and walked down the hallway to his room. Why was Mom making such a big deal about the fireplace? And why was Mom so nasty to Dad about it? That bear rug last year was so cool that they almost had to pry Dickey and George off of it to get them to go to bed. He had no idea what his Dad was talking about when he said something about Kodak. Maybe it was the type of bear the rug mas made out of. And the silver tree was pretty neat, even though the entire house smelled like turpentine instead of pine. All Dad was attempting to do was to make Christmas fun.

Dickey entered his room and sat down on his bed, head in his hands. Tears that he had been holding back finally began to make tracks down his cheeks. He wasn't crying for himself, but for his Dad, who tried so hard each year to make the holidays great. He couldn't let them see him crying or that would just start another round of yelling. Dickey dried his eyes, wiped his nose on his shirt sleeve, and lay down on his bed staring at the ceiling. Soon the guests would be coming and he would have to get dressed, stand up straight, and be bored out of his mind. What fun that would be, but it was better, at least in Dickey's mind, than listening to his Mom yang at his Dad.

Chapter III

Most had arrived at the party by about 8:00 p.m. Present so far at the Stonebottom Christmas soiree was Myrtle Whatley and her husband Clem; Sophia and Martin Galfaloon; Ralph and Alice Sweedlepipe; Ed and Trixie Wilson; Fred and Ethel Wafflened; Ricky and Lucy Monfalucci; Morty and Joyce Milled; Paula and Roger Muldew; Edith Plotz, and Flo Hinch. Yet to arrive were Betty's parents, Biff and Helen Wellington, who decided that they were going to bring along their two children, seven year old Norman and seventeen year old Billy.

Dickey could not have been any more bored at this early stage if he had been made to watch traffic signals turn from green to red. Until his uncles arrived, there was not another child in the apartment beside himself and his brother George. At four years of age, George was not much fun, at least until the food came out and Dickey could get him to shove something up his nose or to overstuff himself with food to the point that he'd puke on someone's shoes. The television was not permitted to be on, so there was no diversion from that direction, only the droning of the same lame Christmas records over and over again on the Victrola. Thank God his Mom was not holding the party on Christmas Eve, when she would have the television tuned in to the Yule Log. Imagine the fun; watching hour after hour of a log burning. She could have sat transfixed to the television watching wood burn until Independence Day if someone kept feeding the fire.

Making matters worse was that Mom made Dickey get dressed up for the evening, putting him in a shirt and tie, his hair was plastered to the side of his head with half a tube of Brylcreem. The hair cream had hardened to such a degree that Dad's bowling ball could have fallen off of the top shelf of the closet, hit him on the head and it wouldn't have left mark. Brother George was gussied up in the same fashion, except that he kept yanking off the clip-on tie. Mom would glance up from some conversation and begin a search mission to locate the missing cravat. Being the good brother, Dickey finally hid the tie under a pile of coats so that at least George would be free from the blue noose.

The doorbell rang and in came Dickey's grandparents along with their two sons. At least now Dickey would have someone to play with. Grandma was a nurse at St. Barnabas Hospital, and Pop was a bus driver for the Bronx Surface Transit Company. They lived on East 184th Street and Park Avenue, about a mile away. Pop was fun; he used to take Dickey and Norman bowling, played baseball with them, and took Dickey on vacation so that Norman would have someone to keep him occupied.

"How are you doing, Dickey," Grandma asked? Oh boy, Dickey thought, here it comes. "Are you feeling alright tonight?"

"I'm doing just fine, Grandma." It should be any second now. With a crowd of people standing nearby, this was going to be good.

"What color is you poop," she inquired? There it was the "poop" question. Dickey could count on one hand the number of times that his grandmother had not asked him the color of his poop. Being a nurse, and still, apparently working off the ancient four humors theory, Granny was very interested in the color of stool. She could tell by the color of one's feces what malady Dickey was suffering from, usually diagnosed as the dreaded condition of constipation. Constipation was the scourge of mankind, especially children. The only way that it could be wiped off the face of the Earth was by taking that magic elixir, Fletcher's Castoria.

The Castoria was a sickeningly sweet patent medication that she believed could cure the ills of the world. Have a headache; Fletcher's Castoria was the answer. Did you come down with a cold; then belly up to the Castoria bar. Break a leg? Drag yourself over on your good leg and knock down a shot. No doubt that Fletcher's Castoria could end the Cold War and world hunger. It could also strip the paint off of the Whitestone Bridge. Information was not available as to whether Grandma held stock in the company that made Fletcher's Castoria, or had a warehouse packed to the rafters with the stuff on Pelham Parkway, or if she received an employee discount from the hospital, but she was always carried a bottle of the stuff in her purse along with a spoon.

"By Jeeze, Nelly (Pop always called his wife Nelly, even though her given name was Helen. Maybe Pop thought that she should have given the name back), do you always have to embarrass the kids and everyone else in the room with poop talk?"

"It's okay Pop, I'm used to it."

The rooms of the apartment were now packed with party guests. Most of the men were sitting in the living room drinking their highballs and smoking. There was so much smoke in the room it seemed as if someone had forgotten to open the cardboard flue on the cardboard fireplace. Smoke was becoming so thick that a foghorn might have been helpful for people to navigate their way around the apartment. George kept walking face first into the crotches of the guests. It must have been hell to be that short.

The ladies were gathered around the dining room table, fussing with the food. Dishes and plates were being moved around the table strategically as if they were chessmen. Arrangement of food on the table was everything, each dish having a designated place. Once the men set upon the food, the arrangement and placement would be but a distant memory. Two tables were set up to handle the food but, by far, the largest table was set aside for the wine, spirits, and mixers, all necessary to turn the party into one great toilet-hugging bacchanalia.

The victuals included Swedish meatballs, Italian meatballs, potato salad, and finger sandwiches of turkey or ham, cookies, cakes, pastries and candy. At the end of the table, all by itself in an isolated corner, as if quarantined from all the other jolly food, were the Italian delicacies that Humphrey adored. There was fresh buffalo milk mozzarella ("Moozadell"), provolone, prosciutto ("Prashoot"), marinated mushrooms, roasted red peppers, baked rigatoni and other deli meats ("Gabbaagoole"). Dad had his own language when it came to some things. Dickey already knew that terlet was the toilet; if you berled something then it was boiled. The one that threw Dickey for quite some time was Earl; as in, "I am going to put Earl in the car." For years Dickey wondered who this "Earl" was that he had never seen before. Where was Dad putting him anyway, in the trunk? It wasn't until he was about ten years old that he found out that it wasn't "Earl" that was being put in the car, but motor oil. Dickey didn't know where Dad's words for Italian food came from either, but Dad and his friends from Arthur Avenue seemed to know what they were talking about. Of course, Mom had a different set of words for the cheeses and the gabbagoole, and Dickey knew that he would have his mouth washed with soap if he used any of them. All in all, it was a festive, colorful, and aromatic table. The aromatic feature was the part that irked Mom.

"Oh, Betty, the table is lovely," exclaimed Flo Hinch, who had hobbled up to the table. Flo was somewhere between 80 and 2,000 years old; she was so ancient that her wrinkles had wrinkles. The skin under her arms sagged like large ropes of bread dough. Sometimes Flo would babysit the kids for Betty and Humphrey. When she did, she would immediately head for the couch and fall asleep before her butt hit the seat cushion. Betty and Humphrey would return home to find Flo slumped on the couch, her top denture having fallen out, resting on her saggy table-top bosom.

"Thank you Flo, and thank you for bringing your Jell-O mold."

"Oh, you are welcome, dear. The apartment looks so lovely. I did want to ask you one thing though. What is that red and white thing with the red light in the living room? It looks so strange."

Betty let out a sigh. "It is an artificial fireplace. Humphrey got it to make the apartment resemble a picture of a cold-water flat in Hell's Kitchen. He saw it in Better Homes and Hovels. I think it is hideous."

"Well, nothing could beat the bear rug he rented last year," chuckled Paula Muldew, who had sidled up beside Flo. "Unless, of course it was the Rust-Oleum silver tree the year before he rented the bear rug," Ethel Wattlened giggled.

"I don't know what gets into Humphrey this time of the year. He seems to get these ungodly decorating ideas into his head and goes off without even a thought about what our friends will say. It is embarrassing to have a party every Christmas and have to explain these monstrosities. By far, that fireplace, or whatever it is supposed to be is the ugliest thing that I have ever seen, and the worst he has ever brought home. Now, nobody is going to talk about anything else tonight," Betty whimpered. On that note, she turned and walked toward the kitchen, dabbing her eyes with her silk handkerchief.

Standing unnoticed at the end of the liquor table was Humphrey. He had taken in every word the cackling women had said. He stirred his drink and walked into the living room, a pained expression on his face. Also unnoticed was his small son, Dickey. He had been maneuvering slowly among the bodies to snatch food from the table when nobody was watching. Dickey had also heard every word the women had said. He watched his Dad as the women made fun of him and the fireplace, and he could sense that Dad had been hurt by the mean words. Shifting his glance from his Dad to the fireplace, to the ladies, and back again, Dickey could not understand why they were making fun of his Dad. The fireplace looked nothing like they described, least of all to his pair of seven year old eyes. It made Dickey sad that his Dad was so sad.

He managed to snatch a few more sandwiches and then backed toward the hallway before he got caught. Billy, his older uncle, was also sneaking around, but food was not his target. Waiting until an adult went off to the bathroom or to get some food, Billy would swipe a highball glass left unattended and drain off whatever was in it. He cared less as to the contents, being more intent on the intoxicating substances. Dickey did not know what liquor did, or why it was that only adults were allowed to drink it, but he had been warned never to touch the stuff. It seemed that liquor must be fun to drink because, in a short time, Billy was laughing an awful lot at nothing in particular and he had a difficult time walking without bumping into walls or people. Eventually, his uncle got his bearings and ping-ponged off a couple of walls and down the hallway towards the bedrooms, laughing all the way.

When Billy didn't return in a few minutes, Dickey decided to see what his uncle was up to. Billy was a mischievous sort of teenager, always getting into some kind of trouble. Whether it was pilfering fruits and vegetables from the vegetable cart that passed down the streets every week, or dumping a package of Cool-Aid into the holy water font at church, Billy was a combination of Eddie Haskell and Dennis the Menace minus the overalls. The best way to keep Billy out of trouble was to keep a close eye upon him. And that was no insurance that he wouldn't find something to get into.

The bathroom was unoccupied when Dickey passed, meaning that his uncle had to be in one of the bedrooms. Both bedroom doors were closed, so he chose his parent's bedroom first, figuring that he might find some interesting stuff in there, like the plastic missiles Mom kept in her nightstand drawer that shook when you pressed a botton. "Hmmm, he's not in here," Dickey discovered after a quick search. "He must be in my room."

Opening the door to the bedroom he shared with George, Dickey was met with a blast of frigid winter air. Although the bedroom appeared to be empty, the window was open, flooding the room with sub-freezing cold. Dickey walked into the room, across to the window, and slowly stuck his head out. There was Billy, sitting on the fire escape and smoking what looked like a cigarette.

"What are you doing outside on the fire escape, Billy? It's awful cold to be sitting out there without a coat on."

"I'm just having a smoke, Dickey."

"Why don't you smoke inside? Everyone else is smoking inside?"

"This is a different kind of cigarette. I don't think that they will like the smell of the smoke."

Now that Billy mentioned the smell, Dickey could see what he meant. It did smell different, kind of woodsy, and not dirty and stinky like his parent's cigarettes smelled. He wondered why that was. Billy's cigarette looked different too, more like a submarine than a rounded tube. And it had no writing on it. His parent's cigarettes were called Salem; he knew that because they would send him to Mr. Yellen's candy store to buy them every so often.

The more Billy smoked, the more he laughed. Dickey could not figure out what was so funny, so he asked, "What are you laughing about, Billy?"

"Oh it's nothing, nothing at all. Just that I hid all of the Christmas presents in our house. My Mom and Dad will never be able to find where I hid them," Billy sputtered between giggles.

"I'll bet that Santa will find them," Dickey said, not thinking that the joke was particularly funny. Billy considered giving Dickey an alternate version of who brought gift on Christmas, but thought better of it.

"You know what Dickey; I think that you are probably right. Listen, people will be looking for us if we stay here much longer. Why don't you go back to the party and I'll be back in a minute." Dickey left his bedroom and closed the door. Boy, it was cold in there. As he walked back toward the living room he could hear very loud laughter. Turning the corner, he could see a bunch of the women gathered near the fireplace. So soused were some of them that they were listing to the left about as much as the fireplace was tilted to the right.

"C'mon Betty, let's gather around the ole fireplace and sing us some holiday songs," sputtered Edith Wilson, who then hiccupped and spilled some of her drink on the carpet.

"That sounds like a capital idea, Betty replied. Just let me find myself another drink." Humphrey saw his wife staggering through the partygoers and realized that Betty was one her way to being totally hammered, if she was not already there.

"Don't you think you have had enough," Humphrey asked? What he received in reply sounded something like this: "Nah, iz Chrismesh time, and who doesn't wanna be merry when you have a honesh ta goonesh fireplace burnin? If oney id were really burnin, we cud call da fire deparshmint to pud id out. Lord knows der id enough shmoke in de place."

"You better not get too close Betty, this thing is throwing out so much heat it'll melt your garters," Myrtle shouted.

The women were laughing uproariously. The more they drank, the more they laughed and the more they joked about the fireplace. Through the haze of smoke and alcohol, Betty grinned in the drunken knowledge that she had been right about the ghastly decoration. How could she not be, her friends were all on her side. The same, however, could not be said about Humphrey. He leaned against the entry to the living room with a drink in his hand, the color of his face turning a bright red that was heading north toward his ears. These holiday parties

255

always ended like this, he fumed. No matter what he tried to do to make the holidays more festive failed and he had to endure the drunken humiliation of his wife and her friends. He envisioned himself as if he were removed from his body, getting smaller and smaller as the laughter got louder and louder. There was no place for him to hide with an apartment full of people, and he struggled to keep his composure.

Just as Humphrey was about to lose his temper, he noticed that Billy was standing next to him. Leaving the bedroom, the teenager had heard the cackling women and decided to hang around the living room to enjoy the show. Billy usually found this kind of gang tackling highly amusing. For some reason, even though he did not like Humphrey very much, he felt sorry for him. Yes, the fireplace was pretty hokey, Billy thought, but it wasn't so bad as to embarrass someone in front of all these people.

From across the room, Dickey saw Billy tap his Dad on the shoulder. Dad leaned over and his uncle whispered something into his ear. First, he shook his head, and then, after some more whispering Dad chuckled, nodded his head and followed Billy down the hall. Dad and Billy returned about twenty minutes later, both sporting silly grins on their faces. The room also seemed to be slightly colder than it was before. Miraculously, the women's laughter no longer bothered Humphrey. After all, he thought, tis the season to be merry, isn't it?

Chapter IV

There is something exciting about the last day of school before the Christmas vacation. Anticipation fills the children as they watch the minutes tick away on the clock above the blackboard. It is truly doubtful that any child could have told their parents exactly what they had learned at school that day, so focused were they on the final bell tolling and being set free from their desks.

Dickey sat at his desk, head in his hands watching Sister Mary Debra as she wrote multiplication tables on the board. There were only twenty minutes left until the hands of the clock reached twelve and the beginning of the Christmas recess at St. Simon. He decided to use the remaining time to amuse himself, and any others who were watching, by making faces at the nun while her back was turned. He had to be careful though; Sister Mary Debra had great peripheral vision (and apparently, eyes in the back of her head), and could whip around in a heartbeat and hurl a chalkboard eraser about as fast as Whitey Ford could toss a speedball. It was said that she had a four pitch arsenal: fastball, slider, curve, and a knuckleball. She rarely missed, and as Dickey could attest, an eraser upside the head definitely stung.

Finally, after an eternity in Purgatory, the bell rang, and the doors flew open disgorging the children in holiday frenzy. Quickly mouthed goodbyes were tossed into the cold wind to friends as boys and girls hustled off to their homes, where the aroma of baking sugar cookies and their Christmas trees awaited them. It was the day before Christmas Eve.

Dickey had one task ahead of him before he headed home. Over the past weeks he had saved five dollars of allowance to purchase Christmas presents for his parents. George was out of luck because five dollars could only go so far, even in the 1960s. If George got what he deserved this year there would be enough coal in his stocking to heat Tiebout Avenue for an entire year. Besides, George got so much crap from the relatives he would never miss the present that Dickey wasn't buying for him.

He walked up Valentine Avenue and turned left up Ryer Avenue, walking past Luscher the butcher and Kilduff's Bakery until he reached the Grand Concourse where he turned left. Buying presents for people at Christmas was a new thing for Dickey. He had never bought anything for anyone before, and the amount of choices was staggering. Walking down the street, he looked into store windows and was completely flummoxed by the mountains of merchandise for sale. There were shirts, ties, sweaters, tools, pipes, shoes, and aftershave for men. For women the stores had lipsticks, blouses, perfumes, kitchen gadgets, cookbooks, and some underwear that resembled slingshots. This was not going to be as easy as he thought.

Dickey strolled along for a while, looking but not going into any stores until he came to a shop at the corner of E. 178th Street. Grover's Thrift Shop was a dark, little establishment about the size of a small kitchen located on the ground floor of an apartment building. Peering into the window, Dickey could see some display cases, shelves that had odds and ends such as dusty old mantle clocks and enameled boxes, as well as a couple of magazine racks. He decided that this place was as good as any to start his shopping, so he opened the door and entered.

"Can I help you, young man," the shop owner asked. She was a tall, skinny woman with a long thin neck, resembling a giraffe. On the end of her nose were teardrop shaped eyeglasses, held in place by a beaded chain. She looked down at Dickey from a great height that made him feel as if he were less than one foot tall. "Ah, I was looking to buy some Christmas presents for my Mom and Dad," he gulped, afraid that a long tongue was going to snap out of her mouth and snatch him up for a mid-afternoon snack. "What did you have in mind," she inquired. He had absolutely no idea what he was looking for and was rooted, frozen, to the spot.

"Can I look around a little bit? I won't touch anything. She eyed him up and down for a moment. He was wearing a parochial school uniform, so that was a plus she thought. "Well, you look clean enough, she said. You may browse around. Let me know if you see something that you like and I will take it out of the case for you."

He walked slowly down the aisles, searching very carefully for something, anything that would be suitable as a gift. Clothing was out; he didn't know what size stuff his parents wore. How do people do this, he thought? Kids give a list to Santa so he knows what toys to make and deliver. No problems for him. But parents were another story altogether. Maybe he should have just asked Mom and Dad what they wanted. But if he had done that, they would know that he was planning to buy them something. No, he wanted it to be a surprise for them to find something from Dickey under the tree on Christmas morning.

In the back corner of the store, Dickey found a case that had some interesting stuff in it. There was some woman's jewelry and a couple of pair of men's cuff links. He remembered that his Dad wore those funny shirts that didn't have any buttons on the cuffs when he went to work.

Maybe the cuff links would be a good idea. And Mom wore necklaces, pins and stuff like that. A pair of cuff links for Dad and a necklace of white beads for Mom. That stuff couldn't cost more than five dollars, could it?

"Excuse me ma'am, I see a couple of things that look like they would be good presents for my parents." Miss Giraffe was still a little suspicious of such a young boy supposedly shopping for Christmas presents, even if he was wearing a Catholic school uniform. "Do you have any money, son?"

"I have five dollars," Dickey replied.

She walked over to the case where Dickey was standing. Most of the jewelry was of the costume variety that had little if any value, and was unlikely to ever sell. "Well, what do you like," she asked?

"I think that my Mom would like those white beads, and my Dad could use those things that hold the cuff of his shirt together. How much does everything cost?"

There was something touching and sweet about this small boy trying to act grown up. The owner knew that each item individually cost more than Dickey had in total. However, she knew that the cheap costume pearls and the silver plated cuff links had been gathering dust in the display case for more than a year. Bottom line was that a sale was a sale. "The beads are $1.75 and the cuff links are $3.00. Would you like to purchase them?"

Dickey stood for a moment attempting to do the complex mathematical calculations in his head. Finally he said, "Nah, I don't want to purchase them, but I would like to buy them if I could?"

Miss Giraffe rolled her eyes and stifled a groan. Opening the case with the key she kept in her pocket, she took out the items and brought them to the front of the store. Figuring that the boy did not have a clue how to wrap gifts, she got out a box for each item and wrapped them in festive holiday paper. A bow adorned each box. "Okay son that will be $4.75." Dickey dug into his pocket and placed the few dollars and the change on the counter. It took a few minutes to separate the money from the skate key, bottle caps, and Bazooka bubblegum comics. He carefully counted out the exact amount. He had twenty five cents left, more than enough for a soda or an egg cream on his way home.

"Thank you very much for wrapping those presents for me. That was very nice of you," Dickey said.

"We want our good customers to come back again. And you are a very good customer, young man. You are very nice and polite."

Dickey thanked the woman, turned and walked out of the store and headed toward home. He had a big smile on his face, little knowing that the store owner had one on hers as well. It would be the best sale she made the entire day.

He stopped for an egg cream at the candy store at the corner of Valentine Avenue. It began to snow lightly while he was inside, and it delighted him greatly. Tomorrow was Christmas Eve, and Santa would be coming in his sleigh and leaving presents while Dickey slept. He was just a little confused, though. There was no chimney on the roof of his apartment building. He knew this because he had been on the roof many times dropping plastic bags filled with water off to see if he could hit somebody below. How would Santa get the presents from the roof to the apartment if there was no chimney? Then it dawned on him- Santa would use the fire escape and come in through the window. He knew that he would have a difficult time getting to sleep, but he would will himself to so that Santa didn't miss his apartment. And tonight would be fun. Dad told him about a new cartoon that would be on that evening. It was something called Mr. Magoo's Christmas Carol. Dickey liked Mr. Magoo, and although he had no idea what the Christmas Carol was all about, he was sure he would he would enjoy hanging out with his Dad and watching it.

Right after dinner, Dickey went into the living room to turn on the television to watch Mr. Magoo. No lights were on except for the ones on the Christmas tree, and the red bulb with the twirling piece of tin in the fireplace. He stopped for a moment and just looked at the decorations in the room. The lights on the tree were glowing and blinking, and the only sound that could be heard was the running water of the kitchen sink as his Mom finished washing the dinner dishes. Breathing in the scent of pine made him wish that it was already Christmas Eve. Nothing could be better than this, he thought.

He walked over and turned on the television and twisted the tuner knob to the correct station, then sat in front of the tree to wait for it to warm up. Dickey expected that his Dad would come in to watch the program with him in a minute or so. Sometimes Dad would even get down on the floor with him to watch television. Mom promised that she would make hot chocolate with a candy cane in the mug; another sign that the big day was almost there. If only they had a color television just like his grandparents, the top would have been reached. Unfortunately, things would remain black and white in the Stonebottom family for some time to come.

Over the music at the beginning of Mr. Magoo, Dickey could hear voices being raised in the kitchen. He went to the kitchen door to investigate and was told in no uncertain terms by his Mom to get back into the living room. Not having to be told twice, he scrambled back and flopped on the couch.

"Do you have any idea how embarrassed I was Saturday night? For once, just once, couldn't we have had a Christmas without one of your five-and-dime store ornaments and decorations? People do not come to our parties to see us during the holidays anymore, they come to see what asinine holiday garbage you come up with every year," huffed Betty.

"Let me get this straight, the fireplace was more embarrassing than you getting drunk, dancing like a fool, than getting sick in front of everyone? It'll take more than a cardboard fireplace top your performance. No, let me amend that; it'll take more than a fireplace, a bear rug, a silver Christmas tree, and a family of live moose camping out in our kitchen playing poker to top that."

"Humphrey, I have almost reached my limit with all of this. Spending money on cheap so-called holiday decorations instead of spending money on Christmas presents? You just don't get it, do you? They're ugly! They're crap! I hate them! And to top it off, you look like an idiot and a total loser in front to all of my friends."

Humphrey had had enough. One day before Christmas Eve, and Betty wanted to continue the battle. As hurt as he was, he was not going to give her what she wanted, which was either the satisfaction of letting her know how deeply she had wounded him, or him agreeing to get rid of the fireplace. However, not all of the fight had been rent from him, so he turned to fire one last salvo.

"You know, there is more to this holiday than just giving someone presents. Maybe the fireplace is cheesy. And maybe some people think it is stupid and laugh at it. If you only took one minute away from your self-centered day to see how Dickey's face lights up just looking at that cheap piece of cardboard, then you might have a clue how important people are over things. You are missing all of that. As for our friends, I don't give a damn what they think. I care about what our kids think and how they feel. So if it makes our kids happy and their Christmas more memorable to have a bear rug, or a cardboard fireplace, then it makes me happier. That is the best gift I could ever receive and the best present I could ever give them. So that should be your concern, Betty. Not our friends, and not how many or what kind of presents you receive."

"Don't you dare tell me what I should care about…"

Humphrey didn't hear the rest of it, because he already had his hat and coat on and was heading out of the front door of the apartment. There was no reason to listen anymore. Granite was no match for the hardness of his heart at that moment. Humphrey could see nothing more than the door, the hallway, and the street beyond. Moving down the stairs so quickly, he could not hear something else that was being said in his apartment. It was Dickey calling out, "Dad, Dad, Dad, where are you going? Aren't you going to watch Mr. Magoo with me? Dad? Dad?"

Chapter V

Christmas had come and gone just as it always does. Wrapping paper that was ripped from presents in a child's frenzy was now replaced by toys lying around the living room. The Christmas tree, once so majestic with its lights and ornaments now resembled a stooped over little old man rummaging in a garbage can for soda bottles to return for their deposit. Ornaments bowed down and touched the floor, and every once in a while the weight of one would cause it to come crashing on to the ground and shatter. Any change in air current, such as one passing the tree, caused the conifer to drop a shower of pine needles upon the floor.

For Dickey, it was a happy Christmas, despite the events leading up to the special day. Fortunately, a child's attention span was mercifully short at that age. Santa brought most of the things he had asked for. He got an airplane that ejected the pilot. This unfortunate military hero escaped certain death by a rescue helicopter winching him up to safety. Dickey also received two model airplanes; a B-24 Liberator, and a B-25 Mitchell bomber. A chemistry set was a gift from his grandparents, and one that his mother would not allow him to touch. She was afraid that he would blow up the apartment or devise some potion to make George disappear. And the best gift of all, so far, was that not one more thing was said about the fireplace. It was lit every night at the same time as the tree.

The Christmas vacation was coming to a close, and two days before he went back to school he was visiting his grandparents with his mother. Dad had some things to do around the house, so he did not accompany them on the visit. Dickey spent the afternoon playing with his Uncle

Norman, and then they had an early dinner because Pop had to work the night shift driving a bus. Pop frequently had to work on weekends, so they had dinner around 3:00 p.m. Dickey and his Mom stayed for a little while after Pop went to work then they left to head home themselves. It was very cold and the streets icy as they began their twenty minute trek home.

The apartment was very quiet and seemed a little different as Dickey hung up his coat in the hall closet. For all of the excitement leading up to Christmas, there was a touch of sadness around the Stonebottom apartment. Nobody seemed as cheerful as they had been just a few days before, as if the New Year held nothing for them. Now, moving through the days was like slogging through mud. Even the snow seemed gloomier when it fell, turning to slush as quickly as it turned grey from the dirt of the city.

When Dickey walked into the living room to turn on the television he immediately sensed that something was different. Gone were the lights, the Christmas tree, and all of the decorations. The fireplace was no longer leaning against the wall, and in its place stood the electric Hammond organ that his Mom had received from his Dad on Christmas morning. The living room was back to the same boring arrangement that it usually was for eleven months of the year.

"Where did everything go, sobbed Dickey. Where is the tree? Where are the stockings? Where is the fireplace?"

"It was time to take everything down and pack it away for next year, his dad gently said to him. We couldn't keep the decorations up for the whole year. The tree was getting dry and the needles were falling out."

"But I loved everything, Dad. Why didn't you tell me that you were going to take all the stuff down? Why did you have to hide it from me?"

"Well, I thought that you might feel sadder if you were around to watch me taking everything down and putting it away. I know you are sad, but I promise that next year we'll have an even bigger tree that you are going to help me pick out. And we'll have more decorations too."

The thought of a bigger tree and more ornaments did not make Dickey feel any better right at that moment. Without question, it would not be music to Mom's ears either. The living room looked naked, empty and cold. With no decorations, it was an ordinary living room in an ordinary apartment. He would have to play in his room now, because toys were not permitted in the living room except during Christmas. The rest of the year it was reserved for company and watching television.

It did not take Dickey too long to get over the new, old living room. Children are very resilient that way. Disaster strikes one minute and back to a semblance of normalcy the next. Mom was busy doing something in her bedroom while Dad decided to attempt to cheer Dickey up with the old standby, hot chocolate and leftover Christmas cookies. "When you are finished, Big Guy, would you please take down the garbage.

During the week, the super would ring up and the garbage would be hauled down on the dumbwaiter where the super would unload the trash. On weekends however, the residents would have to take their garbage down to the basement themselves. Dickey hated taking the garbage down at night because to him, and most of the other kids in the building, it was a very scary place. The basement was cold, dark, and creepy. Single light bulbs hung from the ceiling spaced just far enough apart so that there were areas of complete darkness between them. The boiler room was in the basement close to where the garbage cans were kept, and it would fire up unexpectedly, causing one to jump out of their skin in fright. You could always feel the invisible hand of the "basement monster," a legend on Tiebout Avenue, on your shoulder ready to rip your head off and spit out your teeth while he was enjoying your brains as a tasty meal. Was it any wonder why Dickey hated the place? He usually returned from tossing out the trash sweaty from running up the stairs to his apartment, with visions of the "monster" only a few paces behind.

Dickey made his way down the final steps leading to the basement door. His breathing became quicker and his heart beat faster, until it was a symphony of drums pounding in his chest. He reached for the handle of the doorknob as if it had electricity running through it. Slowly opening the door, he edged into the basement. The door slammed behind him, causing him to jump. He always forgot that the door slammed and he always scared himself half out of his wits by letting it slam behind him.

A long hallway and around a corner led to the garbage cans. Every time he made this short journey, he envisioned James Cagney making his last walk to the electric chair in the movie "Angels with Dirty Faces." One would think that Dickey would move faster down the hall to get the terror he always felt over with sooner, but he always moved at the pace of a snail.

When he was five feet from the end of the hall, the boiler ignited, sending him against the opposite wall huddling down in fright. A door slamming and now the furnace scaring the crap out of him; what was going to happen next. He wanted to drop the bag of garbage right where he stood and take off running for his apartment. He knew that he couldn't do that because, one time, the super caught him leaving garbage in the hall and marched Dickey right up the stairs to his Mom. He got off lightly that time, but a swat across the backside with the "Fanny Whacker" would be the penalty for his next transgression.

Dickey closed his eyes and rounded the corner. Maybe he could make his way to the garbage cans without opening his eyes. Unfortunately, closing his eyes and walking was not the smartest idea. He turned the wrong way and walked straight into a row of empty trash cans, tumbling half into one of them. Boy, did it smell?

He opened his eyes, heaved himself out of the can, and picked up the bag of garbage he had dropped when he fell into the can. Some of its contents had spilled, so he bent down to put the boxes and cans back in the bag. Then, out of the corner of his eye while bending down, he could see it. The red color of the object caused him to move forward slowly. As much as he wished that he could just run away, his curiosity got the better of him, and he could not help investigating further. Taking a couple more steps, he was directly in front of the filled trash cans at the end of the basement. Now he could clearly see the one thing that in his short life that was never meant for him to see.

Standing up against the wall behind some garbage cans stood the remains of the fireplace that had once been in Dickey's living room. It was torn to pieces, recognizable only by the red and white brick pattern. The happiness and joy of his Christmas lie torn and discarded in a heap of trash. Dickey could remember every moment of his Christmas holiday in the torn bricks. He knew that it was his Dad that destroyed the fireplace. And from the violence of the ripping and tearing, Dickey was shocked at the emotion and the rage Dad must have felt as he was destroying the cheap holiday decoration. Burned into his memory, he recalled every nasty thing said to his Dad about the fireplace, and every joke that his Mom made. Dad would be remembering it for a long time too. Dickey now understood why his Dad did not want him to be at home when the holiday decorations were being taken down. Humphrey did not want Dickey to see him tearing the fireplace to shreds. He wanted Dickey to remember the way it was on the day he set it up; with the red bulb glowing and the cheap tin turning. He wanted Dickey to remember that Christmas was about memories, and family, not the presents one received. When Dad and Dickey sat together around the imitation fireplace reading holiday stories, it didn't matter whether the fireplace was made out of cardboard, or brick, or stone. Those moments of a father and his son together were the things that would live with Dickey for many years to come.

Dickey is many years older now. He has a wife and children and they live in a nice house in Maryland. His parents have since passed away more than a decade ago. Richard- he is no longer called Dickey- has never had a fireplace in any of the places he has lived since moving from the Bronx more than forty years ago. While he was alive, his Dad never put up another fake fireplace, although he did buy a huge plastic Santa and eight not so tiny reindeer when the Stonebottom family moved to New Jersey, which his Mom hated as much as she despised the fireplace. To the end of his life, his Dad brought home garish Christmas decorations every year. And to the end of her life, Dickey's Mom gave Humphrey a ration of cow pies for every decoration he brought home. At least one thing would change. Eventually, Humphrey purchased an artificial Christmas tree. That gave Betty one less thing to bitch about.

Every year Richard Stonebottom actually does have a fireplace of sorts. It is red and white and it is made out of

270

cardboard. In the place where the logs would normally go, there is a red light bulb and a piece of tin that slowly spins, giving the illusion of fire dancing over logs. Of course, the fireplace leans a bit to the right. It stands in the living room of apartment 5C at 2120 Tiebout Avenue in the Bronx. Richard believes that the fireplace is the best fireplace he has ever seen, and he loves his Dad for putting it up a few days before Christmas when Dickey was seven years old. He tells the story of the Christmas fireplace to his children just about every Christmas. After so many years of having heard it, they can repeat it almost verbatim. With fireplaces available now that give off heat by just plugging them in to an electrical outlet and looking so much like the real thing, the kids can't quite understand why their Dad keeps talking about a crappy cardboard one and doesn't just go out and buy one.

These days kids do not get that it isn't the gifts you receive that either breaks too easily of go out of style too quickly, but that it is the memories that have been created by their parents that they take with them all their lives. When they grow up, get married and have children, they use those memories to create traditions with their family. It continues on through each generation. And while it probably won't be a cardboard fireplace, it will be some magical moment that you create for your family at Christmas that will be imprinted upon their memory that will stay with them always.

Can you smell the aroma of the burning logs coming off of fireplace at Dickey's apartment? I'll bet that you can. I know that Richard does, every 25th of December as he sits in front of the family Christmas tree watching everyone open their presents. There is, however, one tradition from his childhood that he refuses to pass on to his children. He refuses to make them watch the Yule Log on Christmas Eve.